THE WILHELM CONSPIRACY

A SHERLOCK HOLMES | LUCY JAMES MYSTERY

OTHER TITLES BY CHARLES VELEY

The Sherlock Holmes and Lucy James Mysteries:

The Last Moriarty

Novels:

Play to Live
Night Whispers
Children of the Dark

Nonfiction:

Catching Up

THE WILHELM CONSPIRACY

A SHERLOCK HOLMES | LUCY JAMES MYSTERY

BY CHARLES VELEY

THOMAS & MERCER

This is a work of fiction. Names, characters, organizations, places, events, and incidents are either products of the author's imagination or are used fictitiously.

Published by Thomas & Mercer, Seattle

www.apub.com

ISBN-13: 9781503940352 (paperback)
ISBN-10: 1503940357 (paperback)

Cover design by Todd A. Johnson

Printed in the United States of America

TABLE OF CONTENTS

For readers who asked for another Lucy James adventure,
and especially for Anna Elliott

"But helpless Pieces of the Game He plays,
Upon his Chequer-board of Nights and Days;
Hither and thither moves, and checks, and slays,
And one by one back in the Closet lays."

—Edward Fitzgerald
The Rubáiyát of Omar Khayyám, 1859

PREFACE

I have recorded the events of this past September, both for posterity and in order to quiet my mind. But these papers must not be published during my lifetime or in the next century.

John H. Watson, MD
London, 31 December, 1896

PART ONE

A GAME HE PLAYS

1. A VISITOR AT 221B BAKER STREET

My account begins with the events of a cold and rain-filled Saturday afternoon, in the late September of 1896, shortly before Holmes and I learned of the first murder connected with this case. The two of us were returning home after a visit to the British Museum, and as we waited for a vacant cab on Montague Street, the downpour had drenched us both. As we reached 221B Baker Street, I was looking forward to a change of clothes and a restorative brandy.

We were climbing the stairs that led to our rooms and had reached our landing when our door opened from within. Lucy James stood before us, holding a folded newspaper.

Even in the shadows of our upper hallway, I could see the apprehension on her youthful features. Her lovely face bore a subtle resemblance to Holmes's, though with far softer and more beautiful outlines. Beneath her dark eyebrows, her opalescent green eyes held a determined glint.

"Mrs. Hudson let me in." She gave Holmes and me each a brief hug as we entered. "Someday you might think of giving me my own key."

Holmes stiffened under the embrace.

I turned away to conceal my involuntary smile. It never failed to cheer me, to see my friend's determinedly rational—some might even say mechanical—facade come up against the warm but no-less-determined affection and informality of his recently discovered American daughter. Of course, it was a mark of the deep regard Holmes bore for Lucy that he submitted to her embraces at all.

"I've put more coals on the fire," Lucy said. Then she thrust the folded newspaper into Holmes's hand. "Have you seen this?"

Without removing his wet Ulster coat, Holmes spread the paper, that afternoon's edition of the *Times*, onto our sitting room table. Lucy had drawn a thick black circle with one of Holmes's wax pencils around an article on the second page. The headline read:

LONDON BANKER SPENCER KENT FOUND DEAD IN SWANDAM LANE HOTEL. GRIEVING WIDOW CONFIRMS IDENTITY.

"It doesn't say much," Lucy murmured as Holmes scanned the article.

I remembered Swandam Lane, a vile alley that Holmes and I had visited seven years earlier, when my beloved Mary was still alive. But the name Spencer Kent meant nothing to me.

"You recalled Kent's name?" Holmes asked Lucy.

"You told me last November. I tend to remember things you tell me, in case you hadn't noticed."

At my puzzled stare, Holmes said, "The report says Mr. Kent was a prominent banker and that it is not apparent what had brought him to die in such squalid surroundings."

I still could recollect no association with the name. Holmes continued, "We took a million pounds in bearer bonds from him on the sixth of November last year outside the German embassy. You promised never to write of the case."

I shuddered inwardly. As the memories came flooding back, I saw again the doomed members of the Moriarty gang, whose murderous plot we had thwarted last Guy Fawkes Night. I saw again the little British banker, who would have paid the gang one million pounds if they had succeeded in a massive assassination. Hundreds, including three American millionaires and the principal leaders of Her Majesty's government, would have died in a firestorm of incendiary bullets had it not been for Holmes. I saw again the events of the following morning, when outside the German embassy, we had forcibly relieved the traitorous banker of the bearer bonds as he was about to return them to his unknown controller.

The little banker had approached the embassy briskly, full of urgency and hope as he neared it. Then Inspector Lestrade and his men closed in. The banker's shoulders had slumped with despair as he reluctantly drew an envelope containing the bonds from inside his coat and handed it over to Lestrade. I saw again his wary glance at those of us who stood nearby, just before he turned and fled.

Now, nearly eleven months later, the little man's flight had ended.

"So you remember."

"Only I did not know the banker's name."

"Chancellor Hicks Beach mentioned it when we brought the funds to Downing Street."

Lucy said, "And you told me about it a few days later in my mother's flat, when I was helping her pack for Rome."

"You deserved to know."

Lucy's green eyes flashed, acknowledging the compliment.

"And now it would appear that the Germans have found him, killed him, and left him with his identification papers."

"To humiliate his bank and his family."

Holmes nodded. "Now you had best be going."

Again Lucy's eyes flashed, though this time, I thought, with a touch of asperity. Since last November, when Holmes had discovered that

Lucy James was his daughter, and last April, when she had returned from visiting her mother's family in Rome, there had been numerous discussions about the need to keep her apart from Holmes for her own safety. Lucy, determined to help Holmes with his investigations, took the opposite view.

On this occasion, however, Lucy did not renew the argument. She merely said, "I shall," and gave Holmes a brief hug. Holmes's expression did not alter as she embraced him, and his posture remained as stiff as before. However, one long-fingered hand came up and delivered the briefest of pats on Lucy's shoulder.

"Have a care for yourself," Holmes said.

Then Lucy grasped both my hands, said "Try to keep him safe," and turned to our doorway.

"Of course," I replied. "But why now, in particular?"

She opened the door. "Because Mr. Kent will assuredly have told his German captors the name of Sherlock Holmes."

Then the door shut behind her, and she was gone.

2. ANOTHER VISITOR

The next morning, I woke to the sound of rapid and forceful knocking. I heard the click of the latch on our sitting room door. Then came Mrs. Hudson's weary but unapologetic voice: "Messenger said it was urgent. From Inspector Lestrade at Scotland Yard."

"Please bring coffee for Dr. Watson," Holmes replied. The latch clicked shut.

Quickly lighting a lamp and putting on my clothes, I descended my little staircase to find Holmes in his dressing gown, his spare frame hunched over our dining table. Clouds of shag tobacco smoke issued from his pipe as he scrutinized several sheets of typewritten notepaper. His brow furrowed in that tense, single-minded manner that I know so well.

"You asked Lestrade for the police report on the dead banker," I said.

He nodded and held up one of the typewritten sheets. "Last week Mr. Kent came to the Green Dragon Hotel accompanied by several men. They paid cash and took the room in the name of one Jonathan Bull."

"Obviously a false name."

“It appears that Mr. Kent was tortured for a considerable amount of time.”

A sense of foreboding came over me. “To force him to tell who had taken their million pounds?”

“There would have been no need to torture Mr. Kent to obtain our names. He would have recognized Mycroft last November and been only too happy to point to us.”

“So why was he tortured?”

“We have no facts on which to base our suppositions.”

“Perhaps to punish him for his failure,” I suggested.

Holmes said only, “What we know from this report is that his fingertips had been burned away.”

At that moment the doorbell rang downstairs. We heard Mrs. Hudson answer, and her voice was higher in pitch than usual. “Why, Mr. Lestrade! Whatever has happened to you?”

“I need to see Holmes” was the hoarse reply from below.

Lestrade’s tread on the stairs was halting and irregular. Holmes sprang to the door and flung it open. The Scotland Yard detective took the last few steps up to our entryway unsteadily, his narrow, ferret-like features even paler than usual and set in a grimace of pain. He took off his bowler hat to reveal a fresh red abrasion on his forehead, extending upwards, staining his scalp and his thinning black hair.

“Just outside,” said Lestrade. “They were waiting for me. Gone now.” He sagged against the door frame.

Quickly we helped the little inspector to a chair. I retrieved my medical bag from my dressing room and soon Lestrade’s injury was cleaned and dressed.

“My good fellow,” Holmes said. “I see that you were set upon by two—no, more likely three—attackers. Two of them held your arms—the creases remain in the sleeves of your coat—while a third grasped you by the front of your shirt, smudging and wrinkling the otherwise clean and perfectly presentable fabric. Since the third man might have more conveniently held you by the lapels, we may infer that his intention was to be as intrusive and offensive as possible." Lestrade nodded assent, and Holmes went on, "Now tell us what happened."

"They came up behind me when I was about to ring your bellpull. Right out of the fog. Took me by surprise."

"Did they speak?"

"Only one of them did the talking. The big one and the one with the mask said nothing. The one who spoke had a German accent."

"Can you remember the exact words?"

"They had me up against the wall. The big one and the one with the mask held me, by the arms as you said. The one who spoke got right up in front of my face—I could see his crooked teeth and smell beer on his breath. He said, 'Inspector Lestrade, you will inform Herr Holmes that he is not to interfere.'"

"When did they strike you?"

"When I twisted away. Gave the bigger one a kick, I did. Then he threw me into the wall. I hit my head. The one who did the talking said that this"—his fingertips went gingerly to his forehead—"would also be a message for you. Then the big one shoved me down onto the pavement, hard. When I got up, they were gone."

"Did you tell anyone at the Yard that you were coming here?"

"Only the dispatch desk sergeant."

"Did you tell the sergeant you were coming to elaborate on the report concerning Mr. Kent?"

"No. Because I wasn't."

"Indeed." Holmes's brow rose slightly in surprise.

"I came here because I got this." Lestrade extracted a folded yellow telegraph paper from his inside coat pocket and handed it over to Holmes. "From the Commissioner."

Holmes glanced at the paper and then handed it to me. The message read:

> MOST URGENT YOU BRING SHERLOCK HOLMES TO DOVER BEACH. MEET DOVER PATROL SERGEANT STUBBS DIRECTLY BELOW RADNAR HOUSE HOTEL. AWAIT ORDERS FROM LANSDOWNE.

Holmes had already opened our sitting room door and was calling down the stairs. “Mrs. Hudson! Dr. Watson will not be requiring that coffee.”

3. ON DOVER BEACH

It was nearly three o'clock that afternoon when we arrived at the Dover Priory station after a long railway journey. A cab brought us to the Radnar House hotel, a sprawling Gothic structure built atop the famous white cliffs. We walked to the edge of the gravel carriage path and looked down at the beach, nearly three hundred feet below.

A south-easterly wind swept in over the waves of the Channel, driving a light rain. The needle-like droplets stung my eyes. On the dun-coloured gravel and sand below us stood a black-painted carriage, enclosed and with small windows, with no occupants or insignia that I could observe. The horse was stamping nervously at the incoming tide, and its hooves made small splashes in the white foam at the edge of the waves. A few yards away, a helmeted man in uniform stood guard over an object that lay beside him. From this distance it was difficult to see the object clearly. It might have been a large black rock, or the corpse of a large seal, or a closely compacted clump of driftwood.

"A dead man, burned black, with no clothing," said Holmes.

For nearly five minutes we picked our way along the steep chalky path that led down to the beach. The rain and a sea mist slowed our progress. During the long walk I was hoping that the case would be stimulating for Holmes. I believed that he would appreciate the intellectual distraction of identifying a body devoid of all the usual clues and that his constitution would benefit from the fresh sea air.

Holmes and I reached the body, with Lestrade a short distance behind us. Holmes addressed the helmeted man who had been standing guard, raising his voice to be heard over the clamour of wind, rain, and breaking waves. "You are Sergeant Stubbs? We must move this away from the tide." He had already taken off his Ulster coat and rolled it into a long tube. Kneeling behind the body, he snugged up the fabric against the cracked and blackened flesh.

I recalled how the nurses at my university hospital moved their inert patients onto a litter using a rolled-up bedsheet. Beside Holmes, I knelt on the wet gravel, holding my breath against the odour of seaweed and charred flesh. Pressing down on the edge of the coat with our knees, we pushed the roll of fabric forwards and down into the sand, gradually unfurling and extending it beneath what had once been a living person. Then, supporting the body on the heavy cloth, we lifted it, and in an awkward, crouching-sideways fashion, manoeuvred it away from the water. Finally we set the body down on the rain-slick brown stones by the cliff, where the incoming surf could no longer reach it.

Breathing rapidly from the exertion, I looked up to see Holmes with the sergeant, pointing to the waiting carriage. "Who is inside?"

"Army," he replied with a shrug. Clean-shaven, stout, and tall—about the same height as Holmes—Stubbs was plainly reluctant to cede control of the case to outsiders. "Are you Mr. Holmes?"

"I am Sherlock Holmes, this is my friend and colleague Dr. John Watson, and joining us now is the man who summoned us from London, Detective Inspector George Lestrade of Scotland Yard."

Lestrade strode forwards, brushing chalk and grit from his battered bowler hat, prepared to assert himself as the ranking officer. He addressed the sergeant. "Were you instructed not to move the body?"

"So were they," Stubbs said, nodding towards the carriage.

The black door opened and one man stepped out, followed by another and then a third, who clambered up to the driver's seat and untied the reins. All three men wore ordinary black suits, black wool coats, and black bowler hats, rather than Stubbs's blue Harbour Patrol uniform.

"Nice and dry in there?" Stubbs asked, wiping rain from his eyes and forehead with his pocket kerchief.

The taller of the two men gave a tight-lipped smile and looked at Holmes. "Mr. Holmes? Have you seen everything you need to see?"

"I have. You are free to take the body to the Dover Castle garrison. I ask that the examination not begin until Dr. Watson and I can be present."

"How do you know that we are from the garrison?"

"Your boots are all of the same pattern, made of reversed leather, and polished black," Holmes replied. "Also, Sergeant Stubbs said you were Army men. Given the urgency of the matter, Secretary Lansdowne would use the local Army garrison—it is quartered at Dover Castle."

"Right you are, sir," the taller man said, as his companion turned back to the interior of the carriage. The two dragged out a folded military stretcher of stout wood and dull-green canvas, the type I had seen so frequently in Afghanistan. The taller man continued, "I will pass your request along to the medical examiner."

With his companion, he placed the stretcher beside the body and used Holmes's coat to slide the body onto the green canvas. With a quick jerk, he freed the coat and held it at arm's length. "This is yours, sir?"

It was an obvious deduction, since Holmes was the only one of us lacking a topcoat. "Please leave it on the sand—away from the tide." As the man flung the coat away, Holmes went on, "I see you are carrying a revolver. Are you expecting someone to interfere with you?"

"Possibly," the taller man said.

"When and where?"

Giving no reply, the two manoeuvred the stretcher and the body into their carriage.

"We are all in the service of Her Majesty's government, are we not?" asked Holmes.

Again, Holmes's words were met with silence. Soon the two Army men were seated side by side between the open rear doors, dangling their legs over the edge so that their boots nearly touched the beach gravel. Their revolvers were now out of their holsters. The taller man said, "Sergeant Stubbs, please telephone the garrison from the hotel and report that we are on our way."

We watched the black carriage disappear with its passengers and cargo into the mist that lay like a small cloud at the edge of the seashore. Holmes picked up his coat and shook it out.

"You can get that cleaned at Radnar House," said Stubbs.

Holmes glanced at the waves behind him and then upwards at the cliff, where we could see the jagged silhouette of roof peaks, looming over us in the diminishing late-afternoon light.

"Are you ready?" Lestrade asked.

Before Holmes could reply, I heard what sounded like a firecracker exploding somewhere on the cliff above us. At the same moment, Sergeant Stubbs clutched his shoulder, uttered a groan, tottered, and was about to fall when Holmes pulled Stubbs up and propelled him forwards. "Run for the cliff," Holmes said. "Now!"

But then came another sharp report, which I now know was a rifle shot. I turned and saw that Stubbs had been struck again. He staggered back and fell at the edge of the tide, his helmet striking the gravel. Beneath him, blood darkened the wet pebbles and the swirling foam.

4. TOO MANY QUESTIONS

Three hours later Holmes, Lestrade, and I sat in a private downstairs room of Radnar House with Lord Lansdowne, Secretary of State for War. Lansdowne had been one of the leaders of Her Majesty's government whose lives we had saved from the Moriarty gang eleven months earlier. Although he was thin, high-browed, and dark haired like Holmes, Lansdowne's features were more elongated and less angular. Beneath his high-domed forehead, his face bore a luxuriantly thick and wide walrus moustache of dark brown, framed by elongated mutton-chop sideburns. His manner, cordial though never haughty, at least in my presence, showed the effects of a lifetime of privilege.

On the sideboard an afternoon tea of generous proportions lay as yet untouched. Before each of us was a glass of warm brandy. I sipped mine. Lestrade had already finished his. Holmes's glass was on the table before him, ignored.

I still could not fully understand what had happened on the beach. After Stubbs had been shot, we had dragged him to shelter beneath the overhang at the base of the cliff. Holmes had gone up the path to seek help at Radnar House as Lestrade and I waited. I was able to staunch the flow of blood from the sergeant's torso by placing my folded scarf beneath his arm and pressing hard directly above and below the wound. Lestrade and I took off our coats and piled them around his head and over his legs to warm him. His muscles shook with nervous tremors, and from his shallow, fluttering breaths, I knew he was rapidly going into shock.

After what seemed an eternity but could not have been more than twenty minutes, Holmes had returned, grim-faced, accompanied by two men in military uniforms. "These are Lord Lansdowne's officers," he said. "While I was climbing the trail, his carriage arrived, which likely caused whoever shot Sergeant Stubbs to flee."

With the aid of the two officers, we carried the wounded man up to Radnar House and entered at the rear, so as not to alarm the hotel guests. The two attendants and I made our way to the second floor with the inert sergeant. A hotel nurse waited in a room at the end of the corridor with her medical kit. She and I cleaned and dressed the sergeant's wounds as quickly as possible. The injury to his shoulder was not serious, but the lesion in his side, due to the shallow angular entry and exit of the second bullet, required four stitches, and he had lost a substantial quantity of blood. Fortunately the bullet had not struck a vital organ, and soon I was able to leave my patient sleeping in his warm bed with the nurse watching over him. One of his fellow patrolmen, a tall, strapping fellow, stood guard in the hallway outside his room. The nurse inside had my orders to administer claret and send for me immediately if he awoke, for I knew Holmes would have questions for him concerning what might have prompted the attack.

Now, in our private downstairs room, Holmes was leaning forwards in his upholstered armchair, recounting to Lord Lansdowne the "message" from the three men who had waited for Lestrade outside 221B Baker Street this morning. He concluded, "Their words implied that I could expect pain and futility if I interfered with them. I do not know what they meant. I presume you do."

I saw concern and possibly alarm in the wide brown eyes of the Secretary of War. His fingertips went to his eyebrows, as though he was trying to apply pressure directly into his brain. "I am at a loss," he said finally.

"Then, Mr. Secretary, let us review what information we possess. First, we know that the traitorous banker connected to the Guy Fawkes affair has been tortured, murdered, and left by his killers to be discovered in humiliating circumstances and publicized in the newspapers for his wife, children, and the rest of the world to see. I interpret this as a message from his employers to indicate the consequences of failure."

"And quite possibly their outrage, given that Mr. Kent failed to return the colossal sum of one million pounds."

"Within a day of the discovery of Mr. Kent's body, another body washes up on Dover beach. You send for me, via the Commissioner, who orders Inspector Lestrade to bring the message to me. Within a few hours Lestrade is accosted and instructed to warn me not to interfere, by a man who calls him by name and does not trouble to mask his German accent."

"You think a traitor in my organization intercepted my message."

"It was either your message that was intercepted or the message from the Commissioner to Inspector Lestrade. Someone in either your organization or the Metropolitan Police is a traitor. And a most efficient someone, since not much time elapsed between the two messages and the appearance of three men on my doorstep awaiting Inspector Lestrade's arrival."

"I fear that conclusion is inescapable."

"There is one more fact to consider. Shortly after my arrival here, someone shot the Dover Harbour sergeant assigned to guard the body. We must ask ourselves why that attack occurred."

"I have no idea why anyone would want to shoot a Dover policeman."

"He was standing next to me when each of the shots was fired."

"So the shots may have been meant for you."

"And the rifleman might have been an inaccurate or unlucky marksman."

"Do you think the Germans wanted to kill you?"

"They may have. But they have had ample opportunities to do that during the past ten months, so I think the possibility unlikely."

"What, then?"

"The rifleman's aim may have been accurate, and there may be another reason for his desire to kill Sergeant Stubbs."

"Do you know the reason?"

"How could I, when you have not been completely candid with me?"

"What do you mean?"

"Mr. Secretary, I need you to tell me why we are here. Why did you summon me, and why did you travel to Dover this afternoon? I cannot imagine that this was due only to the discovery of a charred body on the beach."

Lord Lansdowne lowered his eyes, and then, as if his mind had finally been made up, gazed directly at Holmes. "Mr. Holmes, we need your help in a matter of the highest consequences, one which could affect the future of the British nation for generations to come."

5. KERREN HOUSE

Holmes nodded calmly, as if such requests were for him an everyday occurrence. "Thank you, Mr. Secretary. Given your position, I expected no less." He picked up his brandy glass for a moment and set it down, still untouched. "I also expect that your request involves the theft of a new and extremely powerful weapon, and that the weapon utilizes electric current."

Astonishment shone on Lord Lansdowne's aristocratic features. "How can you possibly know that?"

"The deduction is a simple one. First, the War Office concerns itself with military conflict and with weapons. You, as its head, would not interrupt your Sunday unless the matter was extraordinary and urgent. If military conflict were imminent, you would be closeted with generals and admirals rather than with me, a lone civilian. That leaves a weapon, which must be new and powerful since you would hardly be interested in an old one. If the weapon were safely held by the War Department, you would have no need of my services and I would still be in London. Therefore a new and powerful weapon has been stolen." He gave one of his brief smiles before continuing, "Also, I must admit that when I signed the hotel register this afternoon, I saw on the preceding page the name of Mr. Nikola Tesla, the famed electricity scientist. He arrived Friday."

Lord Lansdowne gave a small smile. "You live up to your reputation, Mr. Holmes. However, I believe I can point out one thing that you do not yet know. Mr. Tesla is now waiting for us in Kerren House, a few hundred yards from here. I shall explain more as we walk."

The rain had stopped and a stiff north-west wind buffeted our backs as the four of us set out on the gravel pathway that led along the clifftop. A faint crescent moon had begun to emerge from behind the clouds over the eastern side of the Channel and, beyond them, the shores of France. The Secretary and Holmes walked behind Lestrade and me. Lestrade carried a lantern.

"We are concerned with Kaiser Wilhelm," I heard Lansdowne say to Holmes as we picked our way along the shadowy and irregular grey stones. "You will recall the ill-fated raid in the Transvaal conducted by our Commander Jameson last January, and the Kaiser's inflammatory telegram congratulating the Transvaal president for defeating our forces so soundly."

"I recall public fury on the subject reported in the press," Holmes said.

"The Kaiser is also driving all of Germany to work at a feverish pace in order to bring their naval power to a strength greater than ours. And despite his recent conciliatory telegram, Germany's forces do grow stronger with each passing day."

"I take it Mr. Tesla's electrical weapon has naval applications?"

"An understatement, Mr. Holmes." Lansdowne stopped, faced Holmes directly, and lowered his voice, as though fearful of being overheard even out in the open air atop the windswept cliff. "Picture, if you will, a cannon positioned just over there, overlooking the ocean, and a

German warship appearing on the horizon. Picture a bolt of lightning shot directly from that cannon, instantaneously hitting the German vessel. Knowing what happens to a man who is struck by lightning, you can imagine the effects this weapon would have on the men aboard that vessel."

"The current would be conducted through the metal deck and frame of the ship. The men aboard would be instantly electrocuted."

Lansdowne nodded. "Without its crew, the warship would be useless. It could easily be taken as a prize by our Navy, and then used against the enemy."

"Could the weapon be placed on one of our warships?"

"Mr. Tesla believes it is possible to generate sufficient electric power to operate such a weapon from a warship. And since his electrical generators are now providing enough energy to light up the American city of Niagara Falls, New York, our government is inclined to take him seriously. However, as I have mentioned, he is very much focused on scientific matters and less inclined to consider practical realities. You will see this when we meet him."

No one spoke further as we resumed our walk. Farther down the pathway we could see the outlines of a dark brick home constructed in the Gothic style. Electric light gleamed from the front windows, partially illuminating another large black carriage, similar to the one we had seen on the beach, a powerful black horse, and three tall men in military garb, waiting on the circular gravel drive. "There, gentlemen, is Kerren House," said Lansdowne. "And those are my men. We have a need for military protection, as you will soon understand."

As we reached the house, the men came to attention and saluted. One of them silently gestured towards the front doorway.

The door opened before we could ring or knock. In the doorway stood a tall, fair-haired woman, dressed in a long-sleeved, close-fitting white satin frock and cloaked in a white shawl that appeared to be of fine cashmere. Her long hair was pinned in a large swirl just above the nape of her neck, a current fashion which I believe is French. She beckoned us into the entrance hall and then inclined her head towards Lord Lansdowne, plainly waiting for the proper introductions to be made.

Lansdowne said, "Lady Radnar, may I introduce Mr. Holmes, Dr. Watson, and Inspector Lestrade. Gentlemen, this is Lady Radnar. Lord Radnar is the owner of Radnar House, and her brother, Lord Kerren, is the owner of Kerren House, the dwelling in which we now find ourselves."

"Thank you, Henry," Lady Radnar said, referring to Lord Lansdowne by his given name and thereby indicating her own equal social position. "Gentlemen, I am Sophia Radnar." She blinked several times. I could see her lower lip begin to tremble. Her tone became hesitant. "Lord Radnar is in America on business, and my brother is still in Bad Homburg. That skeletal foreigner Tesla is in the conservatory with Harriet, my stepdaughter, and her friend from London. I will take you to them, but first I have a request for Mr. Holmes."

"Of course," said Lord Lansdowne.

"How may I be of assistance?" asked Holmes.

"Mr. Holmes, I—" She broke off and a shudder passed through her graceful frame. "If only my husband were here," she continued after a moment. "He is accustomed to encountering critical moments in transactions of great importance. I am sure he would know what to do. I, unfortunately, do not."

"Of what are you afraid, Lady Radnar?"

She shut her eyes tightly. Then she shook her head as if trying to banish a bad dream. "You are right. I am afraid. Things are changing too quickly for me. I cannot understand all this new science, yet my husband and my brother both say our future—my future—depends on it. My brother has invested all his capital in his project, and my husband has overextended himself as well."

Holmes gave one of his quick, perfunctory smiles intended to evidence sympathy. "But what is it that you fear?"

"I am afraid that the body found on the beach today was somehow connected with my brother's work. I am fearful that a dreadful mistake was made. I have read that in the United States they use electricity to kill murderers, and that there are burns—"

She broke off, looking downwards and pressing her lips tightly together, obviously trying to regain control of her speech.

She took a deep breath and then continued. "My nerves are not what they might be, Mr. Holmes. I have spent the past three months at Bad Homburg attempting to restore them—and without complete success, it would appear. But I am not a fool. If my brother is working on a military project, then some kind of new weapon must be involved. If the weapon has gone wrong, there may have been an accident, and that accident may be what killed the poor person whose body appeared on our shore last night. Such an accident would create a scandal and the Prince, who cannot abide scandal, would disassociate himself from the project. My brother and my husband would be ruined."

"The Prince?"

"Of Wales." She shook her head again and began to usher us towards the rear of the entrance hall. "But I am keeping you too long. My stepdaughter and her friend are with that emaciated foreigner, as I said. They are in the conservatory, which my brother has converted into his laboratory. I only ask you, Mr. Holmes, to clear up this matter as quickly as you possibly can."

And with that she opened the door to the conservatory, motioned for us to enter, and then turned and walked quickly away.

Inside, beneath the tall, wide, and brilliantly lit glass roof of the conservatory, a man and two women were huddled over one end of a huge metallic hemispherical structure that might have been a gigantic kettledrum set down onto a wheeled platform. The wheels rested on the white clay floor tiles. The apparatus must have been twelve feet in diameter. It dominated the room in the way an elephant dominates a circus ring. I had no idea of the inner workings of the great object, but as we drew closer I could see within it six clusters of metallic equipment. Each was similarly configured, connected by wires and metal rods to a circular metal frame suspended above the apparatus. The metal frame was empty, but there were brackets attached to it that could have been used to fasten more equipment into place.

I glanced around the room, trying to observe the details, as I knew Holmes was doing. Farther from the centre and in front of a door that led to outside the conservatory stood a brass telescope supported by a sturdy steel tripod. Along the near wall on one side of the entrance door hung a large tapestry depicting Queen Elizabeth in a somewhat heroic pose. I felt a vague discomfort at this, as I would have expected a portrait of Queen Victoria. But then my attention was drawn to the other side of the entrance door, where along the wall was a grey slate counter and a sink. Above and below the counter was a splendid array of somewhat dusty wooden shelves, filled with glass bottles of various shapes and colours. I wondered fleetingly why this equipment was in the conservatory, and if Lord Kerren was an amateur horticulturalist or chemist as well as an electrical inventor.

Two of the three persons looked up as we entered. I recognized Nikola Tesla, whose elegantly urbane attire, crane-like figure, beady eyes, and spare dark moustache were widely illustrated in newspaper sketches. I had not realized how tall he was nor how appallingly thin was his frame. Had his clothes not been extensively tailored, they would have hung on him like a rain-soaked flag on its pole. Though of height equal to Holmes's six foot two inches, Tesla could not have weighed more than one hundred and forty pounds.

The woman closest to Tesla kept her head down. But a glance was enough for me to recognize her as Lucy James.

6. A LIGHTNING RAY IN THE CONSERVATORY

The other woman was holding a small sketch pad, drawing with brisk, firm strokes using a silver-plated reservoir pen. "Good evening, Mr. Holmes," she said. "I am Harriet Radnar, as you no doubt have deduced."

Miss Radnar spoke in a clear and declamatory manner. She might have been an actress on a stage. The left side of her face was partially obscured by her long blond hair. With an annoyed backhanded gesture, she cleared it away to reveal perfectly proportioned features and a complexion as flawless as a china doll's. Compared with Lady Radnar, Harriet was smaller in both height and bone structure. Whereas Lady Radnar had given me the impression of a large and graceful swan, self-contained and generally serene—other than under the present circumstances, of course—Harriet made me think of a small hummingbird, hovering, radiating energy and intensity, as if on the verge of darting to another spot. And whereas Lady Radnar wore her hair pinned just above the nape of her neck, Harriet's long tresses hung free, held only by a black headband just above her smooth forehead. I recalled that Lady Radnar had said Harriet was her stepdaughter. I wondered fleetingly whether Harriet resembled her real mother.

Putting her sketch pad and pen into her purse, she continued, "I was just making a sketch of Mr. Tesla, here. He has been regaling us with tales of his lightning-ray machine, and some of his other secret adventures."

Tesla cocked his head, bird-like, one hand on his chin while the other, gloved in white leather, smoothed the expensive dark wool of his lapel. "They are such charming ladies. I could not resist telling them. You are Mr. Holmes, I take it?"

"Indeed," Holmes replied courteously. He moved towards the metal structure, away from the ladies. Tesla quickly moved in front of him, as if he were about to point out the features of the apparatus inside.

"Please, Mr. Tesla," said Miss Radnar. "Before you immerse yourself in the scientific details, first allow me to introduce my friend to these gentlemen." She gestured to Lucy. "This is my old school classmate Lucy James. She is also my present-day colleague in the D'Oyly Carte Opera Company."

I struggled to conceal my apprehension. I could only imagine the concern Holmes must have felt upon finding Lucy here, in the midst of a case that had already taken two lives and very nearly a third.

Now Lucy, her lovely face framed by her neatly coiffed dark hair, acknowledged the introduction with grace and poise, obviously not wishing to disclose her relationship to Holmes. The darker, more Mediterranean features that she had inherited from her Italian mother contrasted with Harriet's almost elfin face and bearing. Lucy wore her customary black wool dress over a high-necked white blouse, with no jewellery. I thought her features seemed to glow beneath the electric lighting of the conservatory, with a warmth that Harriet did not possess. Or perhaps it was my affection for Lucy that led to my seeing her this way, or my memories of how the Savoy Theatre's arc lamps had lit up her countenance when I had first seen her on the stage nearly a year earlier.

"Mr. Holmes, I've been an admirer of yours since Harriet and I were at Miss Porter's School in Connecticut." She looked at Lestrade and me, her green eyes wide and innocent. "And you must be Dr. Watson. I've absolutely devoured your stories about Mr. Holmes. And are you Inspector Lestrade? I've read about you too. And Lord Lansdowne, you and I shook hands last Guy Fawkes Night after I sang in *The Mikado* on Mr. Morgan's yacht. You may not remember me, but I remember you. It's not often I come face-to-face with a British Cabinet Secretary."

Lucy's performance seemed impeccable as far as I could tell. I risked a quick glance at Holmes, but his grey eyes betrayed no sign of emotion.

"What brings you to Dover, Miss James?" asked Lord Lansdowne. His manner was extremely courteous, but I thought I detected a note of suspicion in his tone.

"Our company gave a matinee performance at the theatre here this afternoon. Harriet and I are sailing for Germany tomorrow."

At the mention of Germany, I felt the same sense of apprehension that had come over me this morning. But Lucy was continuing as though it were the easiest, most natural thing in the world to enter the domain of the government that had paid Adam Worth to murder us all less than a year ago.

"Our first show in Germany will be for the Prince of Wales and his friends at the Bad Homburg spa," Lucy went on. "His Majesty's on his annual visit to take the waters and, I gather, to shed some weight. Mr. Tesla's going there too, hoping to meet the Prince. He's told us about an electrical cure-all machine that he thinks the Prince might like. Quite the opposite of this deadly contraption, here."

"Mr. Tesla," said Lord Lansdowne. "What have you told the ladies about this machine?"

Bent over the machine, Tesla looked up for a moment to reply, "Only its general capabilities."

"It looks like an enormous kettle," said Harriet.

"Only it holds lightning bolts. Like the key on Mr. Franklin's kite, only bigger," said Lucy.

From a quick look she directed at me, however, I could tell that Tesla's information, whatever it was, had not been nearly as incomprehensible to her as she let on.

Lord Lansdowne nodded. "Ladies, I wonder if you would please adjourn to the living room while we have a private word with Mr. Tesla, here?"

7. TOO MANY REQUESTS

Neither of the two ladies concealed her displeasure at being excluded from the discussion, but they both left without protest. Following their departure, we five men stood a bit awkwardly for a moment, inspecting the perimeter of the metallic structure.

Finally Holmes spoke. "How does the machine receive its electricity?"

"There is a powerful generator in a nearby shed, and a large tank of petrol to provide fuel," Lansdowne said. "My department paid for the installation."

"There is also an electric compressor to provide refrigeration," Tesla added. "Extreme cold is required for the manufacture of argon gas, and argon is a key component for this apparatus. You see these six metal tubes at the centre of the drum, pointing up at the metal ring. These contain argon, a chemically inert gas capable of containing the electric rays so that the energy may be focused for long-distance travel without losing its force."

"You are getting ahead of yourself, Mr. Tesla," said Lansdowne. "We cannot understand you."

"It is not necessary for you to know how the machine works." Tesla's expression grew urgent. "I will explain in due course. But first I must make you understand how you are to help us, Mr. Holmes."

"How?"

"I blame myself, but I have been busy with other matters—you may have read of my wireless transmissions, and of my generators that transform the energy of Niagara Falls into useful illumination. You may also have read of the fire that consumed my laboratory in New York City more than a year ago. Recreating what was lost there has taken an inordinate amount of time. Also I have developed an argon wand that emits energy at the same high frequencies that resonate within the cells of the human body. I credit this device with my own recovery from an accident in which I was struck down in the street by a large vehicle. Dr. Watson, I am sure you will want to know—"

Lansdowne interrupted, "Please come to the point, Mr. Tesla."

Sulkily, Tesla folded his arms high across his narrow chest, hands clutching his gaunt shoulders as though comforting himself. Then he smoothed the lapel of his impeccably tailored jacket and replied, "The point is that no man can work on all things at the same time. So I entrusted my lightning-ray project to Lord Kerren, who is a most competent fellow, if somewhat overambitious. He fancies himself the Kentish heir to the intellectual heritage of his fellow Englishman Faraday, and the Scot Maxwell. He has visited me in New York—in fact it was just before the unfortunate fire that has caused me such difficulty. Now, where was I—oh, yes. I was saying that Kerren has assembled the apparatus here. He telegraphed me that an initial trial had enjoyed complete success."

"Meaning what, precisely?" asked Holmes.

"Meaning that a large sheep tethered outside this conservatory was electrocuted and killed."

"Was the body charred?"

"According to the message I received from Lord Kerren about a month ago, yes."

"What happened then?"

"Lord Kerren sailed for Germany. He planned to meet with His Royal Highness the Prince of Wales, who travels to the German spa at Bad Homburg annually for purposes of his health."

"Why?"

"His Royal Highness is providing funds for this work. Lord Kerren wanted to communicate the initial success and to request additional financial support."

"Did he meet with the Prince?"

"I do not know. Kerren sent me a wire from Germany to say that I should join him. However, I first came here. I arrived on Friday as scheduled, and was pleased to see that all the arrangements I had requested had been made."

"Were these scientific arrangements?"

"They were personal in nature. I require an electric circuit in my room, so that I can operate a particular apparatus that provides electrical current beneficial to my health. Also I need a separate table where I may dine in privacy. Also—"

"Why did you not travel directly to Germany?"

"I needed to see the completed machine for myself."

"But upon your arrival, you discovered that an important part of the machine was missing."

"How can you know that?"

Holmes pointed to the metal tubes in the middle of the machine. "Those tubes—I believe you said they contained argon—have copper wires projecting from their tops. They must connect to something. And there are empty metal brackets on this metal ring above the tubes. That also indicates a missing component. Your expression of concern signified to me that the missing component was a critical part of the weapon."

Seeing Tesla's nod of assent, Holmes turned to Lansdowne. "Mr. Secretary, I now understand. This empty ring is the reason you called for me this morning. Why was this apparatus left unguarded?"

"Lord Kerren had conducted his work in secret. He did not wish to call attention to his laboratory, so he instructed my men to stay away from his home. I supported his instruction." Lansdowne lowered his gaze, embarrassed. "I take full responsibility," he added.

"Mr. Tesla, can you describe the missing apparatus?"

"I cannot. But Lord Kerren will be returning soon. He may have plans or sketches."

"Mr. Secretary, how can you be certain that Lord Kerren did not take the apparatus with him to Germany?"

"My men at the garrison helped him close up Kerren House and drove him to the Port of Dover. This machine was intact when they left the building."

"Very well. Now let us review the position. You, Mr. Tesla, want me to retrieve an electrical apparatus that you cannot describe."

"I may be able to sketch out some possible—"

Holmes continued as though Tesla had not spoken. "Lord Lansdowne, you want me to determine who took the apparatus and whether the Germans have it, and whether they can make a copy and manufacture it to be used against us. If the apparatus is indeed in Germany, you also want me to bring the apparatus back to England if that is possible."

"Yes, I—"

"Lady Radnar wants me to avoid scandal by quickly identifying a body that has been charred beyond recognition, and which, I can tell you from close observation a few hours ago, has had its teeth removed. Further, she will want me to prove that the body has nothing to do with the activities that take place here, even though you, Mr. Tesla, affirm that your apparatus has already brought about the demise of an ill-fated sheep."

He paused, looking at Lord Lansdowne, his tone deliberately restrained. "Am I correct so far?"

"Quite so."

"Then a few additional inquiries are called for." He ticked off the points on his long fingers. "Who was the traitor who learned Inspector Lestrade was to call on me this morning? Who gave the order for him to be intercepted outside my Baker Street rooms? Who carried out the attack on Lestrade? And why were the attackers so helpful as to provide a warning, and to speak it with German accents? In addition, since I was standing beside Sergeant Stubbs when he came to be shot this afternoon, I would like to know who shot him and who gave the order to shoot."

My spirits rose. Even as Holmes issued this rapid-fire litany of questions, all of which appeared difficult or even impossible to answer, I could hear in his voice the quickening of excitement that accompanied his rising to a new challenge.

Lansdowne asked, "Are you prepared to undertake the mission?"

"You ask a great deal of one man, Mr. Secretary."

"You have been of great value to us in the past."

"The traitor within your ranks must be located and unmasked."

"Agreed."

"And I want no further knowledge of the case to be communicated to the ladies we have just met. If they are to travel to Germany, for their own safety they should know nothing of these matters."

Lansdowne's wide brown eyes gave a momentary glance towards Tesla, and then returned to Holmes. "I have a reservation on that point, but I agree to do as you ask."

"Then I shall begin at the Dover Castle garrison, with the investigation of the body recovered here in Dover, and we shall see where that leads us. I am not convinced that I ought to travel to Germany. The missing component may still be here in England, and the warning I received—delivered so heavily laden with a German accent—may have been an attempt to conceal that fact."

Lansdowne nodded. "Very well, though I hope I can persuade you to include the ladies. Now let us return to the hotel."

Tesla found the appropriate switch and extinguished the conservatory lights. He and Lestrade moved towards the exit. Lansdowne hung back, indicating with a glance that he had something further to say to Holmes.

Outside the glassed walls of the conservatory, the twilight sky was now visible. To the south-east, over the Channel, lay the line of dark clouds from the retreating storm and, above them, the small crescent moon. Within the clouds, as though directed by heaven, came the momentary flash of a lightning bolt.

Tesla had opened the door to the front portion of the house. From within the parlour came the ringing of a telephone.

Holmes asked Lansdowne, "Why would you want the two ladies to know any further details of this matter?"

"Because, Mr. Holmes, Harriet Radnar is an agent of the War Department."

Holmes seemed about to reply, but at that moment Harriet appeared in the doorway. "The hotel has just telephoned, Mr. Secretary. Sergeant Stubbs is dead. They say he has been murdered."

8. AFTERMATH OF A MURDER

At Radnar House we took the stairs two at a time and were soon in the second-floor hallway. The door to Stubbs's room was open. On the carpet outside the doorway lay a knitted black wool watch cap, of the sort that could be bought for a shilling or two at any used-clothing store in any British port city. Holmes picked it up as we went into the room. There the nurse sat slumped on the carpet beside the bed, rubbing the back of her skull.

Sadly, a glance at the sergeant was enough to understand that there was nothing I could do for him. From the grotesque angle of his head and neck, it was plain that his cervical vertebrae had been twisted and broken.

"I heard a thump in the hallway," the nurse said, "and then a man was inside here, staring at me through his black mask. He had a gun. He made me turn around, and then he hit me from behind. I think he must have done the same to the guard out there in the hall."

"Was this the mask?" Holmes showed her the watch cap. Several inches above the knitted lower border, two eyeholes had been cut out, leaving a jagged fringe around the two openings.

The nurse nodded.

Holmes asked, "What colour were his eyes?"

"Blue, I think. Or brown. Maybe they were—oh, I can't remember! It all happened so quickly—"

"Would you recognize his voice?"

"He didn't speak. Just gestured with that gun of his—a pistol, I don't know what kind—and pushed me 'round."

"Did you notice anything else about him? His hands? The way he stood? The way he smelled? Try to remember, no matter how trivial it may seem."

The nurse shook her head. "Just the pistol. But I remember those eyes, even though I can't remember the colour. They were cold and hard."

A few moments later we stood at the far end of the corridor, at the top of the staircase. Chill, moist air surged around and over us, bringing with it the salty tang of the sea. We looked down to the bottom of the stairs, where the door to the outside had been left wide open.

I awoke just after dawn the next morning in my room at Radnar House. From my window I could see the dull-grey waters of the Channel and the beginnings of the sunrise. The rain had passed and there were patches of blue sky that promised fairer weather. Closer to the hotel, at the edge of the cliff, I could see a tall, slender figure striding through the high grasses and up to the edge of the lawn. It was Holmes, in his jacket without his Ulster. He carried a rifle.

He looked up towards my window and waved, but did not beckon me to join him.

I dressed quickly, nonetheless. I opened the door of my room.

Lucy James stood before me.

She had raised her right hand, about to knock. Her green eyes were wide with excitement. Upon seeing me, she reached out and took my arm, turning into the hallway to walk towards the staircase. We might have been going to the dining room for breakfast together, although it was nearly an hour too soon for that.

"He's outside with a rifle," she said as we turned for the stairway. "I bet it's the same rifle that wounded the police sergeant."

"Very likely."

"He told Mr. Lansdowne he didn't want to go to Germany."

"How do you know?"

"Mr. Lansdowne told Harriet and she told me. Why doesn't he want to go?"

As we reached the bottom of the main staircase, Lucy led me to a pair of upholstered chairs that were positioned at the edge of the hall, where we could continue our conversation in private. Briefly I described the events of the previous morning, including the threat from the Germans.

"Harriet didn't mention any of that."

"Did she tell you she works for the War Department?"

"Only that she sends reports to Mr. Lansdowne's people from time to time. I didn't ask her to elaborate." She sat up straighter, placed both hands in her lap, and all the light of the morning seemed to dance in those iridescent eyes of hers. I could not help recalling our initial meeting in D'Oyly Carte's office, when she had first so captivated both Holmes and me. Now her youthful bravado had a deeper assurance beneath it, though she still had an air of unguarded vulnerability. I wondered how much of the change was attributable to her accomplishments on the stage since then. I also wondered how much had come from her finally having the certain knowledge that came from meeting her true parents and discovering that her father was Sherlock Holmes. I felt pride for him and for her.

"It's good to sit with you, Dr. Watson," she was saying. "I was in such a rush Saturday."

"It's good to see you too, Lucy," I replied, quite conscious of the fondness I had always experienced for her, and feeling a little uncomfortable at the formality of her addressing me as "Dr. Watson." I know she must have perceived my emotion, for she took a deep breath before she went on.

"So the Germans are toying with him. One afternoon their message is in the papers, and the next morning they are on his doorstep."

"It was an odd message."

"They are showing him they know where he lives, and that they can reach out to harm him at any time."

"You can see why he wants you to stay apart from him."

"Whenever I want to help him he pushes away. He's doing that now."

"He is concerned for your safety. With every case there is risk—"

"I know, and this case looks like it could be a doozy."

"Excuse me?"

"A corker. Difficult. Dangerous. I *will* help him." Her eyes went to the French window alongside the main foyer door. "And I'm not going to take no for an answer."

"I doubt that you are in a position to bargain."

"Oh, that's not going to matter. No bargaining will be required. I'm quite prepared. But look, there he is outside."

She got to her feet and in a few moments we were outside the hotel portico and standing with Holmes on the wide gravel carriage path. He nodded at me and said, "Good morning, Lucy."

"Good morning." She eyed his jacket critically. "You must be freezing. Haven't they cleaned your overcoat?"

"Watson and I will visit the garrison at Dover Castle after he has eaten breakfast. The hotel concierge promised to have my Ulster ready before we leave."

She glanced towards the edge of the cliff. "Breakfast won't be ready for an hour. Did you find footprints?"

"The trail is an indecipherable sludge."

"Because all you men walked up and down it in the rain. What about where you found the rifle?"

Holmes pointed to the grass at the edge of the cliff, some twenty feet away from the trail. He shook his head.

"Is there a depression in the grass where he may have waited?"

"Farther down along the trail there is a shallow impression in the cliff. It has a clear view of the beach where we were standing."

"Were there cigar ashes? Rifle shells?"

"The area had been swept."

She looked at the rifle in Holmes's hand and spoke, almost to herself. "He saw you arrive, followed you, got into position, waited until the Army men had taken the body, and then shot poor Sergeant Stubbs. Lord Lansdowne's men arrived at the hotel, so they would have heard him if he fired another shot. He didn't want to risk that; he dropped his weapon and walked away. The question is, did he come back later?"

Instead of answering, Holmes said, "Please tell me about Miss Radnar. Can she be trusted? And be quick."

"Why?"

"She will be with us in a moment." Holmes gestured in the direction of the hotel. Harriet Radnar walked swiftly towards us with a determined stride, the skirts of her long black dress billowing beneath her black woollen shawl. Her head was bare, save for the black headband. Her long blond tresses streamed behind her on the wind. Behind her, two horses and a black carriage were departing, clattering away on the gravel drive.

Lucy said, "Both of us were shunned a lot at school, she because of her British aristocratic airs, and I because I had no family. So that brought us together."

"Why was she sent to America?"

"She doesn't get along with her stepmother. Her father can't abide it when they argue. She doesn't know about—you and me."

Holmes nodded in acknowledgement as Miss Radnar joined us.

She looked at Lucy for a moment, then at Holmes. It may have been my imagination, but I thought she was noticing a resemblance between daughter and father. She gestured at the departing carriage. "Inspector Lestrade has gone back to London. Another carriage is waiting at Kerren House. Mr. Tesla is inside it. We shall ride with him to the garrison."

Holmes's gaze narrowed. "We?"

"The Secretary wants me there. He has told you that I work for him, has he not? Besides, I have a feeling."

Lucy said, "If you're going, I'm going."

9. AT THE GARRISON

We arrived nearly fifteen minutes late for the medical officer's examination at the Army garrison. Fitzwilliam, the strapping young lieutenant who had met our carriage, had looked quizzically at Holmes at first, clad as he was in his indoor jacket while the rest of us wore overcoats against a wind that seemed to have lost none of the chill it had taken up at its arctic origin. Once introduced, however, the lieutenant had been effusive in his admiration for Holmes. Also, I thought, he was inspired by the prospect of escorting and holding the attention of the two ladies.

I wished Lucy and Harriet were less politely attentive as the lieutenant took us on an unnecessary tour of the Dover Castle perimeter. He paused repeatedly to point out historical features, spending more time than needed, I thought, in explaining how the garrison fulfilled its current mission, which was to guard the coastline against smugglers. Then he stopped us where we had a clear view of the port below. A naval vessel was unloading a cargo of wounded men. Some lay on their stretchers beneath drab olive blankets. Others stood on crutches, their bandaged limbs protruding from beneath their khaki uniform greatcoats.

I recalled the cold, rainy morning at Portsmouth jetty sixteen years earlier that had occasioned my own harsh and lonely homecoming from the Afghan war. Memories of Candahar, my wound, my illness, my weakness—they all returned. My impatience turned to pity. I asked Lieutenant Fitzwilliam where the men had been.

"South Africa or India, most like. You can see the *Victoria* on the horizon, steaming away. These are the lucky ones. They'll go to Buckland Hospital, not far off. On *Victoria* there'll be more, and they'll go to Netley Hospital near Southampton. My brother went to Netley when he lost his leg in the Transvaal."

Tesla spoke up. "They would heal more rapidly if they had the benefit of my electrotherapy machines," he said. "Do you think the British Army would be interested in that, Mr. Holmes?"

Holmes turned and walked onwards without reply.

Finally we crossed the castle moat and ascended the wide stone steps to the second floor of the outer building. There, another young lieutenant saluted crisply and told us "the Secretary himself" was waiting. He opened a heavy oak door and showed us into the great hall, a cavernous stone enclosure, cathedral-like in its breadth and height.

In one of the triangular alcoves built into the enormously thick castle walls, we saw the yellow light of electric lanterns. In this alcove the medical officer in charge of the examination had set up his shop. Red bearded, with a brown leather apron cloaking his barrel chest, he was engrossed in examining the blackened object that lay before him, illuminated by a cluster of floor lamps that surrounded the steel examining table.

Lord Lansdowne saw us first and murmured a quiet word or two into the ear of the industrious medical officer. The man looked up instantly. Lansdowne introduced Holmes, Tesla, and me, but referred to

Lucy and Harriet as "Mr. Tesla's assistants." The medical officer, introduced as Major Dawes, looked dubiously at the two young women.

"Not a fit sight for ladies," he said.

"They will stand back and avert their gaze if they find it necessary," Holmes replied, striding quickly to stand at the foot of the table. He took his magnifying glass from his pocket. "Now, Major, what have you learned thus far?"

In a few terse sentences, the major reported his findings, while Holmes shuffled around the body, squinting at the blackened flesh through his magnifying glass. Beneath a one-inch layer of char, the musculature was intact and not inconsistent with that of a drowning victim. The man had not drowned, however, as the lungs were not waterlogged. The cause of death appeared to be massive crushing of the skull, accompanied by severe damage to the mandible and maxilla. There were no rings on the fingers, and, due to the burning, no identifying scars or other skin markings.

Holmes nodded. "Mr. Tesla, could this burning have been caused by your apparatus?"

The slender inventor was pressing a lavender handkerchief, presumably perfumed, to his nose. "Possibly. If we might examine the sheep that Kerren used for his earlier experiment—"

"The animal was served as mutton in the hotel restaurant. I interviewed the chef this morning," Holmes replied. Holmes turned back to the major. "Have you catalogued the contents of the stomach?"

"They indicate a beef stew, with carrots and peas, recently ingested at the time of death."

"Which was?"

"Judging from the state of decomposition, no more than one week ago."

"Anything else?"

The major shook his head, whereupon Holmes took out the tape measure he habitually carried on his person and spent a few moments bent over the subject, moving to and fro. Then he stood, pocketed the tape measure, and faced us.

Lord Lansdowne asked, "Well, Mr. Holmes?"

"A most singular case. We shall want a list of any persons who have gone missing from the Dover area since the fifteenth of August, the date that Lord Kerren closed up his laboratory."

"But if the time of death was no more than one week ago, I fail to see why we should investigate persons who may have been missing for nearly a month and a half."

"It is as well to be inclusive" was Holmes's only reply.

At that moment we heard raised voices from the great hall entrance, and then someone called, "Henry! I have urgent news!"

Lord Lansdowne looked momentarily startled at the use of his given name, but he seemed to recognize the voice. "It's all right, then, Lieutenant," he said. "Mr. Arkwright may enter."

I was astonished to hear the name of a famous violinist whom Holmes and I had seen on several occasions. For a moment I wondered if this could be a mere coincidence, but then Mr. Arkwright came towards us, removing his hat, and I saw the distinctive shaved head, completely bald, familiar to audiences at concert halls on both sides of the Atlantic.

He strode briskly towards us, eyes flashing as if he were about to deliver in midstride whatever message he brought for Lord Lansdowne. Then his expression softened as he saw the ladies, and his aquiline features crinkled in a delighted smile as he recognized Holmes. "Mr. Sherlock Holmes, I believe? It is most comforting to be in the company of a fellow violinist."

"Dr. Watson here and I have both admired your virtuosity," Holmes replied. "But I hardly qualify as your fellow."

"Though you own a Stradivarius, I believe—"

Lord Lansdowne interrupted. "Adrian, I did not expect you until tomorrow. We were just finishing up here." He turned to the medical officer. "Major Dawes, we will take our leave of you now. If you discover anything further, please notify me at once."

The major nodded obediently. As we turned to depart, I saw Arkwright give a momentary glance at the charred remains. Then he closed his eyes and shuddered.

10. AN UNEXPLAINED EVENT

Minutes later we entered the garrison commander's office. The room had been built into a turret on the north-east side of the castle. The outer wall of the office had been modified to admit a pair of wide French doors. Through their glass panels we could see the familiar gapped stone fortifications that had once sheltered medieval archers as they crouched to fire their feathered missiles. Beyond, to the south-east, we could see the blue waters of the Channel. To the north was the grey line of the beach where we had found the charred remains. Above the beach were the white cliffs, and, atop the cliffs, the shadowy profile of Radnar House.

Lansdowne motioned us to a conference table. "I have asked the garrison commander for a few minutes' private use of his office."

"He has a superb view, doesn't he?" said Arkwright, seating himself opposite Holmes and me and next to Harriet, who sat beside Lucy and Tesla. "I understand he can tell the time on the cathedral clock in Calais if the weather is fair. With binoculars, of course."

"From our hotel you can also see the clock," Harriet said. "You can see this castle too."

"Let us get down to business," Lansdowne said as he took his place at the head of the table. "We all have a single mission here—to find and recover a key component of an electrical weapon. Mr. Tesla here may be able to tell us more about the component. To accomplish this, we must work together. It is imperative that we know and trust one another. Now, except for Miss James, each of you is well known to me, and, Miss James, I believe that Mr. Holmes can vouch for you. I recall that you were of considerable assistance to us last November."

Lucy nodded. I glanced at Holmes, trying to remember if Lansdowne knew that Lucy was Holmes's daughter, and saw him shake his head. The movement was barely perceptible.

"Next, let me introduce Adrian Arkwright to the rest of you," Lansdowne continued. "You may know him as a renowned musician. His performances throughout Europe and America, however, enable him to move in rarefied circles where he is in a position to acquire useful information."

"In plain English, I'm a spy," Arkwright said, with a winning smile. "And if we're trusting each other, I do have that urgent news to report."

"First let me complete the introductions. Mr. Tesla is known by reputation on both continents. He has been working with Lord Kerren, the uncle of Harriet Radnar—"

"'Working with' Kerren is not accurate," said Tesla, bristling. "I gave him access to my diagrams in New York two years ago. Shortly thereafter, all my records were destroyed in a fire. I have seen his work here, but only yesterday. He has assembled six of my electrical resonant transformer coils and connected them to six metal tubes, which are pointed at a metal ring. Whatever belongs on the ring is missing from the apparatus. I cannot describe it or vouch for its performance."

"Have you an idea as to the function of the missing part?" Holmes asked.

"I cannot say with certainty. However, this ring is in a position to focus the energy from the six metal tubes connected to my six transformer coils."

"The way one can start a fire with sunlight using a magnifying lens?"

"That would be an imprecise description of its function, but adequate. Electricity is not like light, and cold glass does not conduct electricity."

"So this missing lens-y thingummy," said Arkwright. "It's made of metal?"

Tesla stiffened, apparently taking offence at Arkwright's casual tone. Then he shrugged, as though refusing to dignify the question with a reply.

After a moment's silence, Lansdowne said, "Let us continue with our introductions. Adrian, this is Lord Kerren's niece, Harriet Radnar. She is one of us. We have recently placed her in the D'Oyly Carte Opera Company."

"That statement is not entirely accurate," said Harriet. "Lord Kerren is the brother of my stepmother. He is not my uncle."

"Thank *you*, Miss Radnar. I seem to be getting my facts muddled this morning. Possibly that is due to the excitement and gravity of the situation. In any event, Miss Radnar, is it accurate to say that you are about to depart for Bad Homburg, where Lord Kerren is now?"

"He is staying there, in the residence that belongs to my father."

"Thank you. Adrian, will you be staying here at the hotel?"

"I will be sailing for Calais this afternoon. I have a concert in Baden-Baden on Wednesday."

Lucy spoke up. "How far is that from Bad Homburg? Harriet and I would love to attend."

"It is less than three hours away. There is a train." He turned to Lansdowne. "But Henry, who is this lovely young lady?"

"I beg your pardon, Miss James," said Lansdowne. "Adrian, this is Miss Lucy James, also with the D'Oyly Carte Opera Company and sailing for Bad Homburg this afternoon. I hope that she also will provide us with valuable information."

"Charmed, Miss James," said Arkwright. "Lovely girl like you, you'll want to keep a weather eye out for the Prince. He's been known—"

"I have heard the gossip," Lucy replied.

"Now, Adrian," said Lansdowne. "What is your news?"

His moment at hand, Arkwright leaned back in his chair, interlaced his fingers, and turned his palms outwards, luxuriating in a stretch. "The Kaiser is staying in Bad Homburg at his castle. Normally he is not there in September, but he has come back. He met with the Prince last Friday. I attended their meeting as the entertainment—they're uncle and nephew and hate each other, as you know, and music hath charms."

"Who asked for you to attend?"

"The Kaiser. He told the Prince that what he called the 'electric cannon' invented by Lord Kerren and Mr. Tesla is in his possession—"

Tesla looked alarmed. "I assure you I have nothing to do with the German government—"

"—and he proposed that England and Germany form an alliance to produce the weapon for their own uses and to keep it away from France and Russia."

Holmes said, "Try to give us his exact words, Mr. Arkwright. Be as precise as you can manage."

But Arkwright seemed not to hear. He was staring out of the wide glass French windows and getting to his feet. "Look out there!" he exclaimed, coming around the table.

We looked around. Outside, hanging in the air over the Channel, about a hundred feet above us and perhaps a quarter mile out to sea, was a military balloon, bathed in the sunlight, as though it were a leading performer lit up by an arc light on a theatre stage. Holmes flung open the French doors and we crowded between them, the better to see.

"Look on the right side of the sphere," said Holmes. "At the lower edge. Smoke."

We came outside for a better view. Leaning over the ramparts, we stared as the balloon drifted out over the ships in the harbour and towards the blue waters of the Channel.

"It's coming up from the gondola," said Lucy.

We watched in fascination. There were indeed wisps of smoke issuing from inside the gondola, a black-painted wicker basket suspended from the balloon. The gondola appeared to be empty, though even from this distance it was apparent that it had sufficient capacity to carry several men and a quantity of weapons.

In the next moment, there was a brilliant flash. Above the gondola the balloon suddenly split apart into fragments. Then it collapsed midair into a heap of rope and fabric, and plummeted, along with the gondola, into the grey Channel waters.

"What in God's name was that?" Arkwright asked.

Harriet pointed to the coastal cliffs to the north of us. "I can see Radnar House over there," she said. "And I saw a flash of light just before the explosion. I think the light came from Kerren House."

"Someone is taunting us," said Lansdowne.

11. RETURN TO KERREN HOUSE

Holmes and I lost no time in returning to Kerren House, pausing only for Holmes to acquire an ordnance map of the area, which he folded and tucked into his inside jacket pocket. Lansdowne and Tesla accompanied us. Arkwright wanted to come along as well, and so did Lucy and Harriet; however, as Holmes pointed out, the boat for Calais would be departing later, and they would need to pack their luggage for the journey to their respective destinations in Germany.

At the entrance, two guards in their smart black uniforms drew themselves up to attention as we approached. The taller man told us they had seen no one on the drive all morning.

Much to their chagrin, however, when we walked around to the rear of Kerren House, the exterior of the conservatory told a different tale. The glass-paned entry door stood wide open, with the glass from the pane above the door's lock neatly cut out in a circular pattern. The glass disc itself lay neatly to one side of the door frame. Close to the open doorway was the empty metallic circle of the apparatus that we had inspected the previous evening. The great kettledrum shape was now angled slightly upwards.

The red-faced guards made their apologies. Lansdowne sent the taller man back to his post, bidding the other remain at the edge of the lawn leading to the cliff, where he could keep watch on the trail below.

Holmes appeared to take no notice of these arrangements. Nor did he look for any footprints that the intruder might have left on the lawn. Instead he entered the conservatory and motioned for us to join him alongside the apparatus.

"Mr. Tesla," he said. "Would you please inspect the wires protruding from the six metal argon cylinders and tell us whether they may have recently been connected."

"The wires have been moved. They are not positioned in the way I left them last night. Also, the brackets on the top ring are at different angles."

Lansdowne asked, "So we can conclude that the machine was made operable, and then once more disabled?"

"There is nothing here that contradicts such an assumption," said Tesla.

"Someone wanted to demonstrate that the machine was workable," I observed. "Whoever it was deliberately left the conservatory without taking the trouble to conceal what he had done."

"Once again, the key apparatus is nowhere to be found," said Holmes. "The question is whether the person responsible is taking it to Germany." His fingertip traced the circumference of the empty metal ring. "This ring is approximately one foot in diameter. If that indicates the size of the missing piece, it could easily be concealed in a suitcase."

Lansdowne's dark eyes blazed. "I will post soldiers at every departing vessel and every departing train. Every suitcase and every parcel of that size will be inspected. We shall do all we can."

"Most commendable," Holmes said. "But assuming the missing piece can be disassembled, our thief might distribute the parts to several people. Those people might leave England by several different ports, and then reassemble anywhere."

"Well, it's no good taking a defeatist tack—"

"However, we can investigate on several alternative lines," Holmes went on. "Interview the hotel staff. Inquire of neighbours or passersby whether they have seen anyone enter or leave this house. Cover the path below. See where the balloon was brought in. Was it launched from the beach? What were the prevailing winds at the time? Was the intention to demonstrate to us while we were meeting at the garrison, and if so, how did anyone know we were meeting there?"

"I think that last is unlikely," said Lansdowne.

"Yet we have established that there is a traitor in your organization."

Lansdowne's worried expression took on an air of defiance. "You need not throw that up at me. I am perfectly aware—"

"You said Harriet Radnar has been working for you," Holmes interrupted smoothly once more, his tone remaining just as bland. "And you indicated that Lucy James would be reporting to you from Germany as well. Why do you need a second actress?"

"The reason is a sensitive one."

I saw a momentary flash of annoyance in Holmes's grey eyes. Then he replied, "Have you ever had cause to doubt my discretion? Or Dr. Watson's?"

After a pause and a long, searching look at Holmes, Lansdowne replied. "The Crown Prince is unpredictable and unreliable. He is an intelligent, well-educated, and headstrong man, who for some years has been thoroughly dissatisfied with the limited influence permitted him by Her Majesty. In consequence, he always seeks to play a more meaningful role, which gets us into difficulty."

"I do not follow you, Mr. Secretary."

"This alliance business that Arkwright has described between the Kaiser and the Prince would be an example."

"Yes, but I do not see where Miss James fits in."

"I shall be blunt. The Prince of Wales fancies Miss James."

"You hope he will tell her something in . . . private."

"At an unguarded moment, shall we say?"

I saw the colour rise in Holmes's cheeks. Yet such was his self-control that this was my only clue as to the emotion he must have felt at seeing his daughter being made a pawn in what surely could be described as a dangerous espionage intrigue. To Lansdowne or Tesla, he must have appeared no more sensitive about Lucy's proposed role than any decent man would about any young woman's being asked to place herself in a compromising position.

"How do you know of the Prince's feelings for Miss James?" Holmes asked.

"He told Miss Radnar, after seeing Miss James in a performance at the Savoy Theatre in June."

I watched Holmes closely. His clear grey eyes continued to conceal the emotion that I knew he must have felt. Although he presented himself to the world as a calculating, machine-like intellect, and I attempted to sustain this impression in all my published accounts of our adventures, I knew this was a deliberate role that he, the consummate actor, had taken upon himself to play in order to protect those close to him.

Tesla smiled in the way of a man in the company of other men. "She is quite attractive. I can understand His Majesty's opinion."

"Indeed," said Holmes, still appearing indifferent. "I believe she has been in the employ of the company for nearly a year. No doubt she has the experience and the knowledge required for her to take care of herself."

"I must be returning to the garrison," said Lansdowne.

12. OUTDOOR INVESTIGATION

A few minutes later we had reached the generator shed, a small rough wooden structure only a few steps from the edge of the cliff. Holmes opened the unpainted wooden door, looked in, and then pointed to the black metal object that thrummed steadily at the side of the shed. "Mr. Tesla?"

"An electrical generator. The metal tank alongside contains petrol, judging from the odour."

A rusted pipe led upwards from the generator to the wooden boards that formed the roof, barely six inches over our heads. From the base of the generator, two sets of wires, each braided into a thick cable and covered with black fabric, led to the roof, several feet from where the pipe made its exit.

A thought occurred to me. "Holmes," I asked, "do you think someone might have used the hot gas exhausted by the generator in order to fill the balloon?"

He was already outside, bent over, walking carefully around the shed. "I see no footprints or markings to suggest the use of a ladder."

"Possibly the ground has been swept."

"However, I do see eleven five-gallon fuelling cans stacked neatly here at the back." I heard the tinny sound of rapping, repeated eleven times. "They all appear to be empty."

The cables from the generator were hung on wooden poles about half as tall and thick as those that carried similar electric wires on London streets. Two of the cables led to Kerren House. A third led to another outbuilding, larger than the generator shed, but also with rough board exterior walls, only a few paces away. This building was silent.

Holmes opened the door to the other outbuilding. It was heavily padded with decrepit-looking pads of some sort of quilting. The same type of quilting had been applied to the interior walls and ceiling. The cotton spilled out of the pads at random intervals, sagging down as if it had been neglected for some time. Inside at the far right end was a tall wooden box, painted white with its own door. The black cable that descended from the ceiling entered the box from an opening at the top. On our left, in puddles of water littered with hay and the remnants of hessian sacking, were blocks of ice, layered on more hessian and stacked in rows that ascended like stairs to the low ceiling.

"Mr. Tesla?"

Tesla, after a dubious glance at the wet and grimy floor and at his sawdust-tarnished patent leather shoes, advanced to the tall box. He opened the door and glanced inside. "This would be a refrigeration compression unit. I expect it was used to manufacture argon to contain the electrical beam, but I do not see any collection apparatus." He looked back at the melting blocks of ice, then at two metallic plates, bulging with tubes that ran from an opening in the wall of the tall box, through the plates, and then back into the box. "The cold fluid coming from the condenser inside this box is pumped through these tubes into these hollow plates—"

Holmes interrupted. He was bent over the lowest level of ice blocks, closely inspecting the fibres of hessian that were embedded in their upper surface. "Could the machine be used to manufacture these blocks of ice?"

"Only with different equipment. Here we have no collection box in which blocks could be formed. Also, ice is commonly available from the commercial icehouses, so manufacture here would not be economical."

Holmes had scraped some of the hessian fibres into an envelope, which he now tucked into his jacket pocket. "Why is the refrigeration machine located here, rather than in the conservatory?"

"You would need to ask Lord Kerren. I suppose he might have placed the machine here for reasons of economy. The plates cool the room, so while he was chilling air in order to extract the argon within it, the cold plates would slow down the rate that the ice melts. And the heat from the compressor, as you see, escapes the insulated box and the room through this metal pipe leading to the roof."

"Yet the refrigeration unit is turned off. And we are three months from winter. Presumably this is the time when delivery from commercial sources becomes most expensive."

"What are you suggesting?"

"No matter. Lord Kerren may clear up the matter for us. Watson, do you detect the scent of coal smoke?" Holmes was exiting through the open doorway. He turned his steps towards the back of the icehouse. I followed him and together we reached the edge of the cliff.

Leaning over the precipice, we saw below us several men manoeuvring a rowing boat down to the water's edge. Closer to the cliff was a gypsy caravan. A thin wisp of smoke issued from a chimney pipe at the back of its roof.

13. FAREWELL AND HELLO

Holmes was keen to speak with the gypsies, so a few minutes later we were crossing the lawn at the rear of Radnar House, about to descend the walking trail that would take us to the beach. At the centre of the lawn, however, Tesla stopped.

"Here I must bid you farewell," he said. "I depend on several extremely busy men to fund my projects, and I have appointments with one of them in Calais. I must not keep him waiting. At this stage of my work, my constant need for capital must be my first priority."

"I am sure many who enjoy the benefits of electricity are grateful to you," Holmes replied.

Tesla's face tightened and he looked away as if he were momentarily embarrassed. Then he turned to me. "Dr. Watson, I do hope you will take the opportunity to visit me in Bad Homburg. As a medical man, you will be highly interested in the advantages of electricity as a mode of therapy for a great number of illnesses. No doubt you can learn much that will assist you in your medical practice."

He held out his gloved hand and I shook it politely. I did not know whether electricity was indeed the panacea that Mr. Tesla obviously thought it was, or whether it was the humbug and quackery that gave so many in my profession occasion to scoff. I wished for a moment that I had kept up with the latest published research on the subject.

But Holmes was speaking. "Mr. Tesla, I hope you will be careful while you are in Germany. If indeed someone there is in possession of the missing component, you may be coerced into helping to make it operational."

Tesla looked away without replying, then turned and strode towards the hotel.

We started down the path a moment later. After only a few paces, however, we halted.

On the path coming towards us was Lucy.

She said, "I was walking down to the beach when I heard your voices."

Holmes looked momentarily puzzled. "I thought you would be departing for your ferry to Calais."

"Oh, that's all changed. We're not leaving until tomorrow."

"Why?"

"Mr. Arkwright sails today, with Lady Radnar. He thinks the Germans are watching him, so he does not want to be seen travelling with Harriet or me. Particularly when we get to Germany."

"That may be a prudent precaution."

Lucy paused for a moment, then smiled with delight. "You think he doesn't want us with him?"

I saw a flash of pride in Holmes's grey eyes. "You are sharpening your powers of observation and deduction."

"Well, I wasn't there to hear him, actually. Harriet told me."

"Where is Harriet now?"

"In Radnar Hall. That's the house just between the hotel here and Kerren House. She said she wanted to look over some of her father's papers. By the way, the hotel porter sent your Ulster coat out for cleaning. The draper in St. Margaret's will have it ready this afternoon."

"And why are you out here on the walking path?"

"Oh, I saw some gypsies down on the beach. From my window at the hotel you can see right up to Kerren House. I saw their wagon, and I saw the smoke coming from a little metal chimney that pokes up out of its roof, and I had a wild surmise."

Holmes raised one eyebrow, but his grey eyes, I thought, shone with pride.

Lucy held his gaze. "So, shall we walk together?"

14. GYPSY HOSPITALITY

A few minutes later, Holmes, Lucy, and I had descended the pathway down to the beach. Holmes was in the lead, with Lucy walking by my side, her face wreathed in a smile of perfect happiness and satisfaction. We approached the gypsy caravan. A young gypsy woman sat knitting on the ledge at the back, clad in the colourful garb of her Romany heritage. She stood up as we came near, straightening the floral scarf that framed her strong, tanned features.

"Away," she said.

"I assure you, good lady—" Holmes began.

"I call my husband and brothers." She indicated several fishermen in a small rowing boat beyond the incoming waves, about a hundred yards from shore.

Holmes reached into his jacket pocket and produced a sheaf of bank notes. He handed over several of them, which were swiftly folded and put away. The woman's manner became decidedly less truculent.

"The lady say we can fish here," she said. "The gentile lady."

"Which lady?"

Her dark eyes went to the trail, and then she tilted her head upwards, indicating the top of the cliff.

"Lady Radnar?" said Holmes.

The gypsy woman gave a nod of assent.

"May I introduce myself? I am Sherlock Holmes, and these are my associates, Miss James and Dr. Watson. We are staying in the hotel next to Lady Radnar's house."

"I am called Drina."

"Do you cook the fish here as well?" asked Lucy.

"A good catch, we cook here."

"On your stove?"

She smiled at the question. "We make tea on stove."

"Do you cook fish on that?" Holmes pointed to a woven wire mattress support, rusted and blackened in the centre, lashed to the side of the wagon along with some thick metal rods and some squares of a metallic mesh made of a thinner wire. The upper part of a hessian sack of coal tilted precariously over the edge of a brown straw basket that hung alongside.

The woman nodded. "You like some tea?"

I caught Lucy's eye. She shrugged, as if to say, "So much for the idea that they inflated the balloon on this stove."

Now that we knew we had followed a false scent, I thought Holmes would decline tea, but he accepted graciously and soon we were each sipping a strong black brew, sweetened with molasses—like coarsely ground sugar. Holmes pointed to the high-water mark on the cliff, where brown remnants of seaweed still clung to the rough white chalk surface. "Where did you go when the storm came?"

She pointed up the coast to the north-west. "We work on farm."

"Near St. Margaret's?"

She nodded. "When the lady tell us, we leave. We come back today."

"Lady Radnar told you the storm was coming?"

"Sun was shining, but she said something fall. Glass something."

"Did you know what she meant?"

"We hitch pony"—she indicated the small Shetland standing placidly downwind of the wagon—"go fast."

Holmes gave one of his perfunctory smiles. "The storm came in the next day?"

"We stay on farm. Till today."

"And today, if your catch is good, you will cook many fish?"

She smiled and shrugged.

Lucy asked, "Did you see the big balloon and its basket a few hours ago?"

Drina's eyes widened with excitement. "It turned to fire!"

Holmes had set down his empty tea mug and strolled aimlessly on the beach gravel, alternating his gaze up to the top of the cliff and then down. Then he came back.

"I thank you for this very fine cup of tea. It has a very pleasant flavour. Is it imported?"

"You are welcome," Drina replied. "It is good tea."

"Where do you buy it?"

"Lady Radnar gave me. She is very kind person."

Holmes nodded politely. "Madam Drina, I thank you again for your kind hospitality. I hope your husband and brothers have great success and that over your coal fire tonight you cook many fish."

15. AT THE DRAPER'S

After we had taken our leave of Madam Drina, Lucy began to walk up the beach in the direction the gypsy woman had pointed. "I'm going to St. Margaret's to pick up your Ulster," she said to Holmes. "The wind's not getting any warmer, and it won't help for you to get chilled. You can come with me or not."

With a bemused smile, Holmes handed over his ordnance map. Lucy glanced at it and put her finger on one corner of the paper. "You see? It's just a cluster of cottages and a chapel. We'll find the draper's and then you can do whatever you've been planning to do, only you'll be warmer doing it."

Following the map, we soon found the sign proclaiming "Lampert, Draper," hung on a modest vine-covered brick-and-stone gabled building. The dwelling had been constructed so close to the edge of the narrow dirt road that a passing cart might have struck us as we waited at the doorway. A small grey-haired woman opened the door to usher us inside. She was plump and energetic, though with a worried cast to her wide hazel eyes. Inside, the room smelled of petrol and fuller's earth. I also caught the scent of boiled beef coming from the kitchen.

The interior walls were covered nearly to the ceiling with wide maple shelves, some holding bolts of fabric, but most empty.

"It's a blessing you're here," she said after we had introduced ourselves. Her name was Mrs. Lampert, and, like the gypsy woman, she did not recognize Holmes's or my name, which was not surprising, given the remote location and the presumable lack of leisure moments for her to read for pleasure. "I promised the man at Radnar House that I'd have your overcoat ready this afternoon, but I had to soak and scrub at it again and again and the fumes—well, I put it outside to air just before lunch. Let me bring it in and you can judge for yourself."

She withdrew to the rear of the little house. We heard the door latch click, and felt a rustle in the air as the door opened. Then we heard her cry out.

Holmes was at her side in an instant, with Lucy and I just behind. In the doorway Mrs. Lampert stood shivering, her hand to her mouth. On a clothes line directly before her hung Holmes's Ulster, slashed to tatters.

"You are not to distress yourself, Mrs. Lampert," Holmes said when we had brought the remnants of the garment inside and settled the trembling woman on a chair in the room adjacent to the one we had first entered. "This was plainly a bit of theatricality, meant as a message for me. I have had many similar in the past. You are not the target of the message, and once I depart, you will never be troubled again by whoever did this."

"How can you be sure?"

"It is my business, good lady. Have you ever had something like this happen before?"

"Certainly not!"

"Is anyone trying to drive your customers away?"

"To the contrary, we are well liked by all our neighbours. My husband's grandfather started this shop, and his father and then he, himself, continued the business. And we have great hopes to begin a larger establishment in Dover. Lord Radnar is arranging the capital for us. He is a regular and loyal customer, and he believes that my husband has a knack for designs that will please the gentry."

"He told you this?"

"Not me directly, but my husband heard it straight from Lady Radnar. Lovely woman, though I would have thought a bit young for His Lordship. But she is his second wife, you know."

"Is she a customer as well?"

"She had a shawl from us about two months ago and was very pleased with it. She had Stanley make up an entire new suit and waistcoat for Lord Radnar."

"She gave the order to your husband?"

"That was the same time she told him that Lord Radnar was prepared to discuss investing in the expansion of our little business. My husband met her in town and returned tremendously excited. He is with Lord Radnar now."

"Travelling in America, pursuing investment capital?"

"You do know things! Yes, investors need to meet personally with the men they are investing in, my husband says. Lord Radnar will introduce my husband to his clients and help him with the bargaining—although I am not to let that get about. Someone else might try to establish a similar business in Dover. It is a good little port, you know, where fabrics can be shipped in and finished goods shipped out to customers everywhere."

"When was the last time you heard from your husband?"

At Holmes's question her smile faded and her eyes took on the same worried expression I had noticed on our first arrival in the shop. "Since he sailed for New York a month ago I have had only one postcard."

"And you have been troubled by this lack of communication?"

"I try ever so hard not to let my imagination trouble me. The ships have to travel long distances and that takes a great deal of time. And my Stanley has never been the sort to look at another woman—he has been to Paris, even, on trips to buy new fabrics. I know I have no cause to fret."

"Please pardon me, but when we first arrived you appeared somewhat agitated. As though you were expecting disturbing news."

"I did not know who you were. For a moment I thought you had come from the government to tell me that my Stanley—well, that he had come to harm. I know it's foolish, but when I heard about that burned-up body on the beach, I had a dreadful premonition."

Holmes leaned forwards and spoke very quietly. "I have been brought in by the military to investigate these matters and have only this morning taken the measurements of the charred body. I can give you certainty as to whether it was your husband's."

Her eyes widened with respect and hope. "I should be ever so grateful, sir. My premonition was bad enough, but this morning the bellman who brought your coat told me about Sergeant Stubbs, and ever since—well, I'm afraid I've let my fears get the better of me."

"What connection do you have with the unfortunate Sergeant Stubbs?"

"Oh, he grew up in St. Margaret's. He still lives—lived—in his parents' cottage just around the corner. We all know—knew—him. When he was made sergeant, we were all glad to see him moving up in the ranks of the patrol, but he was no better than he should be, if you know what I mean."

"Why should his death cause you concern about your husband?"

She shook her head. "It's foolishness. Just foolishness."

"Please, Mrs. Lampert."

"Well, I saw Stubbs in the market the day after Stanley left for New York, and he said he'd seen him."

"You mean he saw your husband after the ship had sailed?"

"No, no—he said he'd seen Stanley getting on the ship. He was on dockside duty that day guarding the boarding line, and he said Stanley had passed right by him to walk up the gangplank."

"Why did that cause you concern?"

"It was his way of saying it. He had this sly look, as if he knew some kind of secret. Though how he could have known about our business with Lord Radnar is beyond me."

Holmes stood up. "Mrs. Lampert, can you show me the book where your husband records the measurements of his customers? Doubtless he makes his own garments. I presume his measurements are in the book there as well?"

"I'll fetch it," she replied, getting to her feet and returning moments later with a black ledger. "These are arranged alphabetically. You'll find Stanley's measurements in the middle."

"What are these?" Holmes held up several sketches of men in military uniforms, though the designs were unlike those of any nation I had ever seen.

"Oh, Stanley is always making little sketches of all sorts. He is very original that way."

Holmes nodded, and then spent a few moments rustling through the ledger and inspecting several of the pages closely. Finally he shut the book. "I am pleased to tell you that Mr. Lampert's measurements are not even remotely similar to those of the body found on the beach Saturday night."

The draper's wife gave a sigh of relief and a glad smile. "Thank you, Mr.—Is it Shamrock? I must beg pardon, for I am very bad at recollecting names. But you have been most kind, where many would not have been, your fine Ulster coat being so damaged and all. I'm afraid it's beyond my skill to repair, but possibly when Stanley returns—"

In the next room, Lucy had been rummaging through the garments hung on a metal rod. She emerged now, bearing a bundle of black fabric in her arms. "A nice tweed Inverness coat and cape," she said briskly, addressing Holmes and holding it up to his shoulders. "Not as trim as your Ulster, but the cape part is bound to fit you, being a cape, and the coat looks like it's long enough. It could be let out or taken in, I bet.

And the black matches your suit. We can't have you freezing. I have money in my reticule to pay for it if you don't."

"Your daughter's right," said Mrs. Lampert, taking the garment and glancing quickly at the paper tag attached to the hem. "I see she takes good care of you. You must be proud."

Holmes ignored the reference to Lucy being his daughter. He said, "Is the garment available for purchase?"

"Well, it is bespoke, but it's for a tall gentleman who is abroad at the moment and will not return for it until October. By then I can easily make another for him."

He nodded, then tried on the coat and cape and pronounced them both satisfactory. Then he took out a ten-pound note from his billfold.

"Oh, that's far too much," said Mrs. Lampert.

"But I require a few additions," Holmes said, placing the note into her hand. He bent and spoke quietly to the draper's wife for a moment.

"I can have those done for you in a quarter of an hour," she said.

At Holmes's direction, the three of us waited outside in the late-afternoon sun.

Lucy asked, "What were the alterations?"

"Pockets to the cape."

"Why did you whisper?"

"I wished to convey my respect. The poor woman has had a shock, and clearly she is distressed about her husband's absence."

"He is everything to her."

"We shall help to ensure his safe return, if we can."

"We?"

"I shall send a telegram to New York when we are away from here."

"What do you make of this destruction of your coat?"

"An attempt to distract or delay us."

"We were not followed. I was watching."

"As was I."

"But the Ulster was hung out to dry well before we arrived. Someone who knew it was coming here to be cleaned could have come here at any time this afternoon."

"And that knowledge—"

"Could only have come from Radnar House."

I saw Holmes's tight smile. I could not tell whether it evidenced his grim anticipation of trouble ahead, or his satisfaction at having led Lucy to the conclusion he was looking for.

"The damage to your coat puts me in mind of the attack on Lestrade yesterday," I observed. "A clumsy warning."

We could see a carriage approaching on the narrow earthen road. We moved closer to the cottage to get out of its path.

Then the door to the draper's shop opened and Mrs. Lampert appeared in the doorway. She held the black Inverness coat and cape clutched tightly to her chest. Whereas earlier she had seemed worried as she greeted us, now naked fear shone in her widened eyes.

Behind her stood a tall, ruddy-faced man, holding a shotgun.

He said, with an undisguised German accent, "Our carriage draws near, Herr Holmes. You will accompany us. Now, put up your hands."

PART TWO

OF NIGHTS AND DAYS

16. STRUGGLE

Holmes turned up his palms and spoke casually, as if facing a loaded shotgun were an everyday occurrence to him. "I am inclined to cooperate," he said. "Provided that you leave my associates alone."

"You are in no position to bargain, Herr Holmes. Now get in the carriage."

"May I at least have my coat? I have paid for it and the wind is cold."

The German shrugged, watching carefully as Holmes accepted the garment from Mrs. Lampert and turned towards the carriage, putting one arm into a sleeve.

In the next moment Holmes spun around and flung the coat over the head of the German, blinding him and pinning his arms so that the shotgun pointed downwards. The two struggled momentarily, but soon Holmes kicked the German's legs from under him, pulled him into the roadway, and threw him to the ground. From beneath the dark folds of fabric the barrel of the shotgun slid into view.

Holmes pulled at the weapon, trying to gain control, but the fallen man threw the cloak aside and lunged at him. I was about to intervene when I heard the carriage and its horse coming to a stop behind me.

Turning, I saw the driver, a blond-haired giant of a man who must have been fully seven feet tall, dismounting to aid his confederate.

I ran at the driver, colliding with his burly frame and crashing into the side of the carriage. We grappled, staggering back and forth. The driver had his huge hands around my neck and was squeezing down hard on my windpipe. Backed against the carriage, I gasped for air, attempting to twist my throat away from the pressure, but his all-encircling grip was powerful and relentless. Then I saw Lucy had pulled her derringer from her reticule and was running towards us. Stopping, she swung the barrel of the little weapon, striking a glancing blow across the bridge of the giant's nose. He blinked, but his hold on my throat never slackened. Then she pressed the tip of the barrel into his right eye. He grunted in pain and ducked his head away, trying to separate himself from the pistol, but Lucy kept the gun always in contact, holding firm. When he paused for a moment, she spoke directly into his right ear.

"My first bullet will blow out your brains," she said. "My second bullet is for your friend. Unless you let go now."

I felt the man's fingers loosen momentarily. Then his muscles tensed and he lashed out with one arm, trying to knock away Lucy's weapon.

As though it were a dagger, Lucy stabbed the butt of the gun hard into the giant's temple. At the same time, I broke free and hit upwards with the heel of my hand, into the tip of his chin, snapping his head backwards. The combination of these two blows only dazed him. Then I spun away and drove my knee into his solar plexus with all my remaining force. He doubled over. Behind him, Lucy kicked the back of his knee and he fell face down into the dirt.

I dropped down hard, putting all my weight onto my knees as they slammed into the giant's back. Lucy clapped the barrel of her derringer to his right temple. "*Please* try something like that again," she said.

By now Holmes had wrested the shotgun from the first man's grip and ordered him to lie facing downwards beside his companion in the roadway dust. While he and Lucy held their guns trained on the two men, I bound the wrists of each behind their backs with their belts. Then I removed their cravats and used them to lash each man's ankles tightly together.

Holmes asked Mrs. Lampert to bring two more belts and more kerchiefs and cravats. As we waited, Holmes said to me, "Search them. Find the knife."

"The knife?"

"The knife that slashed the coat," said Lucy, her teeth clenched, still pressing her gun into the giant's skull.

I searched each man. Strapped to the left calf of the smaller was a six-inch knife in a black leather sheath. I unbuckled it and put it into my pocket.

The smaller man said, "What do you think will happen now, Herr Holmes?"

"I think you will be taken to London and held for the abduction, torture, and murder of Spencer Kent, the banker, at the Green Dragon Hotel, Upper Swandam Lane, London. I believe witnesses will be found to identify you. You may also be held for the attack on Inspector Lestrade, if he recognizes you."

"You are wrong, Herr Holmes. We shall not be charged with any crime."

"And why not?"

"We possess diplomatic immunity, by the authority of the Congress of Vienna. My name is Dietrich, and my colleague here is named Richter. You will find our papers in our wallets."

I extracted the wallets from the inside coat pocket of each man and handed them over to Holmes. Holmes passed the shotgun to me. He pulled folded papers from each and held them up in turn to the fading western light. He said, "Your papers appear to be written in German."

Lying face downwards on the ground as he was, the smaller man was losing his composure. "What other language would they be written in? I demand that you release us! Your ambassador will hear of this!"

Holmes placed the wallets carefully into a pocket of his new coat. Then he turned to Mrs. Lampert and accepted the kerchiefs and cravats that she had brought.

Holmes knelt beside the smaller German. "I shall wait for these papers to be authenticated by your embassy in London. Meanwhile I shall extend you all the courtesy due to a pair of thugs who attempted to abduct me and to murder my friend."

Outraged, Dietrich opened his mouth to reply, whereupon Holmes stuffed one of the kerchiefs into it and then bound it in place with another around the man's mouth and neck. He followed the same process to gag the giant Richter, although this time Holmes needed to hold the tip of the knife very close to the huge man's eye as an inducement for him to open his mouth. This accomplished, Holmes used the two belts to lash each man's wrists to his ankles, so that when he had finished, the Germans were trussed up like a pair of sheep ready to be sheared.

Then he stood, took a five-pound note from his wallet, and turned to Mrs. Lampert. "Madam, I ask the use of your telephone to call the garrison and then Scotland Yard. I hope this will compensate you for that cost, and for your clothing accessories."

Mrs. Lampert's face shone with gratitude and relief. She took Holmes's arm and led him into her little shop.

While Holmes was inside, Lucy came over to stand beside me.

"They will both want revenge," she said. "And if they are indeed connected with the German embassy, they will soon be free."

17. A DISCOVERY AT RADNAR HOUSE

Nearly four hours later Holmes, Lucy, and I were concluding a light supper in the Radnar House private lounge, where we could speak without being overheard. As was sometimes his practice, Holmes avoided any discussion of the case, preferring to confine our conversation to matters such as the state of London's cultural offerings, new forms of transportation and architecture, and Lucy's upcoming role in the D'Oyly Carte Opera Company's next production. This habit of his I found by turns both a relief and a frustration, for the events we had just undergone had unsettled me, and I wanted the secure knowledge that we had a plan to address them.

We had just finished our coffee when the door opened and Harriet Radnar entered, accompanied by a tall, slender man of middle age, who seemed to me both worried and distracted. Dressed in a plain black wool suit, white shirt, and black cravat, he carried himself with a grave demeanour, although he wore his long blond hair nearly touching his shoulders, in the fashion recently popular amongst the literary set. Harriet introduced him to us as Reginald Havener, Lord Kerren, brother of her stepmother, Lady Radnar.

"I've just come from my laboratory at Kerren House," Kerren said. "Lansdowne wired me last night. Harriet tells me you've already seen what's left of my machine."

"The Secretary has asked me to help recover the missing components."

"Well, perhaps I can help you." Kerren took a seat on one of the upholstered chairs. "Do you know, Harriet, it was in this very room that I won that building from your father in a game of baccarat? It used to be the entry lodge for Radnar House. That was a painful night for your father, of course, but the house has been an absolute inspiration for my work on the electric cannon. And if the cannon is a success—well, your father will say it has been a happy outcome."

"Have you heard from Lord Radnar recently?" asked Holmes.

"His wire reached me this morning in Calais, as a matter of fact. Radnar is still in New York."

"I had a wire from him today myself," said Harriet. "He said I should start thinking what to wear to the Queen's Jubilee next year. That's his little joke. He always says we're sure to be 'right up there in the front pews if Reggie can get his lightning bolts in order.'"

"How long were you in Germany, Lord Kerren?" Holmes asked.

"I left here the day before Lord Radnar headed west to New York. Both of us had the same objective—he was seeking American capital while I was pursuing additional funds from the Prince of Wales. I would have remained at the spa, but Tesla wired me to come back and demonstrate the machine for him. I arrived on the afternoon ferry. Where is Tesla, by the way?"

"I'm sorry," Harriet said. "I forgot to mention that Mr. Tesla sailed for Germany at noon today."

Kerren's brow furrowed. "I would have expected him to wait for my arrival."

"Tesla seemed to think the machine would not work," said Holmes. "Although we did witness a demonstration of sorts."

"The balloon. Yes, Harriet told me. But that must have been an illusion."

Holmes's grey eyes glittered. "Please explain."

Kerren hesitated, as though uncertain whether to tell us the details of his invention. Finally he said, "You may think of the missing part as the muzzle of the cannon. It is actually similar to the muzzle of an ordinary gun in its function, though of course not in its design. The complex of electrical equipment inside is designed to spin electrified particle beams into a kind of braid—the way they work together is the core of my invention. Without spinning the beams together, all the energy is dispersed over a wide pattern and useless against an enemy. It took me more than a year of sleepless nights and every combination of—In any event, when it worked, I knew how important it was. I had to give Tesla's plans for the rest of the machine over to the War Office when they paid me. But I held on to the plans for my jewel box. That is what I call my electrical beam–spinning device. The plans are in a notebook, safe in a London bank vault."

"Please describe the box."

This time there was no hesitation in Kerren's manner. "It is an actual jewel box that belonged to my sister, shaped round—like a cylindrical hatbox—and made of silver. About six inches deep and about a foot and a half in diameter. The bottom has six small clamps to take the wires from the argon tubes. The lid is hinged and the surface is engraved—the design is like a snowflake. I drilled a two-inch hole in the centre for the muzzle—the business end of the weapon. That's where the braided beams shoot out."

"And you have the box locked away," said Holmes. As Kerren raised an eyebrow, Holmes continued, "You would appear far more worried otherwise, and you would not have stated so confidently that the demonstration with the balloon had to have been a trick. Now tell us, where is the box?"

Kerren gave a self-satisfied smile. "I did say that perhaps I might be able to help you, Mr. Holmes. And now I shall. The box is in a place where no one would ever think to look. It is not in my lab. It is not in my house. It is here, in this very room, where I enjoyed so much good fortune at the card table."

He stood abruptly and strode to a corner of the Persian rug at the centre of the room. He knelt and lifted one corner of the rug to reveal the smooth parquet blocks beneath. He gave one of the blocks an expert twist. The block came free, and he set it aside, then reached down to what I could see was the dial to a combination lock. "This is a cast-iron strongbox made in Wolverhampton," he said proudly. "I had it set in concrete, and the concrete is set into the foundation of the hotel." His smooth features narrowed with concentration as he spun the dial first in one direction, then in the other.

There was an audible click as the tumblers meshed. Then Lord Kerren lifted up the strongbox lid.

His jaw dropped, and his handsome features flushed scarlet. "Well, I'm damned," he whispered.

The strongbox was empty.

For a long moment Kerren continued to stare at the empty box. Then his eyes, widened at first in shock and surprise, narrowed in resolution. "I must return to Bad Homburg," he said.

18. JOURNEY BY RAIL

Twenty-four hours later, Lucy, Harriet, and I were nearing the end of our journey to Bad Homburg.

Holmes had left us, intending to follow Lord Kerren. We were in a first-class compartment on a French railway train that had just crossed the German border. Thick red velvet curtains covered our windows and muffled the clatter of the wheels on the steel rails beneath our carriage, as did the heavy layer of horsehair padding on our red leather seat cushions. I had been drowsing on and off since we had returned from supper in the dining car some three hours past.

Across from me, Lucy consulted her watch and said, "We're slowing down." She pushed her window curtain aside. "That sign says Saarbrücken. We're early. And I don't like the look of those men."

The train was stopping. Under the dim light of an overhead electric lamp, four figures stood in military posture. Three, tall and powerfully built, wore grey German military uniforms with the familiar spiked helmets that made them look even taller. A fourth man in a frock coat stood before them, grey haired and with a thick grey moustache. He wore a top hat and formal attire, as though he had recently come from an opera or a state function.

"The one in the top hat is obviously the leader," said Harriet.

The train stopped. The four Germans quickly boarded, and within a minute we were moving again.

A few minutes later, as the train rattled along, there was a perfunctory knock at our carriage door and then it opened. A moment later the grey-haired man I had seen on the platform had positioned himself to stand directly in front of my seat. His white silk tie, scarf, and impeccably starched shirt front gleamed brightly in the light from our carriage reading lamp. He might have been in his late forties or early fifties, but his clear skin and stolidly handsome features indicated excellent health. The determined set of his square jaw and the shrewd glint in his bright-blue eyes evidenced his confident assurance that he was in complete control of the situation and intended to have his own way.

Looking down on me, he demanded, *"Wo ist Herr Holmes?"*

Lucy saw my look of astonishment and spoke. *"Auf English, bitte? Der Arzt nicht Deutsch sprechen."*

"But you do," the man replied, in perfect English. "How frequently have you visited Germany?"

"This is my first time. I studied German in school. In the United States. At Miss Porter's School. That's in Connecticut, though I don't suppose you've heard of it."

"Your papers, please. And yours as well, Miss . . ."

"Radnar," Harriet replied.

The ladies handed over their travel documents. After a long minute perusing them he asked, "Your parents, Miss James?"

"My parents are—were—estranged. I was raised in a series of institutions, supervised and funded by a trustee. I am now of age and independent."

"And your parents, Miss Radnar?"

"My mother is dead. My father, Lord Radnar of Kent, is travelling in America on business."

"And your connection with Dr. Watson, here?"

"Lucy and I met Dr. Watson in Dover and realized we were going to the same destination. For different purposes, of course. He is not a member of the D'Oyly Carte Company."

"I am aware of that. Dr. Watson, what *is* the purpose of your journey to Bad Homburg?"

Obviously I could not tell this man that Holmes and I hoped to locate a stolen component of a powerful military weapon and then steal it back from the Germans. I said the first thing that came to mind. "Who are you?"

"My name is Bernhard von Bülow. I am his Imperial Majesty's Ambassador to Rome, and I will ask the questions here, Dr. Watson. Are you acquainted with the Austrian inventor, Mr. Nikola Tesla?"

"I met him in Dover. We were at the same hotel."

"My family's hotel," Miss Radnar added. "It is the premier location in Dover—"

"Dr. Watson. Did Mr. Tesla tell you of his travel plans?"

"He mentioned that he hoped to meet the Prince of Wales in Bad Homburg."

For some reason, von Bülow's manner became a touch less frosty. "Do you know where Mr. Tesla is staying in Bad Homburg?"

"I do not."

"Where are you staying, Doctor?"

"I have a reservation at the Parkhotel. I am told it is conveniently close to the spa."

"The Kaiser-Wilhelms-Bad, you mean."

"If you say so."

"His Imperial Excellency has allowed his name, which is the same as that of his illustrious grandfather, to remain in the carved stone edifice of the Kaiser-Wilhelms-Bad, for all to see. His Imperial Excellency is the all-highest authority in this country, and your presence here makes you his subject as well."

"I understand."

"On his Imperial command, which is his sole and unfettered privilege to dictate, you could be shot." Von Bülow stood calmly, hands clasped behind him and legs spread out, looking very much like a military guardsman. He continued, "Why do you suppose I have travelled from Rome to Saarbrücken and spent my valuable time questioning you?"

"I have no idea."

"It is not to listen to evasions or falsehoods. Now I advise you to be more forthcoming when I ask you again. What is the purpose of your journey to Bad Homburg?"

A safe reply occurred to me. "I plan to meet with Sherlock Holmes."

"For what purpose?"

"He is on an investigation. I generally accompany him on his investigations."

"Who is his client?"

As I hesitated, Harriet intervened. "My stepmother has asked him to investigate a matter concerning their family hotel."

"What matter?"

"An unidentified body found on the hotel grounds," Harriet said. "My stepmother fears a scandal if the matter is not resolved. A scandal would be bad for business."

"From what I know of the tastes of the British public, I should think quite the opposite, Miss Radnar. But let us assume that this answer of yours is truthful, at least in part. We will now come to the point of this interview."

Von Bülow leaned forwards. His blue eyes met mine. After a long, searching look, he continued, "Why did you attack two German diplomatic emissaries yesterday in the village of St. Margaret's?"

The question ought not to have taken me by surprise, since von Bülow had said he was the Kaiser's diplomat, and the two thugs had claimed they were entitled to diplomatic immunity. Still I was taken aback. I realized that von Bülow was confirming that the claim had been genuine. The thought that Dietrich and Richter might even now be on their way to Germany made me pause.

"They attacked us first!" Lucy was saying indignantly. "I was there! One of them had a shotgun, and the other had a knife. He practically strangled poor Dr. Watson—"

"Please, Miss James. I wish to hear the explanation from the doctor."

"It is quite as Miss James says," I replied. "It was plain that we were about to be abducted at gunpoint to an unknown location. We had every right to defend ourselves. The conduct of your country's emissaries, if indeed they were such, was quite inexcusable."

"On the contrary. The two men were bearing an important message. Your conduct made it impossible for them to deliver it."

"You surprise me, sir. What was the message?"

"It was for Mr. Holmes."

"From?"

"From the highest level of authority in Germany."

"I cannot believe you. Why would the Kaiser send a pair of thugs to deliver a message?"

"They were available. The choice was perhaps unfortunate."

"So now you are the messenger from the Kaiser?"

"I am."

"So what was the message?"

"The Kaiser wishes to retain the services of Sherlock Holmes."

"For what purpose?"

"To locate a missing object."

"What is the object?"

"I believe you already know, Dr. Watson. It is the same object that you recently discovered to be missing in Dover."

I sat mute, but I knew I had failed to conceal my surprise. I was sure the expression on my face had told him he was correct.

He gave a satisfied smile. "Now you will kindly deliver that message to Mr. Holmes at your next opportunity. We shall be watching you in Bad Homburg."

With that ominous statement, he withdrew. The door closed behind him.

19. A MESSAGE AND A MEETING

Night had fallen by the time we reached the Bad Homburg railway station, a small structure barely large enough to shelter a dozen passengers. The stone platform was well lit by electric lamps. As we descended from our carriage with perhaps a dozen other passengers, I noticed that the breeze coming across the platform bore a particularly pleasant scent and a clear and crisp autumnal feel. Harriet said something about the natural conditions that created this effect of "champagne air," as it was touted locally, but I paid little attention. Our journey had been long and fatiguing, and I was looking forward to settling into a room at the Parkhotel.

We had entrusted our luggage to the porter and were about to pass through the station to find a cab when another porter stopped us. In a brusque but otherwise respectful tone he asked, "You ladies appear to be English. Is either of you Miss Radnar?"

Harriet identified herself, and he continued, "Then this telegram is for you."

Harriet opened it immediately and showed it to us. The letters formed words that were entirely unintelligible.

"Coded," Harriet said. "I will decipher it when we are in the cab."

Not long afterwards, the three of us settled into a four-wheeler taxicab for the ride into Bad Homburg. In the yellow glow of the carriage reading lamp, Harriet hunched over the yellow telegraph paper, inscribing decoded letters into her sketchbook with an engraved silver pen. Soon she looked up with a satisfied expression. "Adrian has a paid spy in Baden-Baden. The spy says two weeks ago there were reports of strange flashes resembling lightning in the Black Forest outside the village, just after electrical scientists and boxes of electrical equipment had been assembled at the Kaiser's castle there. Then the lightning flashes stopped. Police and the army came in. Civilians were arrested and hauled away for questioning."

We tried to fathom the meaning of von Bülow's imperious visit in the context of Arkwright's message. Taken together, the two seemed to confirm that the Germans had stolen the jewel box apparatus essential to the firing of the new weapon from Kerren's laboratory, and that later a person or persons unknown had stolen the jewel box from the Germans. Assuming that we were correct, then von Bülow's desire to hire Holmes to find the jewel box was likely to be a sincere one. But what if von Bülow had some other purpose in mind? If the two German thugs indeed wanted to deliver a request to retain Holmes's services when they had met us in Dover, was that not in direct conflict with the warning they had delivered to Lestrade at Baker Street? Holmes obviously had to be told in any case, but of course Holmes was nowhere to be found, and we had no way to summon him.

As we rode in the taxicab, Harriet, who had become familiar with the town during several summers here with her parents, pointed out some of the buildings that we passed along the way to our hotel. Lucy gazed out of the window attentively, but to me, the buildings were only shadowed profiles, to be glimpsed through even more shadows of tall trees and shrubbery in what appeared to be an enormous park.

Finally we arrived at the Parkhotel. Lucy and I said farewell to Harriet, who continued in the taxicab, on the way to the flat owned by her father. Not long afterwards I was in my room, a plush, luxurious affair crowded with overstuffed furniture, potted palms, and a double bed with an equally overstuffed mattress. On the dresser and bedside table were several brochures proclaiming the virtues of various potions and nostrums available at the local shops and spas. I barely glanced at them. I was ready for a sorely needed night's rest.

Then someone knocked softly at my door.

Opening it a crack, I beheld a small man, somewhat portly and likely in his midthirties, holding a folded newspaper beneath the arm of his swallowtail coat and clutching his top hat before him. His round, clean-shaven face turned up to meet my gaze, and his small, dark eyes peered searchingly at me from behind gold-rimmed spectacles. The obviously simulated smile he had fixed on his mouth turned instantly to an equally artificial expression of contrition. "I do apologize for disturbing you at this hour after your long journey, Dr. Watson," he said. Then the fixed smile returned for a moment. "May I come in?"

"For what purpose?"

"It concerns something Mr. Holmes wishes to locate."

I bade him enter and soon we were seated on velvet-upholstered chairs, across from one another before the curtains of my window. He held up the newspaper that he had been carrying. "I shall come to the point directly, Dr. Watson. I am here in response to this advertisement placed in this afternoon's newspaper. It is written in German. I believe you do not speak the language? Correct? Then I shall read it to you. It is under the category of 'Personal' and says: 'Those with information concerning a missing electrical jewel box will find it to their advantage to call upon Dr. John Watson at the Parkhotel, Bad Homburg.'"

Again, the artificial smile appeared for a moment. "From your astonished look, Dr. Watson, I take it that you have not been made aware of this advertisement."

I felt a surge of annoyance, both with Holmes for not telling me what he had done, and with this overly unctuous man for raising the point. I said, "I take it you have some information. Would you kindly convey it. The hour is late."

"Of course. The person I represent is in possession of the jewel box."

"Where did he acquire it?"

"In Baden-Baden."

"Where?"

Again the false smile. "I am not able to provide that information. However, I am able to provide the jewel box. The price demanded by my client is one hundred thousand gold marks, or about twenty thousand pounds sterling. To the British government, this would be a trifling sum. Half will be due as an immediate payment, and the other half on delivery."

"I shall have to discuss this with Mr. Holmes."

"Naturally."

"How shall I find you? What is your name?"

"Ah. You will understand that I need to be quite discreet in such a delicate matter, Dr. Watson. You may call me Herr Gruen. And I shall have to find you. I trust you will not make that too difficult a task." Then, with a brief flash of that annoying smile, he stood, bowed politely, and picked up his hat. A few moments later he was gone.

20. AN OUTDOOR DEMONSTRATION

On Wednesday morning I was feeling somewhat rested, for, after a few minutes' tossing about in my bed in futile attempts to determine how I ought best to reach out to Holmes, I dropped into a sound slumber, to awaken only when the bright morning sunlight came streaming through an opening in the heavy curtains of my window.

Lucy and I joined D'Oyly Carte, the dapper impresario of the Savoy opera company, at his breakfast table. Carte had finished his single boiled egg and triangle of toast and had set down his napkin, after delicately touching it to his perfectly trimmed black beard. As usual, he was impeccably tailored, attired for this occasion in a suit and waistcoat of light-grey tweed, with a blue silk kerchief tucked into the breast pocket of his jacket. We chatted comfortably about the performance that the company was to put on that evening and the rehearsal that was to begin in a few minutes at the theatre a short walk away. Neither Lucy nor I mentioned our undertaking to recover the electrical weapon. I was wondering where Holmes would choose to make his appearance known. Lucy, seated to my right, was listening to Carte while surveying the fashionably dressed women and their men at the crowded tables around us.

Then Lucy said, "Dr. Watson. Please keep your head down and do not look behind you."

I kept my eyes on my empty plate as Carte asked, "What are you talking about?"

"Two men that do not know you, Mr. Carte, but they know Dr. Watson and me. Please slowly turn your attention towards the doorway. Do you see a very tall man and his hard-faced companion?"

Carte sipped coffee while allowing his gaze to drift around the room. "Yes."

"Please say what they are doing."

"They are surveying the tables. They do make a most unpleasant-looking pair."

"Two days ago we sent them to a London jail. They are from the German embassy, so they were probably released, and then deported."

"How would they know to look for you here?"

"I don't know that they are. What are they doing now?"

"The tall one has just noticed me and whispered something to the other. Now they both have turned away. They are leaving the room." I took a brief glimpse and saw the two retreating forms. They were unmistakably Dietrich and Richter.

"We must follow them," said Lucy.

By the time we made our way through the crowded tables and reached the hotel lobby, the two men were nowhere to be seen. Lucy pressed on to the front entrance, and we followed. On the steps in front of the hotel, we looked across the boulevard to a vast green expanse of trees, shrubs, and lawns. There was still no sign of the two men. We looked up and down the wide pavement, again without seeing either Dietrich or Richter.

"I won't ask what you're doing, Lucy," Carte said amiably. "Though I take it that it will not interfere with your performance tonight."

"Thank you."

"I suppose we may as well stroll over to the theatre for rehearsals."

We began our walk along the broad boulevard. "We are at the southern border of the *Kurpark*," said Carte. "The main spa, the building where much of the healing business is conducted, is called the *Kurhaus*. I've been here several times, but never taken advantage of all the treatments that so many rave about. You can't see the building, for it's nearly half a mile off and all those monumental trees get in the way. That tower over there is part of the *Schloss*, the restored castle where both the Kaiser and the Prince of Wales stay when they are here."

Carte continued to talk as we strolled along. "The Germans like their parks to be oversized, I suppose. This one is twice as big as St. James's. But still it is arranged in the modern English style, with the trees laid out in a natural pattern."

He stopped. "Hello, what's this?"

Across the boulevard and amongst the line of trees nearest us, a group of soldiers in tight grey uniforms walked behind a single ramrod-straight figure, clad in white with gold braid on his shoulders and sash. Absurdly, I thought, the white-uniformed leader carried a sword in its scabbard at his hip.

Carte said, "Look at the man in white. I believe we are witnessing the Kaiser himself."

"What is he doing?" I asked.

"Inspecting the trees. I've heard about this."

The Kaiser stopped before a tall elm tree. He looked the tree up and down, as though it were one of his soldiers. Then he nodded, turned, and continued on his path, his uniformed retinue trailing him in a cluster.

We watched fascinated as the process was repeated. Stride, stop. Look up and down, nod, and stride again. Then, a moment later, the Kaiser was standing at attention, looking up at a tall elm. He raised his white-gloved right hand and twirled his fingers, or perhaps snapped them—it was impossible for me to tell at the distance. Then he dropped his hand to his side, came to attention once more, pivoted, and moved on.

Behind him, two members of his retinue stopped before the tree. They pulled out a spool of red ribbon. One of them walked around the tree, spooling out the ribbon, while the other held the end. Then the ribbon was cut and tied.

"Marked for doom," said Carte. "That tree will be cut down today."

"Why?" Lucy asked. "It appears to be a perfectly good tree."

"Nonetheless it is doomed, because Wilhelm commands it. Look, he's turning."

Wilhelm and the others were heading north on the street that marked the western border of this part of the *Kurpark*.

"If we followed him, I'm told we'd see him stop again and stamp his foot. That means he wants a new tree planted on that spot." Carte shrugged. "But we turn left here. The theatre's just down this road."

We had rounded the corner following Carte when suddenly from behind us we heard a sudden crack, like the sound of a thunderclap, although oddly muffled. We stopped immediately and turned back to the park.

The tree that the Kaiser's men had marked with a red ribbon had been split apart from above. The tall elm was slowly tearing itself in two, as though an invisible giant had just struck down upon it from above with an invisible axe. Its two halves were each twisting and swaying as they grew farther and farther from one another. The branches crackled and rustled as the weight of the two portions of the trunk bore them downwards towards the ground. Steam or smoke came from the exposed white wood of the trunk. The red ribbon was torn asunder.

We stood transfixed by the sight. "What the devil was that?" Carte asked.

As we watched, three soldiers ran swiftly to the edge of the park and stood at the corner, blocking the path to prevent any bystanders from getting closer. Behind them, we saw two more soldiers closing the rear doors of a large black van. The van was already moving, pulled by four black horses. It reached the edge of the park and turned away from us, heading north in the direction of a large building with a tall white tower.

Lucy and I stared at one another. "Are they demonstrating the electrical weapon?" She spoke quietly, out of Carte's hearing.

"Why would they be so obvious about it?" I whispered. Then an idea came to me. "Perhaps they are only *pretending* that they have it? Although I cannot understand why they would want to do that."

Lucy gave a brief smile. "I suppose we ought not to theorize in advance of the facts."

21. AN INDOOR DEMONSTRATION

We made our way to the *Kurtheater* without further incident. As we entered the foyer, however, a momentary flash of light surprised us. The light came from an open doorway off to the left side of the box office and was accompanied by excited voices, primarily those of women. Entering through the doorway, we found the source of the commotion. Nearly all the members of the Savoy chorus, in their street clothes, were gathered around Mr. Tesla, who stood beside one of the chorus ladies. Tesla held a glass wand of about one inch in diameter and about five inches long, against the lady's forearm. The wand, connected by a wire to a complicated apparatus behind Tesla, emitted a violet glow.

"What's all this?" asked Carte. "Why are you all not on stage?"

Harriet Radnar stepped forwards from behind Tesla. "Mr. Carte, this is Nikola Tesla, the electrical inventor. He has rented this part of the theatre in order to demonstrate his inventions. Something of a sideshow, one might say. Mr. Tesla, this is Sir Richard D'Oyly Carte."

Tesla beamed happily at Carte. "Sir, your reputation precedes you. I am delighted to make the acquaintance of the first impresario to light his theatre with electric light. I was just demonstrating my electric transformer coils, which I have here connected with my violet ray wand."

He addressed the woman from the chorus who had been standing beside him. "Madam, does your wrist feel better?"

The woman beamed. "Much warmer, and the sharp pain has gone away altogether."

I wondered whether the same effect would have been achieved with a hot compress, but kept my doubts to myself.

Tesla was speaking. "The electrical currents agitate the cells, promoting circulation, which we know to be a benefit to health. However, the currents produced by my machine are set to vibrate at different frequencies, just as a violinist alters the frequencies of a vibrating violin string by placement of his fingers, in order to produce different notes. Some of the frequencies also produce ozone that oxidizes the toxic wastes associated with illness, turning them into harmless gaseous compounds that the body can readily expel. The violet ray is useful for hair loss, poor circulation in the extremities, varicose veins, warts—"

Carte interrupted. "Yes, yes, this is all very well. I certainly admire your inventive genius, Mr. Tesla. However, ladies and gentlemen, we do need to begin the rehearsal. Our stage tonight is barely two-thirds the size of what we have at the Savoy. We have less than two hours to accustom ourselves to its strictures. The Prince of Wales expects a dazzling performance, as does the Kaiser, and as, I am sure, do all of us. You will kindly prepare for the opening of act one."

People scurried to obey Carte's directive. I expected Carte to follow, but his attention now appeared to be focused on a silver globe set atop a five-foot-tall column of polished metal. The globe was about the size of a grown man's head, and the diameter of the column only slightly smaller. About two feet away stood another globe and column of identical shape and size.

"I think I have seen pictures of those," Carte said.

Tesla beamed with pleasure. "Allow me to demonstrate," he said, and pressed a button. At that moment, a large bright spark about the size of a yardstick flashed between the two polished globes. The cold white illumination cast Tesla's sharp features in harsh relief. I realized we had found the source of the flash of light that we had seen moments earlier.

"Quick as lightning," said Carte.

"It *is* lightning, sir," said Tesla. "Though on a smaller scale than that found in nature. Mankind is not yet capable of—"

Carte interrupted. "Is it safe?"

"It is as safe as the electric arc-lamp spotlights that are used in nearly every theatre today. Those, I might add, are also my invention. I have demonstrated this one many times before many audiences. If you stand near my transformer coil, which gives the apparatus its increase in voltage, you will feel an unmistakable sensation of health and well-being. You see, Mr. Carte, electricity represents our very essence of life—"

"Never mind that. How would you like to bring your invention out of this little room and show its power to an entire theatre audience, including two monarchs—this very night?" At Tesla's nod, Carte continued, "Then I'll tell you how we'll manage it. In our first act we have a scene requiring thunder and lightning. We provide the thunder by twisting and shaking a flexible sheet of metal. Your apparatus will provide the lightning. Also, we have a faery queen in the show, and your violet rod that glows can be her magic wand. Oh, no, I see a wire connects the wand to the machine. That would spoil the magical effect. But with proper screening, I think those shiny steel globes could create remarkably realistic flashes of lightning."

"They *are* flashes of lightning. As I was saying—"

"Quite so. Will you do it? Permit the use of the machine? Imagine the effect on the Prince of Wales and the Kaiser when they learn that you have created this awe-inspiring power. Both men will be attending tonight's performance, you know."

"How will my machine be protected?"

"The same way all our equipment is protected. Our stage manager will keep it safe."

"I will need to remain close by during the performance. Backstage, of course."

Carte agreed. Tesla remained in the anteroom tinkering with his equipment, while Carte led me into the theatre auditorium. "I must attend to things backstage," Carte said. "You are welcome to stay for as long as you like." He motioned to the seats at the back of the auditorium. "Oh, and I see your friend is here as well. Please say hello to him for me."

I drew in my breath. There in the back row, his fingers steepled beneath his chin in that familiar pose, sat Sherlock Holmes.

22. OBSERVATIONS WITHOUT CONCLUSIONS

"Holmes," I said quietly, taking a seat beside him. "The Kaiser wishes to hire you to find—"

"In good time, old friend." He held up his finger for silence. "Let us see what we can of the rehearsal. We may not be able to attend the performance tonight, so let us take this opportunity to appreciate Lucy's talents." So saying, he sat up straighter in his seat, steepled his fingertips together once more, and fixed his gaze on the stage before us.

I have often remarked on Holmes's ability to concentrate his attentions on the artistic realm, despite the urgency of professional matters. On this occasion his behaviour generally ran true to form, although the performance was frequently interrupted for adjustments to the staging. The placement of the twin globes of Mr. Tesla's lightning machine for maximum effect, I recall, took up a good deal of time. Holmes merely closed his eyes, waiting until he heard Lucy's voice. Then he would come awake, leaning forwards in his seat and watching intently as she performed in that effortless manner of hers, by turns coquettish, innocent, adoring, and fiery, as the story required. He spoke only once, leaning towards me and murmuring, "For her this is still as natural as breathing."

The hands of my pocket watch stood at nearly one o'clock when the rehearsal ended, and Carte told the company they would find a light luncheon waiting for them at the Parkhotel. I had expected that this would be my opportunity to report, and in particular to recount my conversation with von Bülow, in the privacy of our relatively isolated spot at the back of the auditorium. But Holmes stood up abruptly. He withdrew an envelope from his jacket pocket and handed it to me. "This was waiting for you at the front desk of the hotel," he said. "I took the liberty of opening it."

The message read: *KURHAUS* #51. 2:00 TODAY. Gruen.

"Who is 'Gruen'?" Holmes asked.

"He came to my room last night. He says he has an associate who has the jewel box. His price is one hundred thousand gold marks. By the way, Arkwright telegraphed us from Baden-Baden. His report indicated that the Germans had the jewel box for two weeks, only to have it stolen away by an unknown party. Presumably that is the associate of Gruen."

"Well done, Watson," Holmes said. "We shall meet this most helpful fellow together. Eventually."

He led me outside, to the stage door entrance. We waited in the cool air until Lucy and Harriet emerged. Holmes congratulated them on their performances, making small talk while leading us along the pavement in the direction of the *Kurpark*. Above and behind us, the early-afternoon sunlight filtered through the still-green leaves of the tall trees, casting odd bits of light and momentary shadows. To the north-west, I could see dark clouds.

When we were out of the hearing of the other actors and musicians, Holmes asked, "What news, ladies?"

Harriet was the first to speak. "I had a wire from Mr. Arkwright this morning," she said. "His concert has been cancelled. He will be joining us this afternoon."

"Did he say why?" asked Holmes.

"I recall the entire message," Harriet said. Her eyes widened as she recited, like a proud schoolgirl, "'Concert cancelled by Lansdowne's order. Will join you at Parkhotel this afternoon.'"

"Most interesting," Holmes remarked.

"Also we have a message from one von Bülow, a German diplomat. He entered our railway carriage when we had crossed the border yesterday. But no doubt Dr. Watson has already given you that information."

"The Kaiser wants you to find a missing object," I said. "I did not have time to tell you—"

"It is no matter," Holmes said.

"Von Bülow said those two German embassy thugs had been sent to hire you," Lucy said. "By the way, we saw them again this morning."

"Let us set that aside for the moment," said Holmes. "Anything else?"

"This morning we also saw the Kaiser himself, marching with his soldiers. He ordered a tree to be taken down. A short while later it was split in half, apparently by lightning. To induce the lightning, they apparently employed some apparatus hidden in a large military van."

"Where?"

"It was just over there, in the park."

We looked across the wide boulevard. Where the tree had once stood, only a low stump remained.

"So we have four incidents of interest," Holmes said. He held out one hand, tapping one finger after another as he continued. "First, on Sunday the Germans send thugs to warn me not to interfere with them. Second, on Monday the same thugs attack us in Dover. Third, yesterday they send a diplomat to say that the attack was a mistake and that they want my assistance to recover a missing object, which we may assume is the same weapon that we are seeking. And fourth, this morning they demonstrate quite publicly that they apparently have the weapon in their possession after all."

"Quite a puzzle," said Lucy.

"What are we to conclude from all this inconsistency?" asked Harriet.

"I recommend," Holmes replied, "that we conclude nothing at all."

Lucy gave me a knowing glance. Her lips silently formed the words *I told you so.*

23. ESPIONAGE

We walked with the ladies as far as the Parkhotel, where they left us to join the rest of the company for luncheon. Holmes and I continued across the boulevard and entered the *Kurpark*, that wide expanse of encapsulated nature wherein several hours earlier we had seen such a remarkable demonstration of man's ability to intervene.

Holmes set out immediately and with assurance along a path that led, as nearly as I could discern without a compass, due north. Across the rolling lawn to our right, we saw white-clad players on distant tennis courts, and far beyond them to the east, barely distinguishable figures that might have been golfers playing on smooth green fairways. Our path was somewhat uphill, so I was unable to discern what lay on the other side of the green slopes and shrubberies that lay before us.

"You do know the way, Holmes," I said as we walked.

"I have visited the *Kurhaus* once this morning. If I am not mistaken, Lord Kerren and Lady Radnar are there at present. You will recall I had assigned myself the task to follow Lord Kerren, and I have not confined my activities solely to rest and recreation."

"How did you proceed?"

"I knew the address of Lord Radnar's flat from Lansdowne. I reasoned that Kerren, being short of funds, would want to take advantage of his sister's hospitality. So I made the flat my destination. I was there soon enough to watch Kerren arrive. The weather being fine at present, Lady Radnar left the windows open and I was able to hear her telephone to make the appointment for her brother. If I heard correctly, his doctor is named Olfrig."

"It sounds so straightforward when you describe it that way."

"I am sure you would inject more drama if you were recording this incident for your readers. However, considering the military and diplomatic circumstances of the case, I trust you will not do so."

"You may rely on me, of course," I said, feeling somewhat nettled.

After a few more minutes, we crested the hill. About fifty yards before us, the path led directly to the *Kurhaus*, a monumental building of brown sandstone, built along the lines, I thought, of St. Paul's Cathedral in London, though only about half the size of that famous structure. Atop the building was a tall copper-clad dome. As we drew closer, I saw that beneath the stately brown columns at the front portico, the tall double doors were open into the rotunda.

Entering, we paused for a moment to take in our surroundings. Above us, the crown of the dome soared possibly a hundred feet or more over our heads. Around us, beautiful classical sculptures of Grecian goddesses looked down from arched niches in the curved wall above the wide marble floor. Two long hallways extended from the rear of the rotunda on either side. Between them, a uniformed nurse of middle age and stern appearance was observing us from behind a desk.

Holmes strode up to her. *"Guten tag. Doktor Olfrig, bitte."*

The woman did not need to consult her directory. *"Funf und zwanzig,"* she said, and pointed to the corridor along our left.

"Haben sie besten dank," said Holmes, and we set out in that direction. Moments later we stood before the doorway to number 25. On the door was a brass plate bearing the doctor's name.

"Now we will continue to number 51."

"Why did we stop?"

"I wished to observe the lock," he said as we walked further down the long hallway. "It is a Chubb. The information will be useful when I return tonight." Then he stopped. Holding his hand up in a gesture for caution, he said softly, "The door to number 51 is open."

I stayed behind him as we entered office 51, too apprehensive to notice the name of its occupant. We soon saw that gentleman, however, or the man I assume was he, for on the carpet face down lay a man in a white physician's smock. At Holmes's nod I felt for a pulse beneath the ear. There was one, and the breathing was regular, though the man was plainly unconscious. A large red welt was visible at the back of his head where he had obviously been struck down.

Holmes whispered, "Do you recognize him?" and I shook my head. Holmes moved silently to a door on the far wall. As he opened it I felt a rush of cold air and saw another office, this one an empty examination room. Afternoon sunlight streamed in through a door open to the *Kurpark*.

Looking out alongside the building, we saw the retreating forms of Dietrich and Richter. They walked rapidly in a hunched-over fashion, dragging the limp figure of a third man and keeping close to the outer wall. Each held one of the man's outstretched arms. The toes of the man's shoes dug wavering grooves in the gravel.

When they had very nearly reached the end of the building, they stopped. Dietrich used a key to open a door. Then Richter bent over, picked up the limp form without apparent effort, and hoisted him over one shoulder, enabling me to see the man's face.

"Holmes," I whispered. "That is Gruen, the man who came to my room last night."

The men disappeared from our view, closing the door behind them. We followed as silently as we could. Holmes tried the door through which the men had gone with their unconscious victim. It was locked.

We could hear nothing from within. Holmes tried the adjacent window, but it too was locked, and the heavy curtains did not allow us to see inside.

I bent to the keyhole. Keeping my voice low, I reported what I saw. "There are several lit electric lamps and tables, with shelves that appear to contain electrical equipment. On my right someone is moving, but I cannot quite make out who it is or what—"

He interrupted. "Thank you, Watson. Now would you please stand back."

He had taken off his coat and wrapped it around his right hand. In the next instant, he had broken through the window glass and was manipulating the lock above the frame. In seconds, the window was open and he was climbing through. I was about to follow when the door opened and he stood before me.

"Please see to Herr Gruen," he said as he put on his coat. "Others will be here in a moment to investigate the noise. When they arrive, tell them we are acting on the Kaiser's behalf. Von Bülow will confirm that the All-Highest is indeed our client."

Then he turned to the inner office doorway and, a moment later, was gone.

I looked around the room. On my right was the man who had called himself Herr Gruen. His arms were outstretched, his wrists strapped to a metal rack fastened to the wall. He slumped forwards limply, but his eyes were open. No longer present on his round face was the fixed smile I had seen the previous evening. It had been replaced by a pained grimace and an accusing stare.

He said, "You betrayed me."

24. A MUSICAL INTERLUDE

It was nearly two hours later when, feeling somewhat the worse for wear, I returned with Holmes to the Parkhotel.

My mind still whirled with the events that had just occurred. I had attempted to persuade Herr Gruen that we had not betrayed him, to no avail. Holmes had pursued Dietrich and Richter, also to no avail, returning shortly afterwards with news that the two had had a carriage waiting and had last been seen driving west on the road bordering the *Kurpark*. As Holmes had foreseen, however, the *Kurhaus* staff were impressed by the name of von Bülow and of course, the Kaiser, so they were willing to overlook the expense of a broken windowpane. Also fortunately, Herr Gruen left almost immediately, refusing to make a complaint against his attackers, and we were not detained long after we gave our explanations of what we had seen. However, we were no further along in our quest to recover the jewel box. In fact, we had lost ground, for Herr Gruen had declared he would no longer use me as an intermediary. I recalled his haughty tone with some indignation. "Either you are untrustworthy or you are incompetent," he had said as he bade me farewell. "In either case I cannot afford the risk that would ensue from our association."

As Holmes and I entered the hotel, I noticed a pleasant light musical air being played by a piano and a violin. The violin, I thought, had a particularly masterful and intriguing tone about it, but I listened only for a moment or two.

The voice of the clerk at the registry desk had interrupted my reverie. "Mr. Holmes," he called. "You have messages." He turned to the tall array of mahogany pigeonholes built into the wall behind him. "And one for you, Dr. Watson." He lifted two cream-coloured envelopes from two of the pigeonholes and handed one to each of us. Both bore the royal crest and seal. "Oh, and there is a telegraph message for you as well, Mr. Holmes," the attendant said, reaching under the desk and pulling out the yellow envelope. "From New York."

"That one is of interest," said Holmes. After opening it, however, his face fell. "I had expected another," he said, holding up the yellow message paper. "This telegram is from Lord Radnar. He wishes me to state my fee for investigating the case that Lady Radnar requested us to look into. A prudent, businesslike request, although I fear I cannot comply. It seems I am already working for two governments on what may prove to be the same matter." He folded the message and tucked it into his waistcoat pocket. "Now, Watson, do these two royal envelopes contain what I think they contain?"

"We are each invited to the royal box at the theatre tonight."

"I ask that you will make an excuse for my tardiness. Now let us attend the performance being played out for us here at this very moment. Judging from the virtuosity, I believe the violinist is Mr. Arkwright."

A short while later we were in a reception room opposite the dining room, where chairs had been set up and an audience of perhaps twenty guests had gathered. Harriet sat playing a small piano, singing in a clear soprano, and Arkwright stood at her side, his violin tucked beneath his chin. They were performing a slow, melancholy piece in which the soloist expresses powerful emotions of longing and despair to an overlooking moon. At the end of the piece there was polite applause, so we took the opportunity to settle ourselves in the back row of chairs, where Lucy was already seated.

Arkwright bowed to acknowledge the response from the audience, a glad smile wreathing his handsome features. With his shaven head, he looked almost cherubic. He nodded at the audience and spoke casually, as if the music had been part of a seminar on his musical craft. "These legato compositions are the most difficult. The temptation is always to press down hard as the note is sustained. But with a Stradivarius the technique must be altered. One cannot press a Strad too tightly, or it won't give you what you want. I know at least one of our number who is well aware of that."

He gave a brief bow in the direction of Holmes and then continued. "Now as our final number, Miss Radnar and I would like to offer you a new and original selection, setting to music a newly published poem from one of the foremost young classical scholars at our University College in London. But not to worry," he went on, with a conspiratorial wink. "It's a lighthearted little piece. Just a bit of fluff and fun."

Beside me, Lucy leaned close to my ear. "I'm afraid Harriet's all spoony about Arkwright."

"Spoony?"

"Mad about. Infatuated with. See how she looks at him all starry-eyed."

Harriet began to play, in waltz tempo, a very simple series of notes and chords in the lower register. After a few bars, Arkwright's violin came in with a light touch that was at once both sweet and—notwithstanding his introductory remark—melancholy in that ineffable sense that transports one to some distant realm of the imagination. Then

Harriet sang, in a most wistful and longing manner, these somewhat ironic words:

Oh, when I was in love with you,
Then I was clean and brave,
And miles around the wonder grew
How well did I behave.

And now the fancy passes by,
And nothing will remain,
And miles around they'll say that I
Am quite myself again.

The performance lasted barely a minute and a half. For those few brief moments, I felt somehow transported to another realm, one that I realized was only in my imagination, but which felt as though it were a different plane of existence. I know not whether it was because of Harriet's yearning expression, the haunting notes of Arkwright's violin, or the words themselves—although those might, in retrospect, be taken as somewhat cynical—but my thoughts turned to my beloved Mary. I wondered whether she—and, indeed, all other souls who had ever lived—was still in existence somewhere, still imbued by some mysterious creating power, alive and intact. Were we all made of the same invisible electrical energy with which Tesla was so familiar, only each of us organized into its own unique individuality? Were we independent of the matter in which we operate on earth, just as a bolt of lightning is independent of the thunderstorm from which it springs? The notion was comforting, somehow. Then my eye was drawn to Holmes's inscrutable profile. He was looking at the two performers in a most carefully scrutinizing manner, as if attempting to understand their inner thoughts. I wondered whether Holmes also had a concern for Harriet, whose affections for a man of Arkwright's background and experience would surely go unrequited. But such is the power of music that even while pondering the romantic prospects of the young lady singing before us, my thoughts also seemed to hover in some timeless and distant realm of memory, far, far away from our own.

Then the music ended and the room was filled with applause.

Beside me, Lucy leaned closer and whispered, "I wonder if the words are his message to tell her it's no use."

Someone called for an encore, but Arkwright shook his shaven head. "Must save ourselves for the theatre tonight, you know. I'll be substituting for the first violinist, by the way, if that will induce any of you to purchase a ticket." There was polite laughter, and then he went on, "Now I will take a question or two, if anyone's curious about our new little confection."

To my surprise, Holmes spoke. "I saw you had no printed music, Mr. Arkwright," he observed. "Had you memorized your composition?"

"Oh, well, I wouldn't say memorized. I go by touch and feel."

"Could you repeat the same notes if Miss Radnar were to repeat her part of the song?"

"I doubt it. Improvisation rarely produces the same results. By definition."

I have no idea whether Holmes would have continued this line of questioning, for Kerren had pushed forwards to stand beside Arkwright and chose that moment to pull him aside for a private conversation. I could not hear what they said, but I could see that Kerren was smiling broadly.

25. AUDIENCE WITH THE PRINCE

At this point I must remind myself that by the time anyone reads these words, more than a century will have elapsed and historians will doubtless have brought to light the various defects and virtues of the man who is to become King of England in a few years' time. I am reluctant to disparage the royal family, and I know that Holmes, who is engaged from time to time by many of the royal houses of Europe, has only rarely allowed me to disclose any information whatsoever concerning such cases or clients. However, I also want to set down what happened, and I shall be as objective as I can.

I climbed the theatre stairs alone and arrived at the royal box as instructed, fifteen minutes before the Savoy Company's performance was to begin. A uniformed attendant examined my invitation and motioned me forwards. Behind heavy brown velvet drapes I saw a man's face partially concealed, observing me. Then the drapes were parted and I saw Kerren standing at the entrance to the royal box. He appeared to be expecting me. Behind him sat the Prince of Wales.

"Dr. Watson is here, Your Majesty," he said, over his shoulder.

"Where is Holmes?" asked the Prince, in a reedy tenor voice.

"He will join us by the second act," I said. "He is following up a clue."

"My invitation plays second fiddle, does it?"

"The clue concerns the case that he is working on for your government."

"Oh. That's different, of course. Far more important. Well, do come in. Don't just stand there. You know Tesla. Here, sit beside Sophie, where I can see you."

The box had two rows of seats, four and four. His Royal Highness sat alone, in the second seat of the upper row. Lady Radnar sat at the left end of the first row, and Tesla at the right end. Each of them had to turn around somewhat awkwardly to see me and, I realized, to address the Prince. I took my seat as instructed. Kerren sat between Tesla and me.

The Prince, as everyone knows, comports himself with great dignity and purpose, which I felt at the first moment I met the appraising gaze from his determined brown eyes. At such close quarters, I also could not avoid being impressed by his perfectly trimmed beard, and by the expensive fabrics of his beautifully tailored clothing. I could not tell how tall he was, of course, because he was sitting down, but his girth—the subject of ridicule at times—was evident. His rotund belly bulged from beneath his tight waistcoat and came to rest on his upper thighs. I wondered fleetingly what enormous proportions would result if the Prince's weight were not kept in check by his annual pilgrimages to Bad Homburg. I wondered if his wardrobe contained many different sets of clothing to match the variations in his measurements that would occur during the time he was undergoing his treatment, or later, when the excesses of his ordinary diet caused him to gradually regain the weight he had lost. His immoderate bulk notwithstanding, he is a known favourite amongst the ladies, being greatly affable and charming when he wants to be.

He stared at me for a moment, his jaws clamping down on a fat unlit cigar. As he pulled it out to speak, he gave a grimace of a smile, showing teeth that were both crooked and tobacco stained. At that moment I recalled what Lansdowne and Carte had said about his having taken a fancy to Lucy. I resolved to do whatever I could to prevent him from being alone with her.

But he was speaking, and my duty was to listen.

"I wanted to get you all together, including Holmes, so you could tell me what I need to know of this electrical weapon. Kerren and Tesla, you want to sell it to me, so your views are tainted. Sophie, Kerren is your brother, so on this subject I can't trust you either. I can rely on Holmes to be objective, but he is otherwise engaged. We have ten minutes, and then I want you out of here so my guests can be seated before the curtain goes up. Dr. Watson, what does Holmes think?"

"He does not yet know whether the weapon will work. There is a part missing."

"I know that. Kerren told me just now."

"But I can rebuild it!" Kerren said. He gave a proud glance at his sister, and then turned back to the Prince. "I have the plans clearly focused in my memory—"

"Never mind what you can do, Kerren. Dr. Watson, does Holmes think the thing is worth pursuing? If it does work?"

"I believe so."

The Prince went on, "Wilhelm says they have the thing in their possession and can demonstrate it."

"We saw a demonstration this morning," I said. "In the *Kurpark*. The Kaiser pointed out a tree, and his men destroyed it."

"How?"

"It appeared to be split in two by lightning. Only I did not see a flash."

"Indeed. Well, Wilhelm has challenged me to a duel. Of sorts. Next week on Dover beach. His electrical weapon against mine, shooting at a military balloon anchored on the beach, with the two of us observing from the top of the famous Dover cliff."

The Prince paused and looked beyond us, beyond the busy musicians tuning their instruments in the orchestra pit and across the theatre. Directly across from us, there was activity in the box that faced ours. The box curtains parted and Kaiser Wilhelm appeared, uniformed in crisp white and gold braid, with a white plumed hat tucked under his right arm. From the audience below there came a sudden outburst of cheering and applause. Behind the Kaiser, the members of his party were taking their seats, the men dressed in the usual black evening wear, the contrast of their dark apparel making the Kaiser's white uniform appear even more distinctive. The others sat, while the Kaiser stood at attention, basking in the crowd's acclaim. Then, after seating himself and turning conversationally to his wife, who sat on his right, and then to von Bülow, who sat on his left, he looked across at our box. With a beatific smile, he pointed with his right forefinger at the Prince, lifting his right thumb and curving the other fingers as though he were miming the shooting of a pistol.

"Do you see that?" said the Prince. "This is the man who proposes an alliance between our nations." Though he spoke in a hushed tone, his voice took on a new intensity as he continued, "If I accept Wilhelm's challenge with a flawed piece of weaponry, that strutting little popinjay will have no need for an alliance. He will keep his version of the electrical cannon and take it back to Germany. His scientific men will improve it and make it portable and easy for soldiers and sailors to operate in all types of weather. They will manufacture thousands and thousands of deadlier and deadlier machines. Before we know it, Wilhelm will have the weaponry to threaten England with extermination." His gaze went from Kerren to Tesla and then back. "I shall do all in my power to prevent that, gentlemen."

Both men nodded solemn faced. Plainly they realized the importance of the Prince's words.

"I want to be doubly sure that our machine will work," the Prince said firmly. "I want to witness the machine in operation before we accept Wilhelm's challenge. And before I see the machine, I want to hear from Sherlock Holmes that he has personally witnessed its success."

Below us, the conductor was stepping up to his podium, to the polite applause of the audience.

"Now, my guests are waiting to join me," the Prince continued. "There are five seats reserved for you below. Dr. Watson, when Mr. Holmes returns, have him come up here and report to me."

26. A GRIM DISCOVERY

I left word at the theatre's main entrance to tell Holmes where we were seated. To my relief, he arrived safely about one hour later, taking the empty aisle seat on my left. A white handkerchief covered the knuckles of his right hand. It was stained red in a few spots.

We were witnessing the last minute of the first act. From the stage and orchestra pit before us came waves of music, reverberating at peak volume. Faeries in their colourful costumes waved menacing magic wands at a group of peers, who knelt before them, pleading in their crimson robes. Lucy's character, rejected by her tenor counterpart, was stumbling towards the two lords who yearned for her. The timpani thundered. In the instant just before each thunderclap, Tesla's equipment produced lightning flashes that shimmered brilliantly over all, to the delight of the audience.

Holmes whispered, "Where is Kerren?"

The curtain fell. The audience roared its approval. I looked over to where Kerren had been sitting, at the other end of the row beside Lady Radnar. The seat was now empty.

We made our way in the direction of Lady Radnar. When we reached her, Holmes asked where her brother had gone.

She shook her head in bewilderment. “He left during the performance. I don’t know why, and I don’t know for where.”

“How long ago did he leave, Lady Radnar?”

“About ten minutes ago. He stood up and left. He walked straight up the aisle. Everyone was looking. People behind us whispered. I was mortified.”

“Was Tesla seated with you?”

“I have not seen Tesla since we had our audience with the Prince. I think he went backstage. He said something about checking on his equipment.”

Holmes thanked her and we took our leave. As we pressed through the crowded centre aisle, moving against the tide of the audience members on their way to the foyer for their interval refreshment, I hurriedly told Holmes of what the Prince had said about Kaiser Wilhelm’s challenge, taking care that those around us could not hear. Holmes merely nodded. Then, as the last spectator moved behind us, I asked, “What did you learn at the doctor’s office?”

Holmes kept moving forwards. “I found a file with Kerren’s name. The file was empty; however, I was able to discern Dr. Olfrig’s special field of practice. And an attendant accosted me, as you may have deduced from the handkerchief I have applied to my knuckles. On the whole, the visit was most instructive.”

We went, unchallenged, through the pass door between the auditorium and the stage, climbed some stairs, and found our way into the area where the actors were preparing for the second act.

Before us there was a flurry of activity. A backcloth painted to depict the Houses of Parliament and Big Ben was being slowly lowered from the flies above, while stage staff wrestled with the palace guard scenic piece that would be used at the opening of the second act. This guard box, built along the lines of the small peaked-roof structures within which a guard could take shelter outside Buckingham Palace, stood on a low wheeled platform, and the two men were heaving it off the platform to place it into its proper stage position.

"Where is Tesla?" Holmes asked one of the two men. He merely shrugged. *"Wobei die elektrisch maschine?"* Holmes asked. At this the man nodded, pointing towards the wing space at the left of the backcloth.

We found Tesla a few yards off the stage, on his knees, securing a canvas drape around the base of another wheeled platform.

"Have you seen Kerren?" Holmes asked.

"He was here only a few minutes ago. He came in during the performance with a strange expression on his face and bent over the first coil of the machine, as if he wanted to see it up close. He had both hands behind his back but I kept him away, of course."

"What did you say to him?"

Tesla blushed. "I may have been less polite than I ought to have been. But I couldn't have him tinkering. He might have hurt himself, or spoiled the effect of the lightning. He seemed to understand, because he nodded and went off."

"Where did he go?"

"I have no idea. I was busy with the machine."

"Was the machine still making lightning flashes?"

"Not while he was here. I was waiting for the very end of the act, just before the curtain falls. The flashes resume then."

"And how are the flashes produced?"

"There is a wire connected to the machine to supply electricity, and a switch that I hold in my hand to create the sparks."

"You had that responsibility?"

"I insisted on it. The stage manager gave me a hand signal, and I moved the switch."

"Were you looking at the machine?"

"No, I was looking at the stage manager. But I could see the light from the spark all around me, and I could hear the crackling sound that the spark produces."

"So you made lightning with the machine, Kerren arrived, you warned him to stay away, and he departed. Then you worked the machine again, just before the curtain fell. Does that describe the sequence of events?"

"Precisely."

"Did Kerren say anything to you?"

"Not while we were here. The noise from the performers was too great to allow for conversation. But he did speak very freely to me before the performance began, just after our audience with the Prince. He was very excited."

"What did he say?"

"He wanted us to work together to quickly reconstruct his apparatus. He said he had the plans in a London bank vault and knew just how to get them. He thought we could be ready to demonstrate the machine to you in Dover by the weekend. He was sure it would perform properly and then you could send a telegram to the Prince to come see it for himself. He said he was sure it would be the equal or the better of any machine that Wilhelm's people could have produced, and that when the challenge demonstration took place, our machine would emerge victorious."

"Have you any idea where he might be now?"

Tesla did not.

Neither did D'Oyly Carte, whom we found watching the preparations for act two. At Holmes's request, Carte brought us to a long table where many of the ladies were seated in front of mirrors, working on their makeup.

Lucy, seated beside Harriet, caught sight of us in her mirror. Her green eyes widened, but only for a moment, and she did not turn around, nor did she speak, other than to whisper something to Harriet.

Led by Carte, we approached to within an arm's length of the ladies.

"Ladies, I wonder if you could help this gentleman," Carte said, with a nod towards Holmes. "He has a question for you, and I would be grateful for your assistance."

"We are looking for a middle-aged man," Holmes said. "He may have become disorientated by the electrical flashes towards the end of act one. He is of medium height and build, and is otherwise quite unremarkable, save for his long blond hair, which he wears at shoulder length. I am hoping that this may have registered in your memories. Can any one of you recall seeing him?"

There was only an awkward silence. None of the ladies, it seemed, had anything to tell us, so we took our leave. For the next few minutes, Holmes questioned everyone else that we could find near the stage. No one could recollect seeing Kerren.

Finally it was almost time for the second act to begin. As the stage manager called for the faeries and Private Willis to take their positions for the first scene, I reflected that we still knew nothing more of Kerren's whereabouts.

"Shall we take our seats, Holmes?" I asked, but he only shook his head.

The actresses playing the faeries, Harriet amongst them, waited with us in the wings as the actor playing Private Willis, in his scarlet guardsman's uniform jacket, marched up to his sentry box and donned his tall black fur busby helmet. From beyond the curtain we heard the audience applaud as the conductor entered the orchestra pit.

Then the overhead lights came on, bathing the stage in the electric glare that was intended to simulate the daylight setting of the second act. The actor playing the part of Private Willis turned to enter his sentry box, so as to be in his proper position before the curtain went up. He opened the door.

A man's body tumbled out onto the stage, clad in black. At my side, Harriet gasped as the body landed with a muffled thud, rolled once, and came to rest facing upwards. We could see plainly a pair of wide and lifeless eyes. They were framed by a warped halo of tangled blond hair, and a horrible grimace that contorted the once-handsome features of Lord Kerren.

27. THE SHOW MUST GO ON

A moment later Holmes was kneeling beside Kerren's body. He leaned in to within a few inches of the hideously twisted face, and then he stood up. By this time, D'Oyly Carte had appeared, his bright little eyes anxiously looking to Holmes for direction.

"Of course we will stop the orchestra and delay the second act for as long as necessary," Carte said.

"You will not" came another voice from behind me. To my surprise, another figure had emerged from the wings onto the stage. It was von Bülow, accompanied by two uniformed German military officers. "I speak for the Kaiser, and I say that the All-Highest does not wish to have the performance interrupted or delayed. His word is law, so there will be no discussion on that point."

"Mr. Holmes?" asked Carte.

Holmes, standing by the body, nodded assent. "I have seen all I need to see. The body may be moved to somewhere more private."

Carte said, "Please take him to dressing room number one."

The two officers lifted Kerren's body. We followed them as Carte led the way to one of the dressing rooms, where the two officers set the lifeless form down on a couch. Holmes, Carte, von Bülow, and I watched from the doorway. From the stage came the muffled notes of the orchestra and the voice of Private Willis concluding his opening number.

"We should send for Lady Radnar," Holmes said. "She is in the audience and should be informed of what has happened to her brother."

Carte nodded and walked discreetly away.

Von Bülow closed the dressing room door. "It is plain what has occurred here," he said. "Kerren met with an accident at the electrical machine. The results of the electric shock are visible on his face. Tesla, who was operating the machine, feared that his healing apparatus would be viewed as a dangerous instrument and that his reputation would be irreversibly stained. So he hid the body in the most readily available place of concealment, the sentry box, which was near the lightning machine with the other props. Tesla then resumed his position and operated the machine to produce the effects needed at the end of the act. Our men will search for Tesla and hold him for concealing evidence."

Suddenly I felt a tug at my sleeve and turned to see Lucy behind me, in her shepherdess costume. She whispered, "I must speak with Holmes."

Holmes was speaking to von Bülow. "I do not believe that electricity was the cause of Kerren's death. Behind Kerren's right ear is a small red puncture mark. I believe Kerren was injected with a powerful vegetable alkaloid, the effects of which have produced the rictus of death that you see on his face."

"We shall find and detain Tesla nonetheless, Mr. Holmes." Then von Bülow caught sight of Lucy. "What are you doing here, Miss James? Are you not required to be on stage?"

"Not for another two songs," she replied. "About six minutes."

"Why are you not waiting in your dressing room?"

"Everyone's talking about the body that fell out of the sentry box. I came to see what had happened."

"Why you, in particular? Why are the others not here?"

"I can't speak for them."

Von Bülow gave her a long, searching look. "Where were you at the end of the first act?"

"On stage, with everyone else. It's the act one finale. We're all out there."

"In the confusion you might have briefly left the stage, however, and then reentered—"

Holmes interrupted. "As any one of the actors might have done. Also, after the curtain fell and people were returning to their dressing rooms, anyone in the company might have met with Kerren. So that would indicate we may need to interview the entire company. But as you have indicated, the Kaiser does not wish to have the performance interrupted. We must therefore wait for the performance to conclude. I suggest that Miss James go to wherever she is assigned to wait to make her next entrance so that the remainder of the performance can run smoothly."

Von Bülow nodded. "She may go," he said, with a glance at one of the two officers, wordlessly conveying his authority.

Lucy whispered to me, "Tell Holmes the Prince wants to meet him after the performance. He told Carte that he wants me to be there as well." Then she left us.

Moments later Carte arrived, supporting an ashen-faced Lady Radnar. "Where is he? Where is my brother?" she whispered, clinging to Carte's right arm. Then she turned to Holmes, and her voice took on a piteously accusing tone, "How could you allow this to happen?"

28. ROYAL COMMAND

The Prince of Wales stared unhappily at Holmes. The performance of *Iolanthe* had concluded, and we were in the same theatre anteroom where Tesla had first demonstrated his machine, barely twelve hours before. Holmes, Lucy, and I were seated on three chairs, and the Prince sat on the sofa, puffing his lit cigar. He had not offered a cigar to either Holmes or me, which I took to be a sign of his displeasure.

He turned to Lucy. "Miss James," he said. "Lansdowne tells me you can be trusted."

"I am honoured to be invited," Lucy replied. She did not appear distressed by Kerren's death, or overawed in any way by the royal presence. Attired in her usual plain black wool jacket and skirt and her unadorned white high-collared blouse, she sat calmly beside Holmes, observing the Prince with no more apparent concern than if he were a zoo gorilla behind heavy steel bars.

"So, Mr. Holmes, where do we stand?" asked the Prince. "And don't tell me we must capitulate to Wilhelm and admit we cannot meet his challenge."

Holmes's voice was steady and determined. "Your Royal Highness, we must find Kerren's killer."

"Leave that to von Bülow. We are on German soil. You have no authority to investigate."

"I think the chances of von Bülow telling us the truth are remote. Sir."

"Of course, they're remote. Von Bülow likely had Kerren killed, to keep him from making the weapon for England."

"Possibly."

"We must not lose sight of the objective," the Prince said, with a show of irritation. "How do we get the machine to work?"

"Either we must find Kerren's plans and reconstruct his apparatus, or we must find the missing apparatus itself."

"How do you propose to find the plans?"

"Kerren said he stored them in a bank vault. Our first task must be to identify the bank amongst the hundreds in London. For that purpose, I propose to call upon the assistance of the Chancellor of the Exchequer. Sir Michael can cast a wide net of inquiry, and his name will compel cooperation."

"I shall have a word with him."

"I believe there will not be need of that, Your Majesty. I was able to do him a small service last November."

"A personal service?"

"Purely professional on both our parts. It resulted in a substantial addition to the Treasury and he expressed his gratitude. I believe he will remember me. However, if he does not, I will certainly request your support."

A grunt of assent issued from the Prince. Then, "What about finding the missing—what do you call it?"

"Kerren called it an electrical spinner. He also referred to it as his 'jewel box,' because he used his sister's jewel box as a container for the apparatus."

"What is your plan to locate this . . . jewel box?"

"I have advertised for it."

"With what result?"

"None of material consequence as yet. However, the advertisements were placed only two days ago, and some of the responses may not yet have reached me."

"Could Tesla build the device contained in the missing jewel box?"

"With the plans, assuredly. But if he were capable of doing so without the plans, I believe he would have told us. He is not shy about letting people know his capabilities."

"Question him about that anyway."

"If I can. Von Bülow is looking for him."

"Let us assume that you will be successful in recreating the machine by one means or another. Now, let us think about how it will be demonstrated for you, and how it will be demonstrated for me. We can then work out the manner in which it will be safeguarded until a week from today when Wilhelm arrives."

There followed a discussion of the distance between the machine and its target, the size and shape of the military balloon, the length of cabling that would be required to transmit electricity to both the British and the German machines, and whether a second electrical generator ought to be employed for that purpose. Finally the Prince said, "I suppose that is all we can do here for the moment," and started to lift himself from the sofa.

Then he sat down again. His glinting eyes flickered towards Lucy for the briefest of moments before looking once again at Holmes. "But I should like to become better acquainted with this young lady." He turned to address Lucy directly, and his tone became decidedly more courtly. "I admired your performance tonight. You were highly entertaining."

"Thank you, Your Royal Highness," said Lucy.

"She is more than an entertainer," said Holmes. "On several occasions she has served me well as my personal bodyguard."

"Bodyguard? I would hardly have expected such a—"

"To date she has saved my life on two occasions. She is highly trained in the Japanese art of *baritsu* and several other systems of physical combat. Considering Lord Kerren's murder and the other circumstances of our present situation, I believe you would do well to consider availing yourself of similar personal protection."

The Prince paled, got to his feet, and strode to the anteroom door without so much as another glance at Lucy. With his hand on the doorknob, he paused. "My associates will have gathered outside by now. My carriage and a late supper await me. Please delay your departure until the corridor outside is empty, so that we may avoid setting tongues to wagging unduly."

After the Prince had gone, Lucy turned to Holmes. "Was that necessary?"

"It will help us avoid further complications in a situation that is quite complex enough as it now stands."

They continued in their conversation and I moved to the door, intending to look out discreetly and determine whether the corridor was clear. I was eager to leave, for I was tired and the day had been long. But before I could touch the doorknob, there came a loud, powerful knock and the door swung open in one swift thrust, very nearly knocking me off balance.

Before me stood three German military officers in close-fitting black uniforms and polished high leather boots.

"The Kaiser requires your presence," said the tallest of the three. "Immediately."

29. INTERVIEW WITH THE ALL-HIGHEST

Still dressed in the white and gold-trimmed uniform that he had worn to the theatre earlier that evening, Kaiser Wilhelm II stared down at us from a polished and intricately engraved wooden throne. He sat ramrod-straight, his right hand on his knee, his left hand on his lap, as motionless as if he were sitting for an official portrait. To look him in the eye was somewhat uncomfortable, for the throne was raised so as to require us to look up to him, even though we were standing. On the right side of the throne stood von Bülow. He had just announced us after the three uniformed officers had escorted us into the high-ceilinged room within the *Schloss*, a tall building constructed around the high tower of a centuries-old castle at the western end of the *Kurpark*. Nearby was an enormous stone fireplace, large enough for a man to stand inside. On the walls hung thick tapestries. From their faded condition, I thought they could have been woven centuries before, depicting scenes of knights on their warhorses, thrusting at dragons with their spears. As we drew closer to the throne, I caught the unmistakable scent of pine oil and camphor. The dim light of the electric sconces around the walls cast shadows on the Kaiser's high-cheeked features.

"Mr. Holmes. Dr. Watson. Miss James," he said, nodding formally to each of us. Unlike von Bülow, he spoke without a trace of an accent. "I know the hour is late, and you were not expecting this interview. However, my plans have been altered, so yours must be as well."

Holmes gave one of his brief, perfunctory smiles. "How may we assist Your Imperial Highness?"

"First, I should like to know whether Dr. Watson has conveyed my request for assistance to you, Mr. Holmes."

"I have," I replied, adding hastily, "Your Imperial Highness."

"Will you accept, Mr. Holmes?"

"I will," replied Holmes. "Provided certain conditions are met."

"We will discuss those later. Now, Dr. Watson, what does Tesla think of Kerren's weapon?"

I was completely unprepared for this question. Ought I to say anything at all? Would not whatever I said be a treasonous revelation?

"Come, come, Dr. Watson. If my uncle can speak to me on the subject, surely so can you. He and I have discussed the merits and potential of Kerren's weapon on several occasions, the most recent of which was this evening, barely two hours before Kerren himself was found dead under such dramatic circumstances."

"Mr. Tesla did not express an opinion to me."

"To you, then, Mr. Holmes?"

"Tesla wanted to see it in operation before committing himself."

"As do I. But now I wonder if I shall have that opportunity, now that Kerren is dead and his jewel box has gone missing."

"Your Imperial Highness knows a great deal about the situation," said Holmes. "More than I, it appears."

"I believe the apparatus presents our two nations with the opportunity to make history, and to control the future governance of Europe. Perhaps we can control Asia as well, if my young cousin Nicholas can be brought into our alliance."

"You have a vision for an alliance between Germany and England?"

"For nearly six decades England has been ruled by my grandmother. Both our nations are descended from the same Saxon ancestry. An alliance would be the most natural thing in the world. However, only recently has my country been in a position to operate as an equal ally from a military standpoint. But now that my naval force has been strengthened, Germany can and must be recognized as an equal partner. Together our two nations can accomplish great things—far greater than if we continue to oppose one another."

"Undoubtedly, Imperial Highness," Holmes replied. I could not detect any trace of scepticism or irony in his tone. "But I was under the impression that you intended a competition of sorts regarding Kerren's weapon."

"Strictly speaking, it is *my* weapon."

Holmes allowed his eyes to widen and his eyebrows to rise enquiringly.

"I bought it from Kerren less than a month ago. He delivered its key component—the jewel box—to me personally, in Baden-Baden."

"He told us the jewel box had been stolen."

"As would be expected. His government, having paid him substantially, would naturally not have approved. So strictly speaking, from the perspective of Her Majesty's government, the jewel box was indeed stolen. Only Kerren was the thief."

"And now the jewel box has again been stolen, this time from you, which is the reason for my presence here. But prior to the second theft, you brought in experts in electricity and engineering to examine it. They made a copy, which you intend to demonstrate in Dover, and which you used for a demonstration in the *Kurpark* earlier."

Wilhelm's eyes flickered momentarily towards von Bülow. Then a tight smile appeared beneath the dark shadow of his distinctively upturned moustache. "You live up to your reputation, Mr. Holmes."

"The conclusion is an obvious one."

"You mentioned certain conditions in connection with your acceptance of my request."

"Your Imperial Highness must know that I am presently employed by my government for the same task. I cannot serve two masters."

"But if they were united in their desires?"

"The question would be what I would do with the jewel box when I had secured it. My government would wish me to bring it to England. Would your government wish the same?"

"Yes, if the arrangements my uncle and I have discussed were to remain in place."

"The arrangements to meet in Dover?"

"Correct. By the way, my engineers made more than one copy of Kerren's jewel box apparatus while it was in our possession, Mr. Holmes. Allow me to demonstrate the capabilities of another version of our weapon."

So saying, the Kaiser stood up before his throne. At this signal, one of the three uniformed officers strode to the side of the room and drew back a heavy tapestried curtain. Behind it was a tall open window. Outside of the window we saw only darkness. But then, moments later, powerful electrical floodlights illuminated an armoured four-wheel military vehicle about the size of a freight truck and bearing the muzzle of a large artillery gun at its front end.

"You will notice a vehicle outside. Yes? You see it? It bears armour and artillery comparable to that of an *Eclipse*-class protected naval cruiser."

The uniformed officer moved quickly away as the Kaiser strode to the window and stopped. He drew himself up to attention, bringing his polished boots together with a sharp click. He raised his right hand. With the same exaggerated gesture we had seen from a distance as he strode in the *Kurpark*, he snapped his fingers.

The electric lights around us dimmed. Outside, the light from the floodlights also grew fainter.

Then the military vehicle burst into flames.

30. A DIPLOMATIC BARGAIN

The electric lights outside and around us in the throne room came back to their full brightness. Fascinated, we watched the spectacle of the burning vehicle for a few moments. Then the Kaiser turned around, executing a perfect military about-turn, as though he had been on a parade drill, and marched back to his throne. The uniformed officer drew the heavy curtain shut.

Wilhelm resumed his position on his throne, obviously pleased with the effect his demonstration had created. "We do not know," he said, "whether either of our copies can produce a result as powerful as the original. I shall bring this latter version with me to Dover, as scheduled, a week from Sunday next. Its performance can then be compared with that of the original jewel box—which by then you, Mr. Holmes, will doubtless have recovered."

"You would place your version of this potentially priceless weapon within the borders of England?"

"Just as you have placed your own priceless personages within the borders of Germany. Just as my uncle does, year after year, and as my grandmother the Queen did before him. If our nations are to work together, they must trust one another."

"Very well, then," said Holmes. "Let us discuss my fee."

"Name it."

"One million pounds. In bearer bonds."

I gasped involuntarily. Holmes was referring deliberately to the sum taken from Kent, the traitorous banker, the previous November. But by his doing so, he was also directly, and most undiplomatically, referring to the outrageous use intended for those funds, which, had it been made public, would have surely brought our two nations into an immediate war.

Wilhelm blinked once, but his imperious expression did not change. "Your reasons for naming such a . . . princely sum?"

"I do not ask for the sum to be paid to me, Imperial Highness."

"To whom, then?"

"To no one, Imperial Highness."

"You will kindly explain." Wilhelm sat up a bit straighter on his throne, and his gloved right hand clamped down on his withered left hand as though he were bracing himself.

Holmes continued, "It has come to my attention that nearly one year ago your government sent one million pounds in bearer bonds to a London bank, and that the bonds were lost. I ask that this transaction—that obligation of the London bank, to speak with precision—be overlooked and forgotten. Such an action would accord well with the proposed new spirit of cooperation between our nations."

"I have no knowledge of such an obligation. Do you, von Bülow?"

"Not in the least, Imperial Highness."

"So is it possible for me to overlook and forget an obligation which I never knew of in the first place? That would be a question for philosophers to debate, I suppose. But we are practical men here. So my answer is that I accept your terms. Von Bülow, see that Mr. Holmes receives cash for his expenses and that his luggage is packed and brought to the railway station from his hotel."

"The latter has already been accomplished, Imperial Highness."

Wilhelm smiled in satisfaction. "Mr. Holmes, you will accompany von Bülow and me to my private railway car, where we shall travel together to Baden-Baden. We will arrive shortly after three a.m., at which time you can conduct an interview with the guard who allowed the theft of my jewel box. He may have been complicit in the theft, or he may merely have been incompetent. But nevertheless, he failed, and I do not tolerate failure."

"An unusual time for an interview."

"Perhaps, but time is of the essence. The fellow has only recently been apprehended. He suffered some injuries in his initial interrogation. He is not expected to live much longer. Dr. Watson and the lady will remain here as my guests."

Holmes stiffened. "I thought you believed our nations needed to trust one another. I do not think it is necessary for you to hold these two persons as hostages to my performance."

"Merely a precaution."

"Hold me as your hostage, and welcome," I said, "but the lady is not connected with us."

"Detaining her here will serve no purpose whatever," added Holmes.

"Nevertheless she may be useful, in the event we require the cooperation of my uncle. I understand that he is quite taken with her."

And with that, Wilhelm nodded to the three uniformed officers. Within moments Holmes was surrounded. A minute later, the great oaken door to the throne room had closed behind Holmes, von Bülow, Wilhelm, and the three officers.

The door locked with a metallic click. Lucy and I were now alone.

PART THREE

HITHER AND THITHER MOVES

31. PERIL BY NIGHT, PERIL BY DAY

Many questions raced through my mind as I tried to understand what had happened, and why Holmes had acted as he had done. Why had he spoken of the one million pounds in bearer bonds? Would not the reference to the failed assassination have been highly offensive to Wilhelm? Was it Holmes's way of throwing down a gauntlet, of showing Wilhelm that we knew of his treachery?

Or was it a way to prove that, just possibly, Wilhelm himself had been unaware of a plot that his subordinates had instigated? If so, I thought, that might lend credibility to Wilhelm's vision of our two nations working together in an alliance, based on mutual cooperation to develop Kerren's weapon. But did Holmes really believe that Kerren had sold his invention to the Germans? And once Holmes had identified the thief and recovered the jewel box, what was to prevent the Kaiser from extracting vengeance? Or did Holmes already have some protective measures in his far-seeing mind?

Lucy's voice interrupted my musings. In a tone of voice that I thought was unusually clear and distinct, she said, "I don't understand why Mr. Holmes would do such a thing to me."

"At least they are not aware—" I began, in an attempt to offer some encouragement, but she motioned for silence, drawing her index finger across her throat and then pressing it to her lips. She cut her eyes towards the bellpull that hung to one side of the throne. Alongside the wall beside the braided silken rope was a speaking tube. From the end of the tube a cork stopper dangled from a short cord. I realized that everything said in the room could be overheard by anyone at the other end of the open tube. To my horror, I realized that I had very nearly disclosed to the Germans the secret that Lucy was Holmes's daughter.

"I will not accept this treatment," Lucy was saying. As she spoke, she walked slowly and quietly around the perimeter of the throne room, pausing only to look behind the large hanging tapestries, one by one. "It is intolerable for a lady to be dealt with in such a fashion. We have another performance tomorrow. I shall demand to speak with Mr. Carte. He will know what to do."

She beckoned me to where she stood, beside a tapestry on the wall to the left of the throne. Lifting the heavy fabric, she pointed to the wall behind, where I could discern the outlines of a tall window amidst the shadows. She pointed at me, then mimed the opening of the window, then put her finger to her lips once more. I nodded and stepped between the curtain and the wall.

I groped along the window frame to find the latch. Behind me, I heard her voice, muffled by the thick tapestry, continuing her litany of complaints. "Surely someone will be along any moment to escort us to a proper place for us to wait. We are not animals, to be left locked in a room without explanation. The hour is late and we have had no supper, nor have we been offered so much as a glass of water."

At last my fumbling fingers were able to open the latch. I bent my knees, placing the heels of my hands beneath the upper frame of the lower sash, and shoved upwards. There was no movement whatsoever.

"This is hardly royal hospitality," Lucy continued behind me.

I grasped the upper part of the frame and shook it front and back, trying to loosen the grip of the frame upon the sash. I felt a slight give. I did so again as Lucy continued, "This is hardly the behaviour of one who wishes to show the proper degree of respect due to an ally."

Then I bent my knees and struck upwards with the heels of my hands, hoping the impact would further loosen the sash. There was a modest degree of movement. On my next attempt the sash slid upwards, far enough so that my arms could straighten fully, and, more importantly, far enough so that either of us could fit through. Cool air flooded around me. I peered out the opening. I could see the darkness of the lawn and shrubbery, some twelve or fifteen feet below. In the distance were the shadowy outlines of a large stand of trees. I also caught the scent of cooking.

Backing out from behind the tapestry, I turned to beckon Lucy to come to the open window.

To my shock, Lucy was standing in front of a tall uniformed soldier, who held her from behind with one hand. In the other hand was the hilt of a polished military sword, the blade of which he pressed against Lucy's throat.

"He was in back of the tapestry the whole time," she said, defeat and disappointment weakening her voice. The soldier smiled with satisfaction. But I could see her eyes, and they sent me a message of defiance. Instantly I understood that she was about to move, and I knew what I had to do.

Lucy twisted sideways, so suddenly that she fell through the soldier's grip. At the same time I hurled myself at the soldier with all my force. As I reached the man, I lashed out with the heel of my hand, just as I had struck the window sash moments earlier, catching him on the side of his jaw with a sharp cracking impact. The man shrugged off the blow and stepped back, swinging the blade of the sword at me, narrowly missing my face. I dived at him beneath the blade and we fell together, grappling, to the carpeted floor, each struggling to gain an advantage. I knew my only hope was to remain close enough so that he could not effectively manipulate the long sword blade. My fingers were at his throat when I felt a sudden rush of air above me and, in the same instant, heard the hollow impact of a hard object against the top of the man's skull.

The man went limp. As I separated myself from his sagging arms and got to my knees, I saw Lucy above me, holding a brass candlestick. She kicked the sword away from the man's motionless fingers.

Instinctively I bent over him and pressed my fingertips to his neck, feeling for a pulse.

"He's still breathing. Come *on*," said Lucy in a harsh whisper. She bent down and grasped him by the collar, dragging him to the far side of the throne.

From the direction of the tall oak entry doors I heard voices. They were coming closer.

"There's another window behind the tapestry on the far side," Lucy whispered. "Can you open it?"

She drew back the tapestry so that I could see better, and moments later I had raised the sash as far upwards as it would go. I glanced back at her, readying myself to climb out, jump down, and then catch Lucy. But she shook her head. "That one's a decoy. Come back this way!"

As we reached the first window that I had opened, we could hear the rattle of keys outside the oaken doors.

"Jump!" she whispered into my ear after we had slid behind the heavy tapestry. "I'll be right behind you."

Climbing into the window opening, I could hear the metallic click of the door lock. Then I pushed off and fell, trying to pull my feet inwards so as to lessen the impact upon landing, as we Army lads had been taught to do, imagining we were to leap and fall from mountain crevices in Afghanistan. As I hit, I rolled to one side. The sod was still soft from the weekend storms, so I was relatively unshaken as I rolled over onto one knee and looked up.

Fifteen feet above me, Lucy was standing on the ledge outside the window, facing the building. I realized she was attempting to press down the window sash, so as to deceive the Germans as to the side of the building from which we had made our escape. I heard a man's harsh voice within the room, calling out in German.

Then Lucy was falling towards me. The next instant she had crashed into my arms and I was stumbling backwards beneath her, colliding with the earth.

"You're intact?" she asked, getting to her feet, her eyes wide in the moonlight.

I stood beside her and caught my breath. Before us, less than ten yards away, were the silhouettes of tall trees. Beyond them were the moonlit waters of a small lake. Behind us the walls of the building towered above. We had landed at the north-west corner of the building. Light shone through a row of windows above us, and more light shone from windows at our feet. Bending down to look inside, within what was plainly a kitchen below the ground floor, we could see the white-capped figure of a plump cook. She was pulling a tray from an oven.

From the far side of the building, we heard the sharp, eager barking of hunting dogs. "Wait here," said Lucy. She ran directly towards the lake and disappeared from view. I heard splashing in the water. Then, to my surprise and relief, I saw her reappear beneath the trees and come running straight back to where I stood. "A trail for our canine friends," she said. "Now we must find the gate."

Keeping close to the wall, we reached the far corner of the *Schloss*. Lucy, ahead of me, looked around and then stepped back into the shadows. "Arkwright and Harriet," she whispered. "They're at the front entrance."

Hugging close to the cold, rough stone facade, I could see our two allies, waiting, watching the well-guarded gate at the far side of the circular drive as if they expected a carriage to come through. I picked up a small handful of stones from the gravel edge and tossed one in their direction. They paid no attention. On my third attempt, however, Arkwright noticed. He was with us a moment later, Harriet close behind him.

The barking of the guard dogs grew louder. Arkwright inclined his head in their direction. "Those dogs are searching for you, I take it?"

Lucy said, "We were hostages. The Kaiser wants to ensure that Holmes recovers the jewel box."

"Well, the Prince wants the jewel box too. He'll be in Dover Saturday, and he expects Holmes to deliver it to him personally. Where is Holmes?"

"With the Kaiser, on his way to Baden-Baden. The Kaiser's guards locked us inside the throne room."

"Where do you want to go?"

"Baden-Baden."

"Are you sure that is wise?" Harriet asked.

"At the very least, Holmes should know that we have escaped. And we may be able to assist him."

"There is a train tomorrow morning," said Arkwright. "We will need to hide you somewhere until then."

A few hours later I felt a light tap at my shoulder.

Lucy stood above me. The moonlight shone upon her lovely face, her dark-green eyes set in firm resolve. "It's time," she said. "Harriet is already downstairs."

I realized that we were once again inside the *Schloss*, in a vacant second-floor suite that we had reached by way of an open kitchen window. The light came from the setting moon outside of the windows.

"She's had more of a reaction to Kerren's death than I would have thought," Lucy went on, "considering that she never liked him. Very unsteady, all of a sudden."

I struggled into my disguise, the white jacket of a laundry attendant, which had been made for a much smaller man. The cap was too large. "Arkwright said these were the best he could do," Lucy said. "Here are four laundry bags for you to carry. Suitcases are inside—supplied by Arkwright. One of them has your jacket and topcoat. Now, downstairs to wait for the diversion."

The corridor was deserted at this predawn hour, as were the stairs and, thankfully, the short kitchen hallway that led to the delivery entrance. We could see two white-clad women within the cooking area, both busy over steaming pans and kettles. We were soon outside. The air had a dank chill about it. We walked down the steps that led to the paved drive. As I clutched the iron railing, the cold, wet morning dew clung to my fingers.

We looked around for Harriet, who was to have stood watch at the corner, but we could not see her in the shadows.

"What time is it?" Lucy asked.

Before I could retrieve my watch from my trousers pocket, we heard the wail of a fire alarm siren coming from the north-east of where we stood. The sky in that direction was too dark for me to be certain of what had happened, but I thought I detected a faint orange glow above the trees to our east.

"Arkwright's completed at least one task," Lucy said. "They've discovered the fire in the casino."

Then we heard the distant clip-clop of hooves and the rattle of wheels on pavement. At the same time, from around the corner we saw Harriet running towards us.

"He's coming!" she said quietly. "I could see him after he passed the guard station."

Moments later, two black horses and a dun-coloured laundry wagon came into view. Seated on his driver's perch, Adrian Arkwright hauled on the reins, and then clambered down as the wagon came to a stop. Under his limp brown canvas uniform cap, his face twisted in a wry grin. "Five minutes' ride coming up. All aboard," he said.

Inside, I shoved my canvas sacks between the others already stacked neatly on either side of the wagon's interior. I then crouched down beside Lucy. Harriet climbed in behind us. "I hate the dark," Harriet said as Arkwright shut the door.

I felt the cart turn around, lurch forwards, and then stop. "This will be the guard station," whispered Harriet.

We waited. Then came a man's voice, distracted and fatigued. *"Ja, fort."* We lurched forwards.

About five minutes later, we stopped again.

"Welcome to Bad Homburg's busiest laundry," Arkwright said, pulling open the door. "I have to return this wagon, but over there is the hansom cab we can take to the station. Doctor, you and Lucy can shed your whites and put on your topcoats. Then you might help me get one of the nags switched over to the hansom."

"Is it far to the station?" Harriet asked.

"They'll be watching at Bad Homburg. We're going to Frankfurt, the next stop down the line."

Soon we had changed into our own clothes and appeared to be respectable travellers. Arkwright handed me a small satchel of cheap, well-worn brown leather stuffed with German currency and gave me instructions as to where I should go when we reached Baden-Baden. Then he pressed the torn half of a business card into my hand.

He was about to explain, but at that moment we heard the sound of an approaching horse and carriage.

Before we could hide, the carriage had come into view. My heart sank as I recognized the driver.

It was Richter, the flaxen-haired giant who had attacked us in St. Margaret's and abducted Herr Gruen at the *Kurhaus*.

32. A CHANGE OF PLAN

The door to the carriage opened and the man called Dietrich climbed out, while Richter climbed down from his driver's perch. The two stood before us. "Hello, Mr. Arkwright," said Dietrich.

"Gentlemen."

"Dr. Watson and Miss James must come with us." His tone was formal.

"There must be a mistake," Arkwright said.

"There is no mistake. We have our orders from von Bülow."

"How did you find us?"

"We were to follow anyone who left the *Schloss*. Your laundry cart has been the only vehicle to depart since the Kaiser's last night. Now, Dr. Watson and Miss James, you will kindly get into this carriage."

"That's impossible," said Arkwright.

"I fear we must insist," said Dietrich. In his hand was now a wickedly curved long knife, which he held so that it pointed towards Arkwright and Harriet. "But our orders only pertain to the return of the prisoners. They do not mention those who merely assist in the escape of prisoners. You and your lady friend may remain here or go wherever it pleases you."

Arkwright gave a sigh. "Well, if you put it that way—" He nodded at Lucy and me, indicating we should obey the order.

The next moment Richter and Dietrich were behind Lucy and me, shoving us towards the open carriage door, like a pair of sheepdogs herding their charges into a shearing pen.

I pushed back from the carriage, intending to drop down to my right knee and pull Richter to the ground, allowing Lucy to escape. Lucy also was moving, turning away from me.

But at that instant I heard a hollow, metallic cracking sound, twice, in rapid succession, behind us. Reflexively I turned around. There on the gravel were the crumpled figures of Richter and Dietrich. The larger man had been struck in the back of the head, for I saw a red stain spreading through his blond hair. Dietrich had a similar red stain discolouring the hair around his temple. Both men were still breathing. A Webley revolver lay on the ground beside them, as did Dietrich's curved knife.

Standing above the two men, Arkwright was gazing down on his upper right thigh. His trouser leg had been cut open. Blood was soaking the fabric. Harriet was bent over beside him, staring in horror, her hands on her knees.

"Get into the hansom. Now!" Arkwright said. "Hurry, before these two thugs wake up!"

I put Lucy and Harriet into the hansom. Turning back, I saw Arkwright with his belt now tied around his red-stained trouser leg, crouching over the sprawled and unconscious Dietrich. He picked up the Webley and the knife and tucked both weapons into his coat.

Within twenty minutes, we were at Frankfurt central station. Even at that early hour, the plaza outside was crowded. Arkwright manoeuvred our cab into the queue and then, when we had climbed out, motioned me up to his driver's seat. He pressed a wad of German notes into my hand. "Pay for three round-trip tickets to Basel; first class, of course, so you have your own compartment. You will get off the train two hours before Basel, at Baden-Baden. Harriet's German is passable. She can tell you what to say to the ticket clerk and to the others on the train."

"Harriet?"

"She *must* go with you. Remember, they're looking for a middle-aged man and a young woman. Not a middle-aged man and *two* young women. I'll join you when I can. Don't let anyone touch that satchel unless he shows you the other half of that business card."

Several hours later our train reached Baden-Baden, stopping amidst clouds of steam and a harsh screeching of the engine's brakes. The afternoon sun had sunk below the dark line of the mountains to our west. As we stepped down from our carriage to the wooden platform that ran alongside the tracks, the wind bit with a sharpened quality that foretold the harshness of the oncoming winter. On other tracks on the far side of the train, a northbound express thundered through, rendering us motionless with the sheer force of its mechanical power. Then it was gone.

I walked with Lucy and Harriet down seven stone steps, through a small pedestrian tunnel beneath the tracks, and up seven more steps to the northbound platform. I glanced around, trying not to appear anxious, as we entered the station. My heart was racing and my breath came shallow in my chest.

We passed through without incident and reached the far side of the building. Many carriages were lined up on the crowded station approach to collect passengers and luggage from the arriving train. With a sweating hand, I gripped the satchel with its precious cargo. I moved through towards the cab line, intending to hail the first cab and give the driver our address. Then I remembered Holmes's advice. He had said never to take the first cab that presents itself, nor the second.

I chose the third. The driver stood beside his horse. "Driver!" I called, raising my right hand and pressing forwards through the crowd.

Then I saw that the driver was Holmes.

He held up his hand in warning.

Something hard and heavy smashed into my back, and, before I could turn, smashed again on the back of my head. The crowded pavement seemed to spin and diminish into an ever-shrinking circle, framed in an ever-growing ring of darkness. Then the cobblestones rushed up to collide with my falling body, and I saw only a black void.

33. ANOTHER VISIT

I awoke to the sound of a man's voice. His words came in a German accent. "We will ask your friend as soon as he awakens."

I opened my eyes. Kneeling beside me was Holmes, and beside him, getting to his feet, was a tall military man in a close-fitting black uniform. The man's greatcoat was embroidered with gold threads. His boots had been polished to a hard gloss, as bright as patent leather.

Holmes was speaking. In my fogged condition, his voice seemed to echo. "I did not want to leave you, Watson. Colonel Brandt here is assisting me in our mission. His men are pursuing your attacker."

"What happened?" I managed to say. I struggled to stand, but the darkness surged in around me once again. I sank back down to the cobblestones.

"You were struck from behind. It was difficult to recognize your attacker. He used a small sandbag, and took your satchel as you fell. That was perhaps five minutes ago. The blow was expertly applied. I believe you will make a rapid recovery. It would be useful if we knew the contents of the satchel."

My fingers explored the back of my head. There was swelling but not the sharp pang that would have indicated a fracture. Nor was there a wound.

"What was in the satchel, Dr. Watson?" asked Brandt.

"Fifty thousand gold marks," I replied. Then I remembered that Lucy and Harriet had been with me. I sat up too abruptly and felt sharp pain inside my forehead. But I was relieved to see the two young ladies standing a few feet away, peering at me from the edge of a crowd of onlookers.

"We can wait until later for more questions," said Holmes. "It is growing dark. Do you think you can stand and manage a ride in my cab? My hotel is the Villa Stephanie, only a short ride from here. Colonel, we shall report to you in the morning."

"Regrettably, I have orders to take Dr. Watson and one of these ladies—the one named Miss Lucy James—into custody."

Holmes's reply was polite but firm. "You might wish to consult with von Bülow. These are my associates and I require their safety. If they are permitted to take shelter with me, then I shall be able to continue in my mission for the Kaiser."

"And if they are not?"

"Then you shall have to take me into custody too. But that would significantly impair my ability to complete the Kaiser's mission."

The Colonel nodded. "We shall have our discussion in the morning. I shall call on you at your hotel at nine thirty." He snapped his fingers, and a soldier standing behind him came forward. "This man will drive your cab and see that all of you are comfortably settled. You will not be permitted to leave the hotel."

"Holmes," I said, when the four of us were inside the cab, "are you sure we ought to stay at your hotel? Arkwright told us to go to a different place."

"Nonetheless we must change our plan. It is apparent from the attack on you that, once again, someone has penetrated our communications and is not hesitant to remind us of his capability."

"Our communications?" asked Lucy.

"I placed an advertisement in the papers this morning. The telegraphed response directed me to meet the afternoon train from Bad Homburg, to present myself as a cab driver, and to watch for you. I congratulate you on your cautious selection of the third cab, of course."

"Might the attacker have merely been an observant street thief who thought the satchel might contain something of value?" asked Harriet. "I saw the fellow, and he was certainly dressed shabbily enough to maintain that impression."

Holmes lowered his voice. "I was not entirely truthful with the Colonel when I implied that I did not recognize the attacker. I am certain that beneath the battered bowler hat and the tattered overcoat was our friend Mr. Gruen."

We reached the hotel shortly thereafter. As we secured our rooms, I noticed that our military escort had settled down in the lobby to wait. "We shall be observed leaving or entering," Holmes said. "I plan to depart by another exit soon, with my appearance substantially altered. Let us meet tomorrow morning for breakfast before the Colonel arrives."

"I will go with you," Lucy said.

"The best thing you can do is to stay here until we can obtain a safe passage for you tomorrow."

"I am not leaving until we have the jewel box," she replied, and I saw in her green eyes the same determination that I had witnessed on previous similar occasions.

Holmes replied, "We can discuss that in the morning."

Harriet said, "I want to send a telegram to London. I feel I ought to seek guidance from Lansdowne. I believe I am under his direction, not yours, Mr. Holmes."

"As you wish," Holmes replied. "I am sure the concierge can help you with the arrangements." Then he left.

Harriet, Lucy, and I met for a light supper in the dining room. Despite my efforts to keep up my side of the conversation, I am certain they both realized I was feeling the ill effects of my injury, so our time together was relatively brief. I went to my room with the intention of preparing for sleep.

As I opened the door, I felt a cool draft of outside air. I switched on the electric sconce light and saw that the curtain on the far wall was drawn back. The door to my balcony stood open to the night. I heard a familiar, overly courteous voice. "Please close the door behind you, Dr. Watson."

Stepping into my room from the balcony was Mr. Gruen, dressed in the swallowtail coat he had worn on the occasion of our first meeting, and carrying the same top hat. With precise little bird-like movements, he closed the door behind him and drew the curtain across. Once again the false expressions of friendship and apology appeared sequentially on his round, cherubic features. "I owe you a thousand apologies, Doctor. I will not keep you long. I ought not to have intruded upon you, but if you will allow me a moment's explanation, all will be made clear. You see, I am your only true friend in all this sad affair of the electrical weapon."

His little dark eyes were wide with forced sincerity.

"You were the man in the shabby coat and bowler hat."

"A necessary bit of camouflage, which I have discarded. As I hope you will discard any animosity that you feel towards me."

"How is it that you know my hotel room and are able to enter it?"

"Commerce, sir. Perfectly simple commerce. Information is a commodity, available for a price. Hotel keys are also readily acquired. If you are wondering how I knew you were staying here, rather than at the location farther away to which Mr. Arkwright had directed you, well, that is simpler still. I observed you from the station, and then I followed you."

"You took a satchel from me. I suppose it provided you ample currency."

"I had no choice in the matter, sir, believe me. I was forced to use the direct approach, for I was being watched. My loyalty is constantly being questioned by my masters. Doing you an injury of sorts was the only way to convince them of my allegiance. Please accept my profuse and profound apologies for that effrontery. By the way, the funds have been delivered to my masters and you have been credited in full for the initial payment we discussed—has it really been only three nights since?"

"Kindly come to the point of your visit, Mr. Gruen."

"Of course. I wish you to understand that I am indeed your one true friend in this matter, because only I am prepared to do what you wish—namely to return the jewel box and its highly complex contents to you and your associates. Others will approach you. They will command you. But they cannot be trusted. They will never deliver."

"Are you referring to the people who accosted you in Bad Homburg?"

"They are some of the pawns in the game, sir. But yes, they are employed by those to whom I refer."

"And why am I so fortunate to have your friendship?"

The fixed smile reappeared and remained as though it had been baked onto his round visage. "Because I, sir, operate from the purest of motives. I work for cash. I have no politics. I do not consider the vast military and political and economic powers that will ebb and flow between nations, depending upon whose armies and navies possess the new weapon. I do not consider the advantages to be gained by breaking a promise to one monarch and so putting him out of humour and altering his abilities to negotiate with his counterpart. I amass what stockpile I can, and when my assets have grown to a sufficient degree, I shall vanish. By the way, here is my token of sincerity."

He extended his hand and I saw in it the torn edge of a business card.

I took the torn card that Arkwright had given me from my vest pocket. I inspected the edges. The two ends fitted perfectly with one another.

"How are you and Arkwright connected?" I asked.

"I am not at liberty to disclose any connections with anyone. Now, to business. You will receive instructions from my masters in letter form. I would urge you to obey them for the sake of appearances and, in fact, for my own protection. However, any funds you advance in accordance with those instructions will be wasted. Make whatever excuses you must, but bear *that* in mind. Tomorrow night you will hear from me before midnight. At that time, I shall have the jewel box in my personal possession and will be in a position to make the exchange. You and I will not be watched this time. You will, of course, have another satchel ready, containing another fifty thousand gold marks."

"Which you do *not* intend to deliver to your masters. Whoever they may be."

"You grasp my meaning perfectly, Doctor." So saying, he got to his feet with a nimbleness I would not have expected considering his bulk. "Until we meet again, Doctor. Here is the key to your room."

The following morning, I awoke with a clearer mind. I drew back the heavy curtains in front of my balcony door and saw dark cloudy skies, brightened just above the darker ridge of pine-forested mountains by the pale aura of the rising sun. I wondered what Holmes had done while I had slept. I recalled that the Colonel would be joining us this morning, to take Lucy and me into his custody. I recalled Mr. Gruen's glib assurance that he would have the jewel box in his possession before midnight.

Turning away from the window, I noticed a white envelope on the carpet before the door. The envelope was addressed to me. The letter inside was printed in black ink, employing block capital letters that were obviously meant to disguise the handwriting of the sender. The letter read, "Trinkhalle. 7:30 tonight. Come alone."

34. LETTERS

Holmes, Lucy, and Harriet were already at our table in the dining room when I came down for breakfast. I asked Holmes how his researches had gone, but he gave an evasive answer. Naturally I told him of the visit from Mr. Gruen.

"He would not be the first criminal to attempt to cut out his associates from their share of the spoils," said Holmes. "Still, any communications from him will bear consideration. He may be telling the truth. He may indeed be able to deliver the jewel box."

"He predicted that letters would come from his masters," I said. "That part of his story has now come true." I showed the letter I had received. Holmes scanned it in a moment and passed it along to Lucy.

Lucy's eyes widened. She pulled a letter from her reticule. It was printed in the same capital letter hand. The message directed her to come to room 504 at the hotel, also at 7:30 p.m.

Harriet wordlessly showed us a similar letter, directing her to come to room 604 at the same time.

Holmes gave one of his wry smiles. "It seems I have not been neglected in this wave of correspondence. Here is the letter that arrived in my room early this morning. 'First payment acknowledged. Bring Tesla to the Friedrichsbad. 7:30 p.m. No one else.'" He turned up his palm. "Apparently they know Tesla is here in this hotel. The maître d'hôtel informed me that he arrived last night."

"It appears they want to divide us," said Lucy. "The question is whether we comply with their request."

"I do not like this," said Harriet. "Someone is making it plain that they know where we are and that we are under their command."

"I think we must tell the Colonel," said Holmes. "If the instructions of these letters are to be obeyed, then he must permit each of you to go where you have been directed. He cannot take you into his custody."

Holmes's assessment of the Colonel's position proved to be correct. The Colonel agreed to allow Lucy and me to remain at liberty, although he did enjoin us to stay within view of himself or his men. The next step was to notify Tesla that his presence would be required that evening.

The Colonel, who had escorted Tesla from the railway station upon his arrival the previous evening, led us to Tesla's room on the sixth floor. Clad in a black silk dressing gown, Tesla recognized the Colonel and, of course, the rest of us when we knocked on the door. Calmly inviting us inside, he perched on the arm of an overstuffed sofa. On the low table before him was a silver tray with a half-eaten rusk and a half-empty china teacup.

After Holmes had explained the situation and shown Tesla the letter he had received, Tesla appeared puzzled. He said, "I do not understand why my presence is required at some clandestine rendezvous."

"Possibly because your expertise is necessary to verify the authenticity of the jewel box," said Holmes. "Whoever wrote this note evidently believes that neither of the governments seeking its return will pay for an unauthenticated device."

"But the contents are Kerren's invention. I can make no assurances that his device will work in the way he described. My mind operates in a different fashion. I have considered the problem, of course, for several years. I had even, as I may have mentioned, set down to writing some of the visions that had come to me—"

"Quite so," said Holmes, interrupting. "But we are here to recover Kerren's jewel box and we need you to accompany us."

"We would prefer that you do so voluntarily," added the Colonel. "You will do so, yes?"

Tesla said, "If I were to be suitably compensated—"

"I will discuss compensation with my superiors," said the Colonel. His face was impassive, and I tried to read in his eyes whether he was telling the truth. I was beginning to feel oppressed by the knowledge that we were all under continued surveillance. I felt certain that we could not trust the Colonel, who clearly had no interest in protecting me. I felt sure that he and his men only wanted to stay close to us in order to recover the jewel box, and that as soon as it was in the Kaiser's possession, the plan for a trial of the weapon on Dover beach would be abandoned. I felt the alliance proposed by both the Prince and the Kaiser was only a chimera of hope, an illusion each man was creating so as to lull the other into complacency. I reminded myself that I ought not to allow my emotions to colour the facts.

"Where are we to go?" Tesla was asking.

"The Friedrichsbad," said the Colonel. "It is a popular destination for foreign cure-seekers who wish to purify themselves."

Holmes said, "The time indicated on the letter is 7:30. That is well past sunset. Is there lighting in this Friedrichsbad?"

"The facility is closed to visitors at that hour. But I can arrange for lighting."

"I remind you that the message I received did not say I was to arrive with a military escort."

"It is imperative that you and Tesla be protected. We do not know who will be waiting there for you. And, Herr Tesla, whoever has the jewel box may wish to abduct you. We cannot rule out that possibility."

"Why would they want me?" Tesla folded his arms and shook his head.

"To force you to use your genius for their purpose. Or to keep you from doing so for others'."

"I am not afraid." Tesla turned away from the Colonel. "I shall accompany Mr. Holmes and we will address any difficulties when they occur."

"Then I would suggest," said the Colonel, "that we take advantage of the remaining daylight hours to visit the Friedrichsbad and acquaint ourselves with the terrain. The knowledge may prove useful when we return."

Lucy said, "Harriet and I will come with you."

I said, "And I as well, of course."

The Colonel gave a fleeting smile. "We shall all visit the Friedrichsbad. My men and I will keep to ourselves, but we will be close enough to see you at all times, and to intervene if there is any reason to do so."

Harriet said, "I will not go. That message says Holmes and Tesla are to come alone. I will not contribute to a failure by disobeying the clear instructions that we have received. If these people are serious—and the attack on Dr. Watson ought to tell us that they are—you will spoil the opportunity to recover the jewel box. And I for one do not want to have to explain why I was part of the failure."

"I take it you have not had a reply to your wire to London," said Holmes.

Harriet shook her head.

“What will you do?” asked Lucy.

“I may go out for a time. There are architectural features here that I would like to memorialize in my sketchbook. At 7:30 this evening, I shall obey the instructions I received.” She got to her feet, her eyes downcast, toying with her purple scarf. “I shall wait for you in the foyer, following whatever transpires in room 604.”

35. A COMPULSORY INVITATION

Shortly afterwards, we approached the Friedrichsbad, the centre of medical treatment activity at Baden-Baden. A massive and ornate sandstone structure, it resembled Buckingham Palace, at least to my untrained eye. Along the broad front walkway, people were waiting to enter. Some appeared weary and forlorn, bereft of hope, while others moved with expectant looks. I wondered how many of each group had been helped by the procedures they were about to undergo and how many were taking the hot baths and other "cures" for the first time.

The Colonel and Holmes were about forty feet ahead of us. I saw the Colonel stride confidently past the line of patients, up the wide granite front steps, and through the broad entrance. Holmes, however, joined the queue with Tesla, who had drawn his hat down over his forehead so as to avoid being recognized by any of the visitors who might have seen his photograph in the papers. Holmes turned as we came up beside them. We waited in the queue for a few minutes. Then Holmes said, "The Colonel is beckoning to us."

"So much for his remaining out of view at all times," Lucy said under her breath, as we walked past the disapproving stares of the waiting patients.

The Colonel fairly beamed with pride as we joined him. He motioned us to walk with him into the Friedrichsbad. The interior resembled the spa at Bad Homburg, but was far grander and more ornate. When we were out of earshot of the other visitors, the Colonel stopped and turned to me.

"Dr. Watson, I am instructed to convey the Kaiser's personal apology for the rough treatment you endured at the station yesterday. I have arranged—the Kaiser has ordered—that you be given a therapeutic treatment for your injury."

"I am perfectly well, I assure you." In fact, my head still throbbed, and the back of my skull, where the attacker's blow had struck, was quite tender.

"Nonsense. The Kaiser insists. He wants your opinion concerning the efficacy of the clinicians and staff. Your medical opinion. He also wishes to make it plain that he has graciously forgiven you and the lady for escaping from his quarters at the *Schloss*."

The idea came to me at once that the Kaiser still wanted us as hostages for Holmes's performance, and that it was now perfectly plain that he had us under his control once more. We *were* hostages, and had been so since we entered the town less than twenty-four hours earlier.

Holmes took my arm and led me out of the hearing of the others. "This cannot be as benevolent as it appears," he said.

"At least they are not holding Lucy."

"They may try to extract information from you."

"I shall tell them nothing. Perhaps I can learn something."

Holmes nodded. We returned to the Colonel. Holmes said, "I shall resign from this case if any further harm comes to Dr. Watson."

"You need have no concerns on that score, Herr Holmes. We have arranged for Dr. Watson to occupy the Kaiser's personal treatment suite. While he is there, you and the lady and Mr. Tesla are to be given a tour of the facility, and any treatments that you wish will be provided at no charge to yourselves, with the Kaiser's compliments."

"I require no treatment," said Tesla.

"Nor I," said Holmes and Lucy, almost simultaneously.

The Colonel shrugged, and then nodded towards a tall bronze door directly behind us. The door squeaked on its hinges as a uniformed officer pulled it open. A tall man in white coat and trousers stood within. He said with a bright, professional smile, "This way, Dr. Watson." He led me into a white-painted corridor decorated with a row of portraits, presumably of past administrators of the facility. "Our treatments employ the hot-water exercise methods that were pursued by the Romans nearly two thousand years ago," he continued, dropping back to walk at my side. "But we also employ the hot-air techniques invented by a renowned Irish doctor—you will pardon me, please, but I do not recall his name. Nevertheless, the combination of the two treatments makes us unique in all the world. Please open that door. It is the Kaiser's personal reception area. His personal attendant awaits you."

The surface of this door was also bronze, shielding the wood beneath, I thought, from the effects of the moist warm air that permeated the windowless hallway and the small room that I now entered. Another white-uniformed attendant, this one a young blond woman, was seated before me, on one of two dark-grey granite benches. Behind her a single large window admitted light through opaque glass. Along the white-tiled wall behind her, a channel for the hot waters had been cut at about waist level, where I could see vapours rising from the continuous flow.

"Welcome to the Kaiser's personal reception and libation area," the woman said with a perfunctory smile and without extending her hand. I heard the door close behind me. The other attendant was gone.

"Do not be nervous, Doctor," she said. "You will not be disrobing here. You will simply imbibe a small cup of the thermal waters—very restorative I assure you—and then you will have your consultation with the doctor in the next room before you proceed with further treatments."

She took down a metal cup from a shelf along the wall and dipped it into the hot flow. "These are oxidizing waters," she said, "coming directly from underground at a temperature of about one hundred and fifty degrees Fahrenheit—not even as hot as a freshly brewed cup of your English tea." She smiled as she swirled the liquid within the cup. "The waters will oxidize the toxins in your system and improve your circulation. This will speed the healing process."

She held the filled cup out before me as though it were a holy chalice. At this close distance, the pungent odour of the waters was quite intense. "I feel fine," I said. "I only have a slight bruising."

"It will be helped by the waters, I assure you."

"This drink smells of sulphur."

"Sulphur is very similar to oxygen in its chemical effects on the human body. Both substances act to burn up materials that have an ill effect on the life forces within us, thus enabling our bodies to perform their vital functions more readily."

"I have heard the same thing said of electricity."

"We here at the Friedrichsbad have decades of experience with these natural waters and believe them more effective than any man-made inventions. I drink the waters daily myself. Come, let us enjoy a toast together."

She dipped a second metal cup into the stream. She swirled the liquid around for a moment, then held it up and clinked edges with mine. The water was nearly scalding hot. I blew upon it to cool it and then drank a few sips.

"The entire cup, please. See, I have done the same."

I did so.

"Wonderful," she said. "Now I can take you in to see the doctor."

She opened the door to the next room. A small, balding grey-haired man, bespectacled and with a shrunken frame, sat behind a desk. He had a very red, flushed complexion that was also apparent in his hands, which he clasped before him on his desk. His wrists, also flushed, were visible beyond the starched white cuffs of his laboratory coat.

"Ah, Dr. Watson," he said. "Please have a seat on the couch, if you will. I have only a few questions to ask before we commence your treatment. Your answers will determine the fine details of the course that we pursue."

He was looking at me with great interest. His bright-blue eyes fairly sparkled behind his metal-rimmed spectacles. "As a medical man," he went on, "you may think it odd that I would attach such apparent importance to a case that involves only a bruising to the skull. Yet when I learned that the Kaiser himself has concerned himself in the matter, and that he values your opinion—" He spread his palms wide. "I am sure you realize that I will do all I can to make sure you are delighted with the results of your treatment here."

The room was becoming warm. It seemed to me that someone had put a kettle on a hidden stove and that steam was filling the room. Yet, I observed, there was no condensation on the doctor's spectacles and his face, though flushed, appeared to be without perspiration.

"We treat the entire patient here," he was saying. "We do not address merely the troublesome symptoms, which are trivial in comparison to the underlying cause. I can see that already you are making excellent progress." He took out a silver pocket watch and held it out, his elbows resting on the desk. The watch swung back and forth on its silver chain as though it were a pendulum.

A wave of dizziness came over me. It seemed as though I had fallen into a pool of water. The light coming from the window and the tiled walls appeared to separate itself, as if the air within the room had the quality of a prism. I tried to look away from the swinging silver watch and focus on his face. I noticed a large red welt at the base of his neck.

He said, "My name is Olfrig."

For the second time in as many days, I lost consciousness.

36. A SECOND ATTACK

When I awoke, I was lying on my abdomen on a hard, cold surface. The air around me was cold. Opening my eyes, I could see the harsh white gleam of floor tiles and wall tiles and realized I was lying on the floor in a corner of a room, still dressed as I had been. I wanted to move but my muscles were reluctant to obey. I had no sense of how much time had elapsed. Within myself I felt a strangely familiar inner emptiness. I tried to identify the sensation. It was a sense of loss. Something had happened, and that something was irrevocable. The feeling brought with it a swirling cascade of memories. Men dying under my care in cold tents as the dust-laden wind howled from the Afghanistan mountains. The roar of the Reichenbach Falls, when I had stood alone at the edge of the abyss, reading the farewell letter from Holmes. The last hours spent in the company of my beloved Mary, when all my medical skills could not defeat the illness that took her from me. Now the same hopeless feeling seemed overpowering. Something had happened. Now it was too late.

What had I said to Olfrig? I could hear his confident, professionally friendly, soothing tones. "Only a few questions."

What a fool I had been! There had obviously been a drug in the cup when the woman had dipped it into the "oxidizing waters." She had swirled the cup to dissolve the powder. There had been no drug in the cup she had selected for herself, but she had made the same swirling motion so as not to arouse my suspicions. The devilish part was that I had no idea what I had said while under the influence of the drug, so I had no idea of what the consequences might be. What could I guard against? What could I tell Holmes?

All these thoughts crowded in on me during the few seconds after I awoke and before I heard the door opening. Then I heard heavy boot steps on the tile. Moments later, strong hands gripped the fabric of my jacket and turned me over.

Above me loomed the smirking face of the blond giant Richter. As he picked me up by the lapels of my coat, I felt his hot, sour breath on my cheeks.

I called out for help.

"The Friedrichsbad is closed. There is no one to hear you," he said. "Where is the jewel box?"

"I have no idea. Let me go."

"I will very soon let you go. I will let you go to a most painful death. Alternatively, if you tell me the location of the jewel box, I will let you go free."

He was dragging me through the open doorway, past a painted wooden sign, into a large open space, cavernous in comparison with the cramped room in which I had awoken. Warm, humid air surrounded me, heavy with the sulphuric scent of the "oxidizing waters" I had imbibed I knew not how long before.

"We closed the bathing pool when you arrived," Richter said. "We turned off the cool water that moderates the temperature sufficiently for patients to bathe without injury. The temperature in this pool is now one hundred and fifty degrees on the Fahrenheit scale. That amount of heat to the human body will cause third-degree burns in roughly two seconds."

He stopped, holding me by the lapels just above the floor. "Now. Where is the jewel box?"

Desperate, I tried to reason with him. "You must have orders not to harm me. The Kaiser himself wants my medical opinion."

"I am tired of following orders. We are alone. And I want the simple pleasure of watching you suffer and die. Where is the jewel box?"

"I cannot tell you what I do not know."

"We know of your meetings with Gruen yesterday."

"He struck me from behind. I would hardly call that a meeting."

"You gave him fifty thousand gold marks."

"Actually he took them and gave nothing in return."

"He met with you in your room last night."

"He still gave me nothing."

He smirked once more. "That is what I hoped you would say. Now you are of no further use to us."

Above me was a great dome with colourful scenes of Roman gods and goddesses cavorting with unicorns and other mythological creatures. Beside me, hot vapours rose from the surface of the shining pool water. He was walking sideways, pulling me towards the edge. My arms and legs dangled limply as he dragged me along, no doubt the waning effects of whatever sedative had been in the drink, though I could feel my strength returning. A plan was slowly forming in my befogged mind. We moved inexorably towards the deadly waters until the skin on my cheeks was in pain from the force of the heat. Then just as he tightened his grip, about to fling me into the scalding waters, I grasped the lapels of his coat and held on for dear life.

He swung around, but he was thrown off balance by my unexpected weight. We spun around in a bizarre dance. Then when he was beside the pool, I lashed outwards and upwards with both arms, breaking his hold on me. Then I fell to the floor, kicking out at his thigh. Overbalanced, he toppled into the scalding waters, hitting the surface with a great splash. I heard his scream of pain as he came to the surface.

I did not see him climb out, for I was already running towards the front entry door as rapidly as I could manage. I burst through into the brightly lit entry foyer, and then out into the night air. From above me, electric lights flooded the plaza, turning the concrete white.

On the plaza, Holmes and Tesla stood alone.

37. A STRUGGLE IN DARKNESS

Both men stared at me in surprise as I came running up before them, stumbling and breathless. "They told us you had been brought back to the Villa Stephanie," said Holmes. He was holding his pocket watch.

"Richter is inside," I managed to gasp. "He is injured. I am all right."

"The Colonel and his men are within earshot. The time is precisely seven twenty-five." Holmes indicated a taxicab stand halfway down the block. "You had best wait elsewhere. Later you can tell us what happened."

I walked away, hoping that my interference had not been seen by whoever had ordered the meeting with Holmes and Tesla. I walked towards the taxi stand, away from the lights, hoping that no one was following me. Then I waited, glancing at my own pocket watch from time to time. As I waited, the hollow feeling that had possessed me when I had first awakened now returned. I was certain I had done something wrong that could not be undone.

Ought I to tell Holmes?

My watch read eight fifteen when I heard Holmes call for the Colonel. Obviously the meeting was not going to take place.

Joining the three men, I explained what had happened in the Friedrichsbad. The Colonel appeared to listen attentively. When I had concluded, he said, "Allow me to go over your statement to be certain I have correctly understood. You say a woman drugged you. What then?"

"There was a doctor. He said his name was Olfrig."

Holmes's eyes glittered. The Colonel appeared puzzled. He said, "There is no doctor at the Friedrichsbad who answers to that name."

"I believe he is from another facility," said Holmes. "In Bad Homburg."

"You say that he asked you questions. What were they?"

"He said he *had* questions. But that is all I remember of him."

"Then you awoke to find the same assailant who had attacked you in Dover and again in Bad Homburg. He threatened to injure you by throwing you into the thermal bathing pool."

"He kept asking the location of the jewel box. He said he knew I had met with Gruen, who I believe is the man who struck me from behind yesterday. I kept telling him that I had no idea. I did not tell him that you were here."

"He is called Richter," said Holmes, "according to his diplomatic identity papers. He is nearly seven feet tall, and he will have been injured by scalding water." He turned to the Colonel. "Your men might look for him at the local hospital."

"We shall handle the matter, Herr Holmes, competently and swiftly. Already I have ordered my men to search the interior of the Friedrichsbad."

"Take me home," Tesla said.

We continued the conversation with the Colonel as we walked in the direction of the Villa Stephanie. The Colonel had lit his petrol torch. In its flickering light his face was shadowed and emotionless. "You blame me for suggesting that we accompany you and Tesla. I in turn could readily blame Dr. Watson for making himself so highly visible just before the meeting was to occur."

"Dr. Watson, in turn, could readily blame you for the attacks he has undergone," said Holmes.

The Colonel's expression remained impassive. "I am of the opinion that there was never to be a meeting at all. It is plain to me that the writer of the letters intends to keep both the money and the jewel box. He ordered you and Tesla and the two ladies to go to various locations at this time merely to create a delay, giving him opportunity to leave the area. He paid Gruen to be his accomplice and retrieve the money. He now has his fifty thousand gold marks, the jewel box, and also the advantage of darkness."

"Or perhaps Gruen was the mastermind and Richter the accomplice. Or perhaps the two had a falling out, after their dispute in Bad Homburg," said Holmes. "Or there is yet another purpose that we do not yet understand."

"All possible, of course. But not entirely useful, Herr Holmes."

We walked on. Holmes went ahead. The Colonel dropped back to join Tesla and his military escorts. I fell into conversation with Lucy as she walked beside me. We began to go over the details of the case after she had satisfied herself that I was unharmed, though I found it difficult to concentrate. My sense that I had made a disastrous mistake still troubled me. I wondered again whether I ought to tell Lucy, or tell Holmes. But I did not see how merely voicing such a vague fear would help, and in truth, I had to admit I was embarrassed that I had been so easily manipulated. The feeling might very well have been the remnants of the drug, I finally decided. Whatever I had done was done. I ought to keep my dark moods within myself and thank my lucky stars for being able to escape from Richter and the scalding waters of the Friedrichsbad.

Lucy's voice intruded on my musings. "I had no luck at all in the hotel. No one answered my knock at room 504. I went up to 604 and knocked there, but no one answered either. The clerk at the desk said both rooms were empty. Harriet wasn't in the lobby, and she didn't answer when I knocked at her door. So I came here."

"I was to go to the Trinkhalle at 7:30. Of course I did not."

"Probably would have been a fool's errand anyway." She thought for a moment. "Did Gruen say how he would communicate with you?"

"Only that it would be before midnight. He did not say how."

"Does he know of Harriet and me?"

"He said he followed me to the hotel. He must have seen you both."

"Then possibly he has already communicated with Harriet. Maybe she went with him."

As we approached the Villa Stephanie, I could see the illuminated windows of some of the rooms within the tall, shadowy outline of the building. Other rooms were dark. Then I felt Lucy's hand on my arm. She was staring intently upwards at the top of the building. Light shone from behind the balcony of one of the upper rooms.

On that balcony two shadowy figures were locked in combat, each struggling to gain the advantage over the other.

"That is my balcony!" cried Tesla.

The shadows twisted and writhed behind the bars of the balcony railing, grappling with one another like two wrestlers in a ring. Now they were inside the room; now outside on the balcony. One of them pressed the other against the low iron bars. Then suddenly he pushed himself backwards and away. He kicked out quickly, swinging his leg in a short, sharp arc. The other figure slumped, stunned by the blow. The man who had kicked him bent over and lifted him upwards. The inert figure toppled over the balcony rail and the next moment vanished into the darkness. An instant later we heard a horrible muffled cracking sound. I knew it must be flesh and bone, colliding with the hard and unyielding surface of the earth.

We ran. The Colonel and Holmes reached the hotel before us. When we arrived, they were holding their lanterns above the body of a man. The body lay facing upwards, twisted and lifeless like a discarded rag doll. It was the man who had called himself Mr. Gruen, the man who had told me that he would be our only ally.

38. A NEW DEMAND

Beside the body, on one knee, Holmes gently tugged at a neatly folded paper that protruded like a kerchief from the breast pocket of Gruen's swallowtail coat. He said, "It is the same paper as the other letters, with the same block capital printing. It reads, 'Tesla's room. 7:30.'"

Above us, I could hear balcony doors being opened, and then after a few moments, hushed voices, followed by the sounds of the same doors being closed. One of the Colonel's men had gone for help to the nearby police headquarters. Another had gone into the hotel and now emerged carrying blankets. "We must cover him and move him away," said the Colonel.

"The man responsible may still be in the hotel," said Holmes. "You should station soldiers at the entrances. Look for men with gloves. Underneath may be telltale abrasions on the knuckles."

The Colonel shook his head. "We must not disturb the other guests with this."

Tesla said, "I cannot stay here." Holding his arms tightly folded against his chest and rocking back and forth, he went on, "I must have another room. I shall not sleep at all after what has happened."

"We shall procure for you a new suite," said the Colonel, his tone reassuring. "First we will go to your old one and you can pack your belongings. Herr Holmes, you will accompany us, yes?"

Holmes nodded. "The rooms may contain clues to the identity of Mr. Gruen's attacker."

"I want to visit Harriet's room," said Lucy. "If she does not answer, I want to enter with a key." Lucy agreed that we should investigate Tesla's suite first, however, since it had been the scene of the crime we had just witnessed.

Two of the Colonel's men were now stationed at the door. They stepped back to admit us. "Please allow me to accompany you, Mr. Tesla," said Holmes. "We can go through the rooms and their contents together. If something appears to have been disturbed, I would be grateful if you called it to my attention."

Lucy and I waited in the doorway as Holmes and Tesla inspected the sitting room, bedroom, and bathroom. From our vantage point, other than the door to the balcony being open, nothing about Tesla's suite appeared to be out of the ordinary. We heard drawers and cabinets being opened and shut. Not long afterwards, they emerged. From their impassive faces we knew that no new knowledge had been gained.

Leaving Tesla to await the arrival of a maid who would help him to pack, Holmes, Lucy, and I walked down the corridor to the stairs. "Please pay close attention," Holmes said. "Mr. Gruen's attacker most likely made his exit down these stairs. He may have dropped something in his haste to get away."

We followed the stairs to the ground floor, and then to the door leading to the hotel lobby. Once again, however, our efforts were to no avail. We found nothing of value to our investigation.

In the lobby we asked the clerk whether he had seen anyone coming from the staircase. He had not. "But there is a message for you, Mr. Holmes," he said, pulling a heavy envelope from one of the pigeonhole compartments on the wall behind him. The envelope bore no writing.

"Who delivered this?" asked Holmes, taking the envelope.

"A Mr. Gruen. He particularly instructed me to tell you that name."

"Can you describe him?"

"Portly, round faced, neatly attired, probably around forty years of age. He wore a swallowtail coat and carried a silk top hat."

Holmes's eyes glittered. He tore open the envelope and held up a key. "This is the key to room 403 at this hotel. There is no message."

"That's Harriet's room," Lucy said.

There was no answer when we knocked at the door. We opened it with the key. Entering, we saw that the room appeared to be in perfect order. The bed had been turned down for the night.

A white envelope lay on the centre of the smooth white bedspread. Holmes picked it up and showed it to us. The envelope was addressed, "To Mr. Sherlock Holmes." The letters were the familiar block capitals written in black ink.

Holmes opened the envelope. Wordlessly, he held up the brief message written on the page inside.

> HER RANSOM IS ONE MILLION POUNDS.
> DELIVER IN BEARER BONDS BY TEN A.M.
> TOMORROW OR SHE DIES.

39. A NEW DIRECTION

The Colonel appeared to be as astonished as we were. "I cannot believe the audacity of this demand. They do not say where the ransom is to be delivered. And how can they expect anyone to obtain such an enormous sum?" He looked at Holmes. "Unless the lady comes from a family of great wealth?"

"Quite the contrary," Holmes replied. "And to assemble such an amount here before ten o'clock tomorrow morning would seem to be entirely impossible. I shall have to send a telegram to London immediately. I must also alert Lord Radnar. Please excuse me."

And with that he left us.

I struggled to understand the message we had just seen. Surely the specific sum of one million pounds and the specific medium of bearer bonds could not be a coincidence. The writer of the demand must have intended us to make the connection to the affair of the past November, the one for which the banker named Kent had recently been tortured and killed. Holmes had referred to that incident in the presence of Wilhelm and von Bülow less than forty-eight hours earlier. Wilhelm had both denied any knowledge of the incident and promised to forget it. Did this demand indicate that Wilhelm had changed his mind and was flagrantly breaking his promise?

Lucy was surveying the room, opening drawers and cabinets in a determined manner, and then shutting them again. The Colonel and I did the same. We drew back the balcony curtains and opened the door, but found nothing there either. After several minutes, Lucy stopped and sat down on the sofa. "It's just like Gruen's room," she said. "Nothing out of the ordinary."

"She may have known her abductor," said the Colonel. "She may have gone voluntarily."

"Gruen obviously knew about this. He was the one who left the key to this room in the envelope for Holmes," Lucy said. "But he was a stranger to Harriet. Why would she have gone voluntarily with him?"

Standing beside the sofa where Lucy was seated, I happened to glance down between the sofa and the far wall. I saw an object there. My heartbeat surged with excitement as I reached down and pulled a woman's leather handbag from behind the sofa.

"That is Harriet's handbag," Lucy said.

"Perhaps she did not leave voluntarily after all," I said. "Perhaps she hid this and intended us to find it."

I handed Lucy the handbag, and she sat on the sofa to open it.

Holmes entered the room, carrying a black silk top hat. "I have sent my two telegrams," he said. Handing the top hat to the Colonel, he continued, "I believe this to be Mr. Gruen's hat, which I asked one of your men to retrieve from the hotel cloakroom. You will recall that the clerk mentioned that Mr. Gruen wore a hat, yet we saw that he was not wearing it when he fell, and we did not find it in Tesla's rooms."

The Colonel nodded. "We have found Miss Radnar's handbag."

"It contains a note," Lucy said, unfolding a cream-coloured paper. "It is dated yesterday morning." She read aloud:

> *"My dear Harriet, I do not wish to encourage false expectations. My professional career demands me to travel where the performances are most readily to be had, and the relationships needed to obtain those performances, combined with the demands of a performer's schedule, simply do not allow for the sort of I life I know you want and which you most certainly deserve. Please accept my apologies for whatever pain this message may cause you. You are a wonderful young person and I wish for you a wonderful future. Adrian."*

"Is there an envelope?" asked Holmes.

"There is not."

"Do you recognize Mr. Arkwright's handwriting?"

"I have not seen his handwriting before."

"We can ask Mr. Arkwright. What else is in the purse?"

Lucy named each item as she removed it.

"Here are two tickets for the Paris theatre in which the company is to perform next week. I have two myself. They are complimentary tickets for us to give to friends and acquaintances. Here also is a blue silk scarf. This is not the one she wore when we last saw her. That one was purple. Here is the cosmetic compact with the powder she uses on her face. Finally here is her notebook with her sketches. Here is a sketch of Mr. Tesla. Here is one of the Trinkhalle. Evidently she used her time this afternoon to go out and see the sights."

"That is all?" asked Holmes.

Lucy nodded. "No secret compartment. Nothing sewn into the lining." She remained seated, holding the sketchbook and looking at the sad little array of items she had spread out on the sofa. "I feel as though I ought to have been here to protect Harriet."

Holmes's voice was kind. "As do we all, I am sure."

The Colonel was examining the hat that had belonged to the late Mr. Gruen. "I see nothing unusual here," he said.

"It should be stored with his other effects, I should think," said Holmes. "And speaking of those, I wonder if anything suggestive was found on Mr. Gruen's person? I also wonder where Mr. Gruen was staying in town, and whether he may have left any clues behind."

"Do you believe that is pertinent to your mission?"

I spoke up. "Mr. Gruen was the man who took my valise yesterday."

The Colonel's eyes narrowed. "And you did not see fit to inform me of that fact?"

"I have not been quite myself since I was struck down. I apologize."

"We have all had a difficult and trying time of it," said Holmes, intervening smoothly. "I wonder if we might be permitted to retire to our rooms and reconvene in the morning? I shall of course notify you if I receive any message from Miss Radnar's abductors."

The Colonel gave his permission. Holmes and I escorted Lucy to her room. To my surprise, Holmes entered ahead of her, turned on the electric light, and examined the room and the adjoining bedroom and bathroom. He then opened the balcony drapes, unlocked the balcony door, looked outside, and then closed and locked the door, shutting the drapes once again. "It is as well to be certain," he said. "If someone abducted Harriet, someone may well intend to do the same to you. Under no circumstances are you to open your door to anyone other than Watson or myself."

He lowered his voice. "Now I have points for you both to think about. First, consider the effect of the ransom demand on my movements between now and ten tomorrow. The message was addressed to me, and therefore I am obligated to make myself available here at the hotel to receive instructions as to where to make the payment. What is to be gained by keeping me here? Second, why make a demand that is so extremely difficult to meet, and with an amount and a form of payment identical to the obligation the Kaiser promised me would be forgotten?"

"It cannot be coincidental," Lucy said.

Holmes nodded. "And third, what are we to do with this object?" He produced a small square of blue pasteboard from his vest pocket. "It is a ticket to the left-luggage checkroom at the railway station."

Lucy said, "You found it in Mr. Gruen's hat."

"It was tucked inside the hatband, to be precise. The problem we must address is how to make use of it, taking into account that I must stay in the hotel and that the Colonel's men will be watching."

40. TO THE RAILWAY STATION

At the first light of dawn, I abandoned my futile attempts at sleep. I dressed and walked down the hotel corridor to knock at Holmes's room. He answered, fully dressed and wearing his Inverness cape. The curtain and balcony door were open. Nevertheless, the room reeked of shag tobacco. Little wisps of smoke hung about the ceiling. The bed was in complete disarray. Both sheets had been pulled off the mattress and lay twisted in an untidy pile.

"I have had two responses to my telegrams," Holmes said. "Lansdowne says the sum is regrettably quite impossible to manage. Lord Radnar's hotel says that in view of the urgency, they have forwarded the message to his destination in Colorado. He is expected there this week."

"So there is no way the ransom can be paid."

"Certainly not before ten o'clock this morning."

"You have been airing out your room after a nightlong consumption of tobacco, I see."

"I would remonstrate with you regarding your deductive methods, old friend, only there is no time. In fact, I was just on my way to see you. Would you kindly go to your room and return with your overcoat and hat. Also please bring the funds given you by Mr. Arkwright for expenses."

I did so without question.

"Perfectly satisfactory," he said, and tucked the fat wad of gold marks into my overcoat. Then he removed his Inverness cloak. To my astonishment, he took from the cloak a ginger-haired wig and false beard.

"Where did you get those?" I asked.

"From the room of the man who was calling himself Mr. Gruen." Holmes sat before his dressing table mirror and began to apply the whiskers to his face. "He had been staying at the Brenners Park-Hotel nearby under a different name. Fortunately, he had stored the requisite spirit gum with these whiskers."

"How did you locate the room?"

"Two nights ago I followed Mr. Gruen after he had called on you. I saw the room number when the night clerk retrieved his key for him. He was not wearing this beard and wig. Presumably, they were part of his disguise for when he was travelling."

"Where are you going?"

"To the railway station, to recover whatever Mr. Gruen stored there when he received the claim ticket. You will stay here. If you receive instructions concerning payment of the ransom, you will come to the station and find me."

"You take my breath away, Holmes. Do you think it possible that you will find the jewel box?"

He gave a last satisfied nod at his bearded and bewigged reflection in the mirror and picked up his battered leather valise. "Assuming the materials associated with the claim ticket still remain and are worth keeping, I shall place them into this valise and bring it back here. But time is of the essence. It is five thirty in the morning. We have less than five hours until the deadline. We do not have a million pounds, but we may have a jewel box. That may give us something with which to negotiate Miss Radnar's release."

So saying, he donned my overcoat, jammed my hat down over his wig, and picked up the valise in one hand. With the other, he swept up the bedsheets, which I saw had been knotted together. A moment later he was on the balcony, tying one end of the sheet to the bottom of the wrought-iron rail. Then he climbed over the railing, holding up one end of the sheets. "Just pull these up after I have landed, would you please, Watson," he said.

He dropped the valise over the balcony to the ground. The faint predawn light cast his figure in shadow as he grasped the sheet and swung away from the balcony, sliding down hand-over-hand, like a circus trapeze artist on a rope.

I had retrieved the sheets and closed up the balcony entrance when there came a knock at the door. I opened to see a bellman. *"Liefurung fur Herr Sherlock Holmes,"* he said, in a gruff, abrupt manner, thrusting a cheap maroon carpetbag at my feet. Automatically I picked it up, noticing that it felt quite empty. I opened it, intending to ask where he had received his instructions, but by then he had gone and the door to the hallway stairs was clicking shut.

Inside the bag was a white paper envelope. On the note inside, written in the familiar block capital letters, was this message:

> PLACE THE BONDS IN THE CARPETBAG. LEAVE BY THE STATUE OF THE KAISER AT THE TRINKHALLE AT TEN A.M. NO POLICE OR SHE DIES.

I had no sooner sat down to try to puzzle out what to do than there came another knock. Lucy was in the hallway. Quickly I brought her in.

"You are safe, at least," she said. "Where is Holmes?"

I explained where he had gone. Then I showed her the ransom note instructions and told her of the messages Holmes had received from Lansdowne and Lord Radnar.

"I had hoped they would change their minds. They cannot expect us to comply with this."

"Holmes thinks if we recover the jewel box it may give us something with which to bargain."

Quickly she took the envelope from me and turned the paper over onto the other side. With a pen from her reticule she wrote: "You must see that we need more time. You have nothing to gain by being unreasonable. We shall deliver the ransom tomorrow at the same time at a place of your selection. S. Holmes."

Lucy put the note into the carpetbag and closed the hasp. "Just before ten I will take it to the Trinkhalle and deposit it under the statue."

"Ought we to tell the Colonel?"

"We can ask Holmes. We have four hours until ten o'clock. Now let us go to the station. Perhaps we can help."

In the hotel lobby the Colonel awaited us, along with two of his men. He asked, "Where is Herr Holmes?"

"He is following up a clue as to the whereabouts of the jewel box."

"We have had men in the hotel since midnight, but we have not seen him. Where are you going with that carpetbag?"

We told him of the note, and of the reply Lucy had written upon it.

"We will have watchmen posted discreetly. The Trinkhalle is a large place. Do not worry. They will not be seen. We also have men at the railway station, checking all passengers leaving town." He looked at the clock above the registry desk. "The first train departs at seven thirty."

"We will go there as well," Lucy said. "I have known her for several years. I may be able to recognize her, even if her captors have altered her appearance."

Fortunately the Colonel did not send his men to accompany us. Lucy and I walked the five minutes' journey to the station under an overcast sky. The rising sun made streaks of dark purple and red along the edges of the morning clouds. As we arrived, the hiss of steam and squeal of brakes cut through the morning air. "The southbound train," Lucy said.

Inside the station, we looked for Holmes. He should have been readily recognizable with the ginger beard and the wig. However, we could not find him amidst the passengers waiting to board and those who had only now arrived and were milling about, getting their bearings and attempting to locate porters to handle their luggage. Nor could I spot any obviously military watchmen, which I took as a good sign, since that augured well for the Colonel's men not being spotted at the Trinkhalle. We did see an old beggar man seated on the station floor against the wall near the street entrance. His legs were stretched out and motionless, protected from the hard cold tiles by a folded blanket of some kind. In the dirty fingers of one hand, he grasped a black felt hat, holding it out upside down to collect coins. With his other hand, he was pressing something tightly to his chest. His weather-beaten face bore an unusually pleased expression. He was staring towards the far end of the station, opposite the entrance to the train platform, where three people stood in a line.

"The left-luggage office," Lucy said, following the beggar's gaze. "We should keep our eyes on that doorway, for it is the one place we know Holmes intends to visit. Now that the first train of the day is in, they ought to open for business."

As if to prove the accuracy of her statement, the top half of the luggage-room door swung inwards, revealing a middle-aged clerk standing behind the counter. We watched the clerk deal with the parcels and suitcases of his three customers. Then a resentful-looking grey-haired man with a crutch limped up, a battered leather valise at his side.

"That's Holmes," said Lucy.

41. TRIUMPH AND TRAGEDY

I saw. It was indeed Holmes, holding his own valise, placing what had to be the left-luggage ticket into the clerk's hand. Yet such was his ability to immerse himself in any role he happened to be playing that I could not help believing he was indeed anxiously awaiting his parcel before boarding his train, all the while enduring the pain from his injured limb.

The clerk accepted the ticket and withdrew into the storage area.

Lucy continued, "Talcum in the hair, black shoe polish to colour the false moustache. Probably had those in his valise. Probably that's where he put what's left of the ginger beard and the wig. He must think people are watching for him. I expect he traded your coat and hat for the crutch." She glanced over at the beggar man. "He probably added a few gold marks to the bargain, judging from the way that beggar's protecting his breast pocket with his free hand."

At the luggage counter, the clerk was handing Holmes a parcel wrapped in brown paper and twine. Holmes tucked it into his valise and then turned towards the open area and the passageway to the platform. I scanned the crowd, hoping to spot any danger before it became a threat to Holmes. Adding to the noise of the crowd and the steady chuffing sound of the waiting steam engine, I heard a distant rumble and the faraway high-pitched whistle of an approaching train. For some reason, I thought of Dietrich and Richter. I watched, particularly alert, but saw no one who resembled either man. The crowd seemed quite orderly and calm, preoccupied with their individual affairs. None of them was looking at Holmes, who was hobbling on his crutch towards the ticket counter. He made his way to the end of the ticket counter line, behind a uniformed nurse pushing her patient in a wheelchair.

The wheelchair patient, a white-haired invalid woman, coughed violently, reacting, I thought, to the wisps of black coal smoke drifting into the station from the waiting steam engine. To her right, at the doorway that led to the station platform just outside the building, two uniformed soldiers were stationed to observe the approaching passengers. Before reaching them, Holmes shuffled sideways to the right, moving out of the stream of passengers. He was now coming in our direction. He approached us where we stood beside the beggar man, hugging close to the inner station wall.

To my astonishment, he passed us, holding the valise close to his side. His stern features gave not even a hint of recognition, save for a cold look and a barely perceptible gesture with his free hand, palm downwards, to indicate that we were to remain in place.

Then he was gone. Lucy and I stood against the wall near the entrance, scanning the crowd. We could hear the distant rumbling of the northbound express. We could see the ebb and flow of the lines of passengers, some coming in from the waiting southbound train and others going out to board it. The nurse and her wheelchair patient evidently had obtained their tickets, for they were moving slowly towards the waiting soldiers at the entrance. The patient had another coughing fit. The uniformed nurse placed a white scarf over her patient's face to protect her from the smoke, and the coughing subsided.

"I know that cough," Lucy said. "It's Harriet!"

I acted by instinct. As the rumbling sound of the northbound express grew ever louder, I made my way towards the wheelchair. If the patient indeed was Harriet, I would have to stop her kidnappers from getting her on the train. Had her cough been an alarm, a call for help? Was the white scarf an attempt to conceal her face from the two soldiers at the entrance? I pressed forwards against the flow of arriving passengers. Behind me I heard a commotion from the street outside. I turned and glimpsed Colonel Brandt and three of his uniformed men coming into the station. I pressed on. Now the nurse and her wheelchair were only a few feet ahead of me, passing under the gaze of the two soldiers. Now I was past the soldiers as well. On the platform, the nurse and wheelchair had paused at the entrance to the underpass steps that would lead them beneath the tracks. I thought the nurse was considering how best to navigate her patient down the steps. From the south came the reverberation of the steam engine, propelling the express train ever closer. I readied myself to stride confidently up to the nurse and lift up the white scarf from the face of her patient. I would call for help from the soldiers if indeed it was Harriet in that wheelchair.

Then the woman in the wheelchair threw off the scarf and stood. The nurse lunged towards her, but the woman spun away, running north along the platform. As she ran, she threw off a white wig. I was looking at her from behind, but I was quite certain that the woman was Harriet. Behind me from the south came a shrill blast from the steam whistle of the fast-approaching northbound express. I started to run after Harriet, but the nurse pushed me off balance. I staggered back, nearly falling off the platform down to the northbound tracks some four feet below. To my horror, I saw the engine of the express train looming out in the distance. It was barely two hundred yards away, belching black smoke and thundering ever closer. The roar of the train increased. Righting myself safely on the platform, I caught sight of the nurse behind me. She was hurrying down the steps to the underpass. The two soldiers were staring at me and towards Harriet. So were Colonel Brandt and his three men, who were just emerging from the station onto the platform.

Turning, I could see Harriet clearly. She was at the edge of the platform, a wild-eyed, dazed look on her face, staring fixedly at the train. Then she leaped from the platform onto the tracks, directly in the path of the oncoming locomotive. She went down on her knees, appearing momentarily dazed by the impact. In the last instant that she remained in my vision, she appeared to begin crawling towards the southbound train on the adjacent tracks. The driver in his locomotive must have seen her, for the shrill blast of a steam whistle cut through the air, followed immediately by the earsplitting screech of brakes. Then the great mass of the black metal locomotive was alongside me, sparks issuing from its locked steel wheels as they skidded along the bright steel rails. The train hurtled past. In the cacophony of the roaring engine and the shriek of brakes I thought I heard a woman scream. The huge locomotive with its trailing railway carriages continued relentlessly down the northbound track. Finally the train came to a juddering stop.

A shadowy stain darkened the tracks beneath one of the carriages, at the spot where Harriet had jumped. The locomotive had passed at least fifty yards beyond.

PART FOUR

AND CHECKS AND SLAYS

42. A HAUNTING MEMORY

About fifteen minutes later, I was standing in the station with Lucy and Holmes, who had returned to us with his hair free of the white talcum, and his sharp features cleared of the false moustache. Immediately he had donned his cape and, with a cautionary nod, stuffed his valise into Lucy's carpetbag, placing it behind her.

I had just told Holmes and Lucy what I had witnessed on the platform.

"Could Harriet have rolled clear of the locomotive?" Lucy asked.

"She was on her knees between the tracks and certainly trying to get to the other side. But she appeared to be confused and faltering. Then the incoming locomotive and the rest of the train blocked my vision."

"The Colonel approaches," said Holmes.

"He will know the outcome. He and his men were on the platform. After they told me to return here, they were about to investigate."

The Colonel's face was sombre. He shook his head, slowly and deliberately. He said, "At the hotel this morning we received an anonymous message. It said, 'Harriet Radnar will be on the 7:30 train.' We came as quickly as we could. My men saw everything. I wish that the two I had stationed at the platform entrance had stopped her, but she sprang up from her wheelchair and ran past them before they could react. Also, their orders were to prevent suspicious persons from going down the steps leading to the underpass and the southbound train."

"And she was running northward along the platform," said Holmes.

"My men and I simply watched her in astonishment, as did Dr. Watson here, though he has no doubt already told you. We saw her leap down to the tracks. Then she stumbled, as though she had been injured. The driver also confirms this. He applied the brakes, of course. Then the train drew closer and the front of the locomotive blocked his view of her, for his window was on the right side. Miss Radnar may have hesitated due to an injury. She may have been paralyzed by the fear of the huge steam engine that was bearing down on her so quickly. But the end result was that the driver could not stop the train soon enough." The Colonel lowered his gaze. "After the initial impact, the locomotive ran over the body. There is very little that remains intact."

We stood silent for a long, nearly interminable moment. Lucy, tight-lipped and grasping her reticule tightly with both hands, turned to Holmes. He was looking out to the platform, where the express train still stood, its locomotive puffing black coal smoke into the air. His hawklike features shone with determination.

"May we see the body?" he asked.

"It has already been removed," the Colonel replied.

"How did you know it was Miss Radnar?"

"Her name was embroidered in some of her clothing."

"We had to do that when we were at school," Lucy said.

"She was also wearing a purple scarf. It has her initials. I have it with me." The Colonel opened a leather dispatch pouch and then a white cloth wrapper to display the scarf. The purple silk was blood-stained and bedraggled, but the initials "HR" were plainly visible.

Lucy looked at it without flinching. "That is hers."

"She obviously was a woman of some spirit. Even drugged, she was determined to get free from the kidnappers. Had she been a few seconds quicker, she would have reached the other side in safety."

Holmes asked the Colonel, "Did you find the nurse?"

"Regrettably, we did not. While my men were staring at Miss Radnar, the nurse apparently passed down the steps and through the underpass to where the southbound train was waiting. A thorough search has been made of the train, but so far it has not borne fruit."

"Was there anything unusual about the northbound express locomotive used on this morning's run?"

"It is the same locomotive I have seen pass through this station on hundreds of occasions," the Colonel replied. "You may rest assured that the investigation will have my full attention, Herr Holmes. Now, may I ask why you are here?"

Wordlessly Holmes held out a yellow telegram. It read:

> I HAVE ACQUIRED THE JEWEL BOX. CONTENTS APPEAR TO BE INTACT. KINDLY ARRANGE MILITARY PROTECTION AND ESCORT FOR TESLA, LUCY JAMES, DR. WATSON, AND ME TO RADNAR HOUSE, DOVER.
>
> S. HOLMES.

As the Colonel finished reading the message, Holmes said, "This morning I sent this telegram to four persons, notifying each that a copy had been sent to the other three."

"And those persons?"

"Ambassador von Bülow, His Imperial Highness Kaiser Wilhelm II, Lord Lansdowne, and Albert, Prince of Wales. I would expect that when you return to your station you will find your orders from the Ambassador."

"Where did you find the jewel box?"

"It was here in the railway station, at the left-luggage counter."

"I shall need to inspect it."

"It is in a safe place. I am reluctant to disturb it," said Holmes evenly. Not for one moment did his gaze flicker downwards, in the direction of the carpetbag barely concealed from the Colonel's viewpoint behind Lucy's dark wool skirt. Holmes went on, "I suggest you consult your orders before insisting on taking any unilateral actions on your own authority."

After the Colonel and his men had departed, I recovered my hat and coat from the beggar, paying him with ten gold marks and returning his crutch, which Holmes had left standing just alongside the entry door. Delighted, the man scrambled to his feet and walked out of the station onto the pavement, to the astonishment of several passersby who doubtless thought he had achieved a miraculous cure.

Holmes's four messages had the desired result. Since high officials on both sides knew that Holmes possessed the jewel box, it was impossible for the Germans to keep it for themselves without overtly breaking their promise to the Prince of Wales. Before the morning was over, we had received the Colonel's assurance that we might safely take the jewel box back to England.

The remainder of the day was spent notifying the appropriate parties and preparing for the journey home. Whatever triumph Holmes might have enjoyed due to his recovery of the jewel box was lost in the sombre aftermath of Harriet's death. Both Harriet's body and the jewel box had to be secured. Lord Radnar and Lady Radnar had to be notified. Fortunately the German and British authorities cooperated on the details of the travel arrangements to ensure that on the morrow we would board a train in Baden-Baden with the jewel box and Harriet's coffin, and then travel safely across the border, across France, and across the Channel.

After supper that evening, and after Holmes had gone upstairs, Lucy asked me to remain with her in the hotel parlour. Her voice had a forlorn tone and there was a little catch in her throat, but the firelight caught the glint of determination in her green eyes. She said, "I feel as though I am overlooking something important in this case."

I felt a rush of sympathy. "This is not the time to analyse all that has happened. You have had a shock. You have lost a friend."

"Please let me explain. There is something else. The thought of Harriet's body—" She broke off with a shudder.

"Of course. It would distress anyone. It distressed me, even though I am accustomed to injuries. There is more tea here—"

"Please. Just listen. It is the association of a similar image that I am unable to clear from my thoughts. For some reason it has put me in mind of another death, or to be precise, two other deaths. The first death occurred at a stable in Connecticut, when I was away at school. The other death was one that you recorded in the story of Silver Blaze."

I feared the shock had been too much for her. "I do not see the connection."

"Oh, you will understand the connection between the two other deaths readily enough. It is the connection with Harriet that I am so certain is of great importance. But I cannot fathom *why* I should feel so certain."

"I do not follow you. But I am prepared to listen for as long as you wish."

"Thank you. I know you are tired and the hour is late. I shall describe the event from my own life first. I alluded to it last November, while we were searching for my mother in London. Holmes wanted me to stay away from the flat that was owned by that horrible man Worth. I told him I was perfectly able to take care of myself, and that a man who had attacked me several years before had not survived the encounter."

"I remember. We were standing together on the pavement on Piccadilly. You mentioned Silver Blaze."

"The man was the master of the riding stables frequented by us schoolgirls one year, the year that Harriet had first arrived. Harriet had been the object of his . . . advances, shall we say. He was a handsome enough fellow, and quite a local lothario, according to the school gossip. She confided in me that she refused to meet with him at the stables after hours, and she thought he was mistreating her horse as a way of getting back at her. The stables were forbidden to us girls at that hour, as was any other place on the campus other than the library or the dining hall or our rooms. So Harriet had good reason not to comply with his request. I suggested that the two of us teach him a lesson. She would pretend to accede, but at the appointed hour when he came to meet her, he would find she had not come alone. I would be with her, and the two of us would confront him. We would go separately to the stables, so that if he were following her, he would not suspect. However, things did not proceed as we had planned.

"The sky was dark after the sun went down, and inside the stables I could barely see the horses. I was a little on edge because Harriet had not yet arrived. So when I got to the stables, I turned on the light switch. But the lights would not go on. I found a spot in one of the horses' stalls where I could see outside. I could see the man as he came near the stables. I could see that he was holding something behind his back. He turned one way and I could see that it was a gun. I groped around in the stall and found a water bucket, a wooden one with a cast-iron band around the bottom edge. I picked it up by the handle. I was afraid, but I was angry too. I kept thinking that he had somehow found out about our plan and that he had done something bad to Harriet.

"As soon as I felt his presence and heard the rustle of his steps in the hay, I swung the water bucket. I caught him right across the shoulder with the bottom edge. It hit with a pretty significant wallop, but he didn't flinch. He held his gun on me. He motioned that I should kneel down in front of him."

Her face tightened, as if she were recalling the contempt she had felt for the man. "I did kneel. But I braced my foot in front of me instead of kneeling fully, and then I grabbed his ankles and yanked his feet out so he went down on his back. I grabbed the bucket by the handle and hit him again—just as he tried to bring up the gun to aim it at me. I got him just above his ear. He dropped the gun. I picked it up and held it under his chin with one hand while I felt under his jaw for a pulse. There wasn't one."

"He did not survive the encounter."

"Exactly." Her eyes narrowed for a moment, and then she shrugged. "As I told you last November, I had just read your story of Silver Blaze in *The Strand Magazine*, and it came to me all at once exactly what I ought to do—I had to make it look as if he had been killed by one of the horses. I scraped up some blood from the floor and smeared it on the front hooves of Vixen, one of the wilder horses, and then I lifted the man's body and dragged it into Vixen's stall. I saw a knife in his belt, so I put that into the hand that had held the gun. Then I dunked the bucket into Vixen's water trough and rinsed off the blood, and pumped in more water to fill up the water trough. I scattered fresh straw around where we had fought. I slipped away. I was grateful I had my black wool cloak to put over my head. I threw his gun into the river. Then I went up to the school chapel, in time for our rehearsal of *Messiah*. Harriet was there, already in the choir box. I sang the soprano solo."

"What did you tell Harriet?"

"She told me that she'd lost her nerve and hadn't come down to the stables. So I told her the same. I haven't said a word about what happened until just now."

"Perhaps talking about it now has done you some good."

"Oh, I don't feel guilty about it, if that's what you're getting at. I know it was a clear case of self-defence, if ever there was one. But what I can't seem to get hold of in my brain is why I should connect that memory with what happened today at the railway station."

"Harriet was involved on both occasions."

"But she wasn't. At least, she wasn't at the stables. Just as I can't get the story of Silver Blaze out of my thoughts, I also keep thinking that. She wasn't *at* the stables. She wasn't *there*!"

Lucy closed her eyes, squeezing them shut, pressing her fingertips into her eyebrows as if to force her memories and associations to comply with her will.

"Perhaps the connection will come to you."

She nodded. "Maybe it has to do with what happened just after. She wasn't there at the stables, but she was at the chapel, where we were singing hymns."

"You are thinking that she is in a better place now."

"She may very well be," said Lucy, "but that thought gives me no comfort. I just keep going back to the stables in my mind, thinking about my waiting for her to come, and her never arriving. Maybe it is because there is so much uncertainty here. Someone is manipulating things. There is a traitor, as Holmes keeps reminding us."

"I agree. Someone is behind this."

"And wherever we look, that someone is not there."

43. SUCCESS AND FAILURE

For the thirty-six hours that followed, I never once saw Holmes relax his vigilance. He remained brooding and uncommunicative, sunk in thought. Yet his sharp grey eyes were ever watchful, whether we were in a train station, a taxicab, or a railway carriage, or on the Calais dock or, at last, the ferry that took us across the Channel waters to the Port of Dover. Even at the port, when we were on British soil once more, he did not relax his vigilance.

Upon disembarking from the ferry, we were met by Lieutenant Fitzwilliam, the robust young officer who had been with us at the garrison. He told us his commander had assigned him to be our personal escort, and that we might call on him for anything we required. No fewer than five soldiers escorted us to our waiting military carriage. They surrounded us and the jewel box as if it contained the actual crown jewels rather than an untried electrical apparatus.

Holmes nodded his approval at these precautionary measures. "Something will happen," he said. "I do not know when, but we must remain on our guard for the moment that it does. I am hopeful—but I will not go into that at present."

We had gathered in the entrance hall of Radnar House. He continued, "Now that the jewel box is under guard in the Kerren House conservatory with its companion apparatus, we have fulfilled our mission for the moment. Tesla is expected to arrive on the morrow. I suggest we get settled in our respective rooms and meet again at breakfast."

There is something peaceful about sea air and being home in one's own country, and I expected to sleep well that first night in England. But I did not. I kept seeing the events of the previous visit to Dover. I saw the explosion of the balloon and its fiery death as it plunged into the sea. I saw the blackened horror of the charred body on the beach. I saw in my memory the sergeant bleeding in my arms. I saw his broken neck as he lay dead where I had left him to heal.

Tesla, too, seemed out of sorts when he arrived at Kerren House just after noon. "I must return almost immediately to New York," he said. "Preparations are under way for the inaugural transmission of electrical power from my Niagara Falls generator to the city of Buffalo. The distance is more than seventeen miles. It will be the farthest transmission of electricity ever created by mankind and will prove to history that my alternating current is far more practical and effective than Mr. Edison's direct current. I must ensure that everything is in order for complete success."

"But you have an excellent commercial opportunity here in England," said Holmes. "Lord Lansdowne is on his way to meet you and to discuss the arrangements for patenting your apparatus—as soon as it is proven successful."

"It is another man's apparatus, not mine," said Tesla.

"But you will help," said Lucy.

"I will help for the sake of the scientific community, and for the promise of a world at peace under the rule of a nation that possesses the world's most powerful weapon."

We walked together into the conservatory, where the jewel box had been placed on a table beside the larger machine. Upon opening the jewel box, however, Tesla's eyes widened with curiosity and surprise. He said, "I see now why Kerren was so anxious to have me at his side. Look here!"

He pointed to the three metal discs, and then to a fourth piece of equipment attached to each. This latter piece was a clear glass tube attached to a metal base. Wires ran from the three metal discs to the metal base. Inside the glass tube we could see an array of thin metal wires and rods.

"This is a ray transmitter tube. See how the end panel of the jewel box is hinged, enabling it to fall open so that the tube is not blocked by metal. This weapon will not produce a lightning bolt at all. It will emit invisible rays, which, if focused and driven by sufficient electrical energy, would be able to penetrate through the flesh and bone of any living creature. This is the mechanism I discussed with Kerren when we were together in New York. It is the very same concept that Röntgen and Marconi have employed in their experimental devices for photography and communications. Without giving me proper credit, I might add."

"So Kerren and you were thinking along the same lines?" Lucy asked.

"That is a kind way of putting it," Tesla said. "However, I very much doubt whether this configuration will work. As I told Kerren when we were last together, when I envisioned this weapon for the first time, its barrel had a length that was thirty feet long, far greater than this one. The longer barrel can focus the rays more intensely, and thus more accurately, in the same manner that a long rifle focuses the path of a bullet more accurately than a short-barrelled pistol."

"Nonetheless, will you use your best efforts and skills to get this apparatus to work?" Holmes asked. As Tesla continued to look sceptical,

Holmes added, "We shall see to it that you receive all the credit that is due you, if this machine can be made to perform properly."

Holmes's promise seemed to sway the Serbian inventor, for Tesla worked diligently over the next few hours. Lucy, Holmes, Lieutenant Fitzwilliam, and I assisted as he tried various combinations and settings of the equipment. He positioned and repositioned the three discs and the firing tube—the radiating wave gun, Tesla called it—in the larger sphere that Kerren had left behind. He rotated them on the metal circle. He fiddled with the connections to the six transformer coils and argon tubes in ways that I did not begin to understand.

With each new configuration, the switch would be thrown to bring in the electricity that flowed from the petrol-powered generator outside the conservatory. The three induction coils in the sphere would emit a throbbing hum when Tesla depressed the switch. Then, when Tesla believed that the charge had grown strong enough, he threw another switch. We stood back each time, watching a metal plate outside the open conservatory doors that had been set up as a target for the beam. Each time we waited. Each time we saw nothing change on the metal plate.

"Touch the plate," Tesla finally said, after switching the machine off. "The energy of the electricity may have transformed itself into heat when it radiated into the metal. But be careful."

Holmes touched the plate with a fingertip. He shook his head. Nothing.

"Perhaps the metal in the tube was damaged when Kerren performed his trial experiments," I said.

"The tungsten metal strip appears intact. I should have to build another tube to determine whether that is really the cause of the difficulty."

"Let us try at a greater distance," said Holmes. We moved the chair and the metal plate to the edge of the cliff.

The results of this attempt were the same as before.

"Perhaps we ought to try it with something living," said Lucy. "Kerren said he had killed a sheep."

Fitzwilliam called to his fellow officers. A sheep was brought to stand just outside the open conservatory doors and tethered there. The animal stood peacefully and contentedly before the machine as it hummed. Nearly five minutes went by while Tesla tinkered with the machine, to no avail.

"I am finished," said Tesla at last. "I can do no more. I will not stand here before the Prince and embarrass myself. I shall make my own travel arrangements at Radnar House. Tomorrow morning I shall be on a steamship bound for New York. You can tell the Prince what you wish."

44. A RISKY MESSAGE

Tesla left the room, saying he preferred to walk to Radnar House alone.

"I do not understand," I said after Tesla had departed.

"Clearly he is not prepared to continue with this enterprise," said Holmes.

"Do you think he may have learned something of Kerren's design and sabotaged the test in some way?"

"There are a number of alternatives that would reflect better on Mr. Tesla," said Holmes. "Perhaps he is simply thinking of the realities of business and is anxious to return to America. That nation is, after all, a larger and more lucrative market for his other inventions. Or perhaps the jewel box apparatus itself is defective. Whoever stole Kerren's apparatus may have tampered with it, either before the Germans copied it or after, when Mr. Gruen placed it into storage in Baden-Baden. Perhaps Mr. Gruen's associates allowed him to take the impaired product, even though he himself thought that he had the highly valuable original. Or perhaps Mr. Gruen's associates have paid or threatened Mr. Tesla to influence his decision to leave. The lack of definitive explanations requires us to take an action that will seem entirely unreasonable."

We looked at Holmes in some consternation as he continued.

"If we simply report that the test is a failure, we will never see the outcome of this affair that the Kaiser's men have envisioned from the beginning."

"What do you mean, from the beginning?" Lucy asked.

"I remind you that Mr. Lestrade was accosted on my doorstep. Those who accosted him knew he had been sent to bring me into this venture. They had that knowledge from a traitor within the organization of either the War Office or Scotland Yard, or possibly both. But we shall never unmask the traitor if we merely throw up our hands and blame Tesla for not being able to get the machine to work. We cannot forget that whoever is behind this has caused the murder of four people, including a British police officer and a British peer."

"And an innocent woman," said Lucy.

Holmes nodded.

"We might report that the test has been a success," said Lieutenant Fitzwilliam.

Holmes shook his head. "I will not bring the Prince here on false pretences."

After some further discussion, Holmes dictated this telegraph message, to be sent to both the Prince in Bad Homburg and Lansdowne in London:

> Jewel box equipment appears to be genuine, but Tesla could not get machine to work. Suggest you come all the same. Suggest Arkwright also attend, if his injury permits. Will explain upon your arrival.
>
> S. Holmes.

Lieutenant Fitzwilliam left the room with the message. There was a brief flurry of voices as he opened the door. Moments later he reentered, accompanied by Lady Radnar, dressed, for her brother's sake, I was sure, in black satin mourning garb.

"She was listening at the door, Mr. Holmes."

Lady Radnar appeared not in the least discomfited to be caught eavesdropping. She stood just inside the room, her stark, proud figure framed by the tapestry of Queen Elizabeth that hung on the inner conservatory wall. Possibly because of this visual association, I had the fleeting impression that her manner resembled that of a queen, comfortable in her realm, even though she was in her brother's house and not her own. "Mr. Holmes, have you solved the mystery of the dead man on our beach? Will the Prince come?"

"My lady, I am very close to the solution regarding the case of the dead man on the beach. To that end, I would ask as a favour that I might be permitted to have access to the room of the late Miss Harriet Radnar."

"Of course."

"You will notify the servants?"

"Of course. Anything I can do to help. Although I fail to see a connection."

Holmes went on, "As to inducing the Prince to come here, I have, as you may have inadvertently overheard, just now done everything I can. But even if the Prince does make his visit, I fear the results will not be the ones you are hoping for."

"You are referring to my late brother, of course. He will never see the success of his invention, and that is quite painful to me. I appreciate your sympathy. His loss is a great one, but we must find someone else to continue his work. It is important work. Possibly Mr. Tesla can somehow be induced to come back and help us. I am sure my husband will know what to do when he returns."

"I regret," replied Holmes, "that I cannot say any more than I have said."

45. A TRAP IS REQUIRED

Holmes insisted on working alone the following morning, leaving Lucy and me to our own devices. She suggested that we take a bit of exercise by walking along the cliff-side path. We headed down to the gravel beach upon which the still-unidentified charred body had been found, and where Holmes and I had spent such terrifying moments under fire from the unknown assailant above us.

About midway down the path, we could see the gypsy caravan on the beach, well in from the tide line, just as it had been positioned when we last visited. We could see wisps of smoke coming from the metal chimney. The two boatmen were dragging their fishing skiff into the waves. One man clambered in and immediately bent to the oars. The other, waist-deep behind the keel, gave a final shove and heaved himself up and into the boat to join his companion.

"Look." Lucy pointed to the caravan, where a tall figure dressed in black was stepping down from the little front doorway.

"Is that Holmes?" I asked.

She nodded agreement. "But we ought not to go to him. Remember he said he wanted to work alone."

We walked back to the hotel, and said nothing of the incident to Holmes when he returned that afternoon to await Lansdowne's arrival.

We were in the drawing room at Kerren House when the Secretary of War arrived at around five o'clock. As he descended from his carriage, his face bore a worried frown. It occurred to me, observing once again his urbane bearing, how difficult to distinguish him from Holmes it would be if one were to view only the silhouette of either man. I thought how different our nation's destiny, to say nothing of my own, might have been had Holmes been born into a family of prestige and wealth such as Lansdowne's, and been directed to turn his energies to political and governmental matters rather than taking the path to which he individually inclined.

"I thank you for all you have accomplished thus far, Mr. Holmes," said Lansdowne once we had settled in the drawing room. "However, I must tell you that I am concerned about the Prince's limited time available for this experiment. I shall have to deal with the complaints he makes via the Prime Minister. Lord Salisbury will not be pleased if the Prince has been induced to journey here for nothing. The courtiers that follow him will gossip. I cannot control what they say. Why have you asked him to come here to witness a test, if Tesla could not get the weapon to work?"

"I am concerned for the Prince's safety."

"As am I, of course. But what of it?"

"You will recall my assertions that there is a traitor within the organization of the War Office."

"I assure you that I have done all I can to identify whoever it was that intercepted my message to the Commissioner last week. But my efforts have not been met with success."

"Let us consider the matter from a different view. You sent for me Sunday morning. You did that because the Prince ordered an independent review of the machine, and because he named me as the independent reviewer. You travelled to Kerren House, where you met Mr. Tesla.

There, you learned that a critical part of the machine was missing. Did anything else occur that prompted you to send for me?"

"Lady Radnar. She telephoned from Dover on Saturday night. She was quite insistent that the mystery of the body on the beach be cleared up as soon as possible."

"When did the Prince give the order for me to be brought in?"

"Why, Saturday night. The Prince wired me from Bad Homburg."

"And Sunday morning three men were on my doorstop, even before I myself knew of my involvement. Sending those men was equivalent to an announcement. They are trumpeting the fact that they have penetrated your—our—organizations."

"And I for one cannot understand why they would do that."

"Their actions are an obvious taunt to both of us. They are challenging us to discover the traitor who gave them the information. They know we cannot countenance a traitor. They know we cannot walk away and forget what has transpired. They know we have no choice but to continue on the path that we have set and that they have enabled us to pursue."

"I do not follow."

"Lord Lansdowne. Please. Think of the challenge that Wilhelm has issued. Think of the fact that Wilhelm's government allowed us to leave Germany with the jewel box in our possession."

"Ah, now I understand. We are being manipulated."

"The Germans are moving their pieces on the chessboard. We are doing the same."

"But as yet we cannot see the move that the Germans hope will produce victory for them."

"We do not even know what victory the Germans have in mind. But we do know that for us, victory will be the discovery of the traitor. The Germans have made that perfectly apparent."

"You are telling me the Germans are setting a trap and we must walk into it."

"Our foreknowledge gives us an advantage."

"And the Prince is to walk into the same trap, so to speak."

"Of course we shall have to warn him. He must make up his own mind on that point. But if I am not mistaken, that is the sound of his carriage on the gravel outside. The absence of any challenge from your men tells us as much."

The Prince entered shortly after, escorted by Arkwright. The violinist limped visibly. Also his facial expression and demeanour appeared far more sombre than on the past occasions. I wondered whether he felt remorse for having led Harriet on, and for having written the note that would have caused her pain in what had proven to be the last few days of her young life. I wondered why he had chosen to break off the romance by a note, rather than manfully facing up to her. Possibly Lansdowne was thinking along the same lines, I thought, as I saw him look disapprovingly at Arkwright.

"I shall speak with you later," Lansdowne said. I wondered whether Arkwright had already signed some official explanation for his superior.

The Prince had by now moved to Lansdowne's side, taking his arm and propelling him towards the conservatory where the machine awaited. I noticed that the grey silk fabric of his waistcoat no longer strained to contain the girth beneath its buttons, and that he moved with a jauntier, more vigorous step. I wondered whether some final treatment at the spa had successfully purged at least some of the toxins from his system. I also wondered whether the dramatic loss of weight had any real benefit. I reminded myself that this was an annual occurrence that evidently did no significant harm.

"So that's the miracle weapon, is it?" said the Prince. He and Lansdowne walked around the machine, each man peering closely at the inner mechanisms. The Prince listened somewhat distractedly while

Lansdowne quickly explained the situation and the course of action that Holmes was recommending.

Then the Prince stopped, turned away from the machine, and looked directly at Holmes. "But has it occurred to you that if someone is indeed leading us on as you say they are, then the same someone may also want to kill the Kaiser? Or kill both of us? There are plenty of enemies to choose from—the French, the Boers, the Irish, and possibly even the Russians. Not the Czar, of course, but there is a whole nest of traitorous snakes in that palace of his. But also someone in Willie's government may want to get rid of *him*. Have you thought of that? Many think Willie is mad, you know. I cannot have it said that an attempt was made on British soil—successful or not successful—to assassinate a fellow sovereign."

"We will be on guard at all times to anticipate any action here that may place either of Your Majesties in danger," said Lansdowne. Holmes nodded his agreement.

The Prince gave Holmes and Lansdowne each a long, sceptical, appraising stare. Then he appeared to make up his mind. "So, Lansdowne, it comes down to this," he said. "You want me to put my life at risk in order to root out a . . . viper in the bosom of our government? Someone you haven't been able to catch on your own? Not even with the help of Mr. Sherlock Holmes?"

Holmes spoke firmly. "I believe it is the only way, Your Majesty."

To my surprise, the Prince nodded. He began to speak, the resolve in his voice growing stronger and stronger with every word. "Nearly every day that I appear in public, I put on the uniform of a military man. All those buttons and medals and ribbons—they take time to arrange, one by one, each in its own turn, and every day I think over and over again about why the devil I am going to such pains to manage what most citizens may view as mere fads and trifles. I am well aware why I do it. It is my job to inspire people to be brave. So I may as well show a spot of real bravery myself." He gave a wink to Lansdowne. "But don't tell the Queen, for God's sake. Now, when can we do this test?"

46. A PLAN

"If you will permit me, Your Majesty," said Holmes, "we need not perform the test today."

We all stared at Holmes. "On this occasion," he continued blandly, "we need only send word to Wilhelm that we are ready for him to bring his version of the weapon, and that we are prepared to proceed with the challenge."

"I agree," said the Prince. Then he gave a wink towards Lucy. "If we say we've done the thing, then for this purpose, it's as good as done."

"Practically, it is done," said Lucy with a smile in return. "As Mr. Gilbert says. Or rather, as his character Ko-Ko says."

Arkwright cleared his throat. "Well, if we want to show up Wilhelm and really make the weapon work, I do see something that we might change."

"You are an electrical expert?" Lansdowne seemed sceptical of his agent.

"Far from it," Arkwright said, his tone modest. "But I was here several weeks ago with Kerren, and he showed me the apparatus, going over the basic components with great pride. It is different today. There is something missing."

"What is missing?" Lansdowne asked.

"I will show you. Kerren put it away here."

He went to the tapestry of Queen Elizabeth and lifted it up like a curtain. Behind the tapestry hung a large, flat black object.

Arkwright took down the object, set it on the clay tiles, and spread it out to reveal that it was composed of not one but four India rubber pads, each about two feet square. I helped him place these four India rubber pads beneath the wheels.

Arkwright looked up when we had finished. "Kerren said he always removed these pads whenever he was away, for safety reasons. The machine will not function properly without them."

"Why not?" asked the Prince.

Arkwright shrugged. "I do not really know, Your Majesty. Kerren said something about the ground draining the electricity away from the weapon."

Lansdowne said, "So did you see the machine work?"

"I didn't, actually. I was visiting Lady Radnar at Radnar House, and Kerren dashed in all excited. He said he had triumphed and that their financial future was assured. Knowing the potential of the weapon, I asked to see it, so the two of us came here."

"You and Kerren," said Lansdowne.

"But something had gone wrong with the electrical generator, so there was no electric current for a demonstration. Also, Kerren was anxious to get away. I helped him remove the pads from under the wheels of the apparatus. Then he hung them up behind the tapestry."

"Odd that Tesla did not notice that the pads were missing," Holmes said. "It had to have been perfectly plain to him that the metal wheels were making direct contact with the ground. He must have understood what effect that would have on the machine's performance. It seems such a simple thing. So easy to understand. And yet we were here for nearly four hours and he did not once mention it."

"He may have focused only on the inside, not the outside," said Lansdowne. "He was keen about the inner workings. They were partially his invention."

"Or he may have been bribed," said Arkwright. "You can't be sure, what with all the other goings-on."

The Prince stood up and spoke in his authoritative manner. "Never mind about Tesla. The important thing is it appears the machine may work after all. So let us proceed. Lansdowne. Where is the balloon?"

"Sir?"

"The target, man! Kerren had spoken of shooting down a balloon. He told me he would wheel the machine right up to the doorway, fly up a helium balloon from the beach below the cliff, and have at it. That is the test he described to me and that is what I told Wilhelm we would do. If we are going to do the thing now, let us do it properly. Then when Wilhelm comes and we are fretting about whatever trap you think someone is about to spring on us—looking for monsters lurking in every corner, so to speak—we shall at least not have to concern ourselves with whether or not the machine will fail."

"Indeed," said Lansdowne. "I shall arrange to have a balloon brought over from the garrison. However, the sky is growing dark. I suggest we reconvene in the morning."

"Meanwhile, we can adjourn to Radnar House," said the Prince. "After my annual stint of abstinence taking the cure at Bad Homburg, I am ready to do justice to some of Lady Radnar's hospitality."

The group began to disperse. I could see Lansdowne take Arkwright aside as they left the room. The Secretary's manner was mollified somewhat, no doubt by the brilliance of Arkwright's observation regarding the rubber pads and the electrical apparatus.

Lucy and Holmes had lingered behind. Lucy said, "I wish Miss Porter's School had given us a course in practical electricity." Looking at Holmes, she went on, "Did you know about electricity going into the ground? Or is that one of the facts that you don't want to have cluttering up your brain attic?"

"It does not matter," said Holmes quietly, giving one of his cryptic little smiles. "Now I must be off. I shall join you both presently at Radnar House."

"Where are you going?" asked Lucy.

"Merely to correct a small oversight on my part. Quite possibly I may revise a conclusion that I drew prematurely. I ask that if you see me again at Radnar House, please do not approach me or point out my presence. I shall be perfectly safe, I assure you." He paused. "And I have one further task to request of you, Lucy."

47. A DISQUIETING DINNER

Dinner was held in the private dining room of Radnar House. Lady Radnar had arranged the seating positions at the round table. She sat at the Prince's right, opposite Arkwright. Lucy sat at the Prince's left, opposite me. The meal was excellent, although there was far too much of everything. The Prince, however, seemed determined to devour as much as he could. He gobbled up lobster bisque, caviar, truffles, quail's eggs, roast lamb, pork, beef, and turbot, washing each course down with glass after glass of claret. The names of these dishes, indicating how each had been prepared, were printed in French on cards beside each of our places when the meal began, but the cards were taken up before the first course and I do not recall them. I was too much disquieted to enjoy the little I ate. Memories came back to me of the two meals Holmes and I had shared with Mr. Rockefeller less than a year earlier. Rockefeller's personal fortune, I was certain from reading the newspapers, far exceeded even the Prince's, yet I knew with certainty that Rockefeller would have been appalled at the profusion of rich dishes arrayed on the table before us. However, it was not my place to comment, either on the economic excess of the meal, or on the deleterious effect it would have on the Prince's health as his digestive system strained to cope with such a heavy load.

The conversation centred on Lady Radnar, how kind it was of her to provide such hospitality after the losses she had suffered, and how difficult it was for her to bear up and see to the arrangements for not one but two family funerals when her husband was away. Lord Radnar's latest communication had indicated he would return as soon as possible from Colorado, where he had been investigating some mining ventures. She had his telegram with her, she said. She had sent him the dates of the funerals and had not yet received his reply. She then attempted to engage the Prince on the subject of the weapon, but the Prince merely shrugged and turned to ask Lucy about her next role with the D'Oyly Carte Opera Company.

Finally I saw Lucy set down her dessert spoon across her sorbet cup, pointing directly at me. This was the signal that she was about to comply with Holmes's request, and that I was to pay particular attention to the reactions of Lady Radnar and Mr. Arkwright. Keeping them both within my field of vision was difficult for me due to our respective positions at the table. I drew back slightly as Lucy began to speak, trying to appear as natural as possible.

"Mr. Arkwright," she said, "I wonder if you would favour us with a bit of music from your violin. I should particularly enjoy hearing a composition you performed in Bad Homburg."

"And what composition might that be?"

Lucy hesitated, and at that moment my attention was diverted. Out of the corner of my eye, on my left, the door from the private dining room into the hotel lobby was opening. In the doorway stood Holmes. A veiled woman, dressed in black, was at his side, leaning forwards as if attempting to see something or someone at our table.

"It was a song from a new poem," Lucy was saying. "I recall you said you had improvised the melody. I believe the first words of the song were, 'Oh, when I was in love with you.'"

A fleeting, involuntary smile flickered on Arkwright's lips but it instantly transformed into an injured look. Across from me, Lady Radnar's features showed nothing more than polite curiosity.

Then Lady Radnar appeared astonished as Arkwright turned to the Prince. "Your Majesty, I pray that you will excuse me from your table. I did not realize Miss James had such a cruel streak in her nature."

He then pushed back his chair, stood, and walked swiftly to the doorway.

The door remained open, but the corridor into the hotel lobby was now clear. Holmes and the veiled woman were gone.

48. A TRAP IS SPRUNG

I did not see Holmes again until I entered the Radnar House public dining area for breakfast the following morning. Holmes was seated with Lucy at one of the tables. They both sipped from coffee cups, but there was no sign that either of them had eaten or was inclined to do so. Each looked at me expectantly as I joined them. Keeping my voice low to avoid being overheard by the half dozen other hotel guests at the other tables, I reported exactly what I had seen of Arkwright and Lady Radnar the previous evening.

"Satisfactory" was all Holmes said. In the public circumstances, of course, I felt it would be unwise to press him for an explanation. I looked at Lucy, but she appeared as uninformed as I.

"We were discussing the poet Keats's views on the season of autumn," she said.

"Miss James is intent on furthering my education," said Holmes. Then he lowered his voice. "I understand that His Majesty is taking breakfast in his rooms. He will be joining us in Kerren House, I believe, just before noon. Mr. Arkwright and I are to meet in a half hour to make certain that all is prepared for the Prince's arrival. Would you care to join us?"

"I'm coming too," said Lucy. "Whatever Mr. Arkwright may think of my cruel nature."

Rather than entering Kerren House by the way we had used on previous occasions, Holmes led us around to the back, following the edge of the cliff. The sky was dark with threatening clouds, and there were whitecaps on the grey waves. The winds from the Channel tore at our coats. I had the foolish foreboding that Nature herself disapproved of the change in the settled order of things that we were about to attempt today. Far below us on the beach, a grey military balloon, of exactly the kind that we had seen disintegrate into fiery fragments less than a week ago, now rose slowly, jerking to and fro in the wind, tethered on stout ropes held by several of Lansdowne's men, as if it were some great elephant being forced to obey the bidding of its handlers.

"Well, the positioning of the target is proceeding nicely," said Lucy. "But what of the gypsies? If I remember correctly, their camp was directly below."

"I have already warned the gypsies not to come here today," said Holmes.

We turned to look at the conservatory. At the centre of its glass facade, the double doors were shut. Inside, we could see the machine. Arkwright was hunched over it. As we drew closer, the four black India rubber pads that we had seen the previous evening were now plainly visible beneath the four metal wheels.

Arkwright looked up when we opened the doors. "Oh, there you are. I was just going over the settings to be certain nothing had been tampered with overnight. You can see for yourself. They are exactly as I remember. I took the trouble to memorize the placement of the dials and the position of the switches."

I noticed that Arkwright did not look directly at Lucy at any time. It was obvious he still felt the embarrassment or shame concerning his callous treatment of Harriet, which Lucy had alluded to in the presence of the Prince. Neither did Lucy look at Arkwright as she and Holmes examined the inner workings of the machine. I did not bother to examine the settings, since I had barely glanced at them during the time that they had been under Tesla's supervision.

Finally Holmes nodded.

Arkwright was putting on his mackintosh. "I'm going to take a look at the generator. We need plenty of fuel, so that we don't lose power. That would be too much of an embarrassment to suffer in front of the royal personage."

We followed him. I recalled the cold Monday morning when we had first walked between the generator building and its companion building, the icehouse. I wondered whether new ice had been delivered. I saw that the door remained unlocked.

All appeared to be in order within the generator shed. The machine hummed within, then growled and rumbled more noisily once the door was open. We could smell the exhaust fumes of the petrol. Arkwright peered closely at the fuel indicator gauge and then gave the tank itself a rap with his knuckles to be sure. The reverberating sound was tight, rather than hollow, indicating a goodly amount of fuel within.

Holmes and Arkwright were both satisfied that all was in order with the generator. By the time we returned to the conservatory, we heard the familiar crunch of hooves and carriage wheels on the gravel drive. We walked quickly to the front to greet Lansdowne as he stepped down from the rear of the black army carriage. The Prince, who looked a bit worse for his evening and a bit unsteady, followed Lansdowne, leaning on the other's proffered hand. The Prince barely took notice of Lucy.

"Are we ready?" asked Lansdowne. Arkwright and Holmes each nodded. Holmes opened the Kerren House front door for the six of us to enter.

In the drawing room, we were surprised to find Lady Radnar waiting for us, dressed in black. She raised her tightly clasped hands, holding them up to the Prince in a gesture of supplication. "Adrian thought you would not mind if I watched the demonstration. It is so important to me and to my husband. And my brother's memory."

"No need to beg, Sophie," said the Prince. "You can watch. But the machine will do whatever it's going to do. Don't try to influence my decision on whether we spend any more money on it. Either the damned thing works or it doesn't."

The seven of us entered the conservatory. Against the murky horizon visible through the glass wall, the machine loomed within, like a dark and shadowy sleeping presence.

"What happened to the lights?" asked Lady Radnar.

"They were on when we left," said Arkwright. "We were just looking at the dials." He went to the switch on the wall and turned it. The lights came on. "There, that's sorted. Now let's see about the aim. If the target's in place, we can fire the machine and put an end to the suspense."

Before us, just beyond the edge of the cliff some fifty yards away, the big grey balloon danced in the wind, straining at its ropes.

"Stable enough, I should think," said Arkwright, his hand on the switch that would turn on the power to the machine. "Lord Lansdowne?"

Lansdowne nodded.

"Then let us have at it," said the Prince, "and chance the consequences!"

Arkwright threw the switch. We all held our breath.

Nothing happened. Within the room the electric lights above us glowed cheerily. Outside, the balloon danced on its ropes over the ocean, as though happy to have had a reprieve from its destruction.

"What the devil is wrong?" said the Prince.

"Yesterday, the machine made a loud humming noise," said Lucy. "Now it is silent."

Arkwright crouched beneath the machine. "I don't see anything different down here. The wires are all connected, just as they were when we left them yesterday. Do you want to take a look, Mr. Holmes?"

Holmes came over to the machine and crouched beside Arkwright.

"The lights are still on, so there can't be anything wrong with the generator," said Lansdowne. "Electricity is obviously still coming into the conservatory."

"I just remembered," said Lady Radnar. "My brother had the men bring in new wires from the generator just to power the machine. Perhaps something is wrong with the new wires."

"Might have blown a fuse or something," said the Prince.

Holmes and Arkwright stood up together. Holmes gave a silent shrug to indicate that he had seen nothing beneath the machine that he could act upon. However, I noticed a familiar glitter in his grey eyes.

"I think the fuse box is right outside the generator shed," said Arkwright. "Shan't be a minute." He took a few steps towards the open double doors.

"I think not," said Holmes. His voice was silken.

Arkwright stopped and turned, eyes widened in puzzlement. "Have you a better idea, Mr. Holmes?"

"I think we ought to all stay here for the time being." He gave a nod to Lucy, who edged closer to Arkwright. "We can await developments."

"Of what sort?" said Arkwright. "The Prince has more important things to do than wait around here, as far as I can see. We ought to get on with it."

"We should indeed," Holmes said. "And now we shall. Lucy, if you please."

At that moment Lucy, now behind Arkwright, drew her derringer from her reticule and clapped it to the back of Arkwright's neck.

"Raise your hands, Mr. Arkwright," she said. "Raise them above your head. Dr. Watson, please remove Mr. Arkwright's coat. See that his hands go nowhere near his pockets."

The Prince gasped in astonishment. Arkwright's eyes blazed for a moment, but then he drew himself under control as I approached. "Holmes, you are making a complete ass of yourself."

I moved beside Lucy and reached for the collar of Arkwright's coat. I felt him tense as if to spin around, but Lucy kicked hard at the back of the knee of his injured leg. He fell forwards, a hand scrabbling for his coat pocket. I stamped down hard on his wrist, pinning it beneath my foot. Moments later, I had Arkwright's Webley pistol in my hand.

"That was a little bit more of my cruel streak," Lucy said. The Prince continued to stare at her. I believe I saw a shudder pass through his rotund frame.

Lucy knelt beside Arkwright, the barrel of her derringer now pressing into his left wrist. "I believe your left hand is of particular value to you as a violinist. What a shame if it were to be injured."

"This is madness," said Arkwright. "Lord Lansdowne, call your men. Holmes and Watson and this woman have gone mad!"

"Once again, I think not," said Holmes, his voice serene. "Dr. Watson, could you please secure Mr. Arkwright? I believe the belt of his coat will do nicely. Please move him away from the machine. As far away as possible, without giving him the opportunity to obstruct my path to the open doors."

"I tell you he is mad," said Arkwright, now kneeling, after I had tied his wrists securely to his ankles using the stout fabric of his mackintosh belt. "Holmes, I have been protecting you, helping you, getting injured for you, getting the machine itself properly prepared for you, and this is how you repay me. Lord Lansdowne, Your Majesty, I have endured danger on many occasions in order to serve you both. You must believe me!"

Holmes advanced towards the machine. His voice was almost kindly. "They very well might have believed you, Arkwright," he said, "if only you had taken the trouble to wipe your shoes. You failed to notice that the edges of your elegant leather soles picked up particles of sawdust from the floor of the icehouse, when you were there this morning."

He reached into the machine. Moments later, moving very slowly, he held up what might have been a small carton of cigarettes, had it not been constructed of shining steel. There was a small black patch on the top of the carton. "This object was affixed by this magnet"—here Holmes pointed to the small black patch—"to one of Mr. Tesla's coils inside the machine. You will recall that there is no doubt that Mr. Tesla's coils work, and that they generate and amplify electrical currents to produce a great deal of electrical energy. All that energy generated from those six coils would have passed through this magnet, directly into this steel carton. As you see, particles of sawdust still cling to it, as do droplets of water. It is cool to the touch, so the droplets are likely to be condensation from the moist sea air. That fact is material, since there is no condensation on the remainder of the machine, indicating that its temperature is warmer than the temperature of the steel carton that I now hold so carefully before you."

Arkwright's eyes blazed with hatred. "Aren't you the scientific expert," he said.

"I do claim a modest expertise in the field of chemistry," Holmes said, now standing at the interior wall of the conservatory and inclining his head towards the shelves. "When I noticed, for example, that there were bottles of sulphuric acid, nitric acid, and glycerine here on these shelves last week, and that the shelves had not been recently dusted, and that marks in the dust indicated those bottles had been recently moved, it occurred to me that a weapon more conventional than this . . . experimental, shall we say, apparatus might be involved in whatever activity we were about to encounter. Sulphuric acid, nitric acid, and glycerine are the ingredients used in the creation of nitroglycerine, which, as you doubtless are aware, is highly explosive."

Lansdowne's face was pale. "Holmes, are you saying that the steel carton in your hand contains nitroglycerine?"

"I believe it to be relatively stable, at the moment," he replied, "since it is still relatively cool, having been stored in the icehouse until Mr. Arkwright removed it this morning and brought it here. While he was doing so, I believe he took the opportunity to shut off the machine's power using the junction box positioned outside the generator shed, so that no electrical power could reach the machine. Had he not taken that latter action, the results would have been very different when the control here on the machine was switched on a short time ago. You will notice that the switch is still in the 'On' position. Had Mr. Arkwright been permitted to go to the generator shed just now, he would not have returned. He would have thrown the switch on the junction box. Electricity would have flowed into the machine and into Mr. Tesla's coils. The powerful energy produced by the coils would have discharged instantly into the steel carton, heating the nitroglycerine and causing it to detonate."

Lady Radnar stared at Arkwright. "And you wanted me *here*," she said, with a terrible intensity.

"Now if you will pardon my departure," said Holmes, "I should like to dispose of this explosive material."

We watched him as he walked slowly and carefully away from us, through the wide-open doorway into the grey shadows outside the conservatory. I shall always hold in my memory the image of Holmes, dressed in his black Inverness cloak, his silhouette framed by the circular globe of the military balloon against the darkening sky. After reaching the edge of the cliff, he looked down to be certain that no one was on the beach below. Then he stood up ramrod-straight and extended his arm so that the steel carton was suspended beyond the precipice. Holmes held the carton for a moment, and then let it fall.

He had turned back and was running towards us when there came the roar of a great explosion. From beneath and behind him, yellow-white light enveloped his falling figure in a strangely beautiful halo. The aura lasted for only a moment. My eyes squeezed shut, involuntarily attempting to recover from the brilliant flash. When I opened them, to my great relief, I saw Holmes getting to his feet. The grey military balloon, its connection to the beach now severed, sailed away on the wind, trailing the shreds of its ropes behind it as if they were so many bedraggled tails.

49. A SECOND SHOT

Pale with shock, the Prince nonetheless stood stiffly at attention. "So this was the trap you spoke of, Holmes," he said. "You had to wait for Arkwright to act in order to be absolutely sure. I see that. By God, what a chaos it would have wrought. The monarchy. The government. And you think Wilhelm is behind it?"

We were gathered in the conservatory. Lansdowne had brought in three of his soldiers, who stood on three sides of the kneeling Arkwright, their pistols at the ready.

"Assuredly we are dealing with someone at a high level in the German government," Holmes replied. "Von Bülow, or possibly someone higher."

"But they'll never admit it, of course."

"Everything they did was designed to accomplish two things: to make us trust Arkwright, and to induce you, Your Majesty, to come here to witness a test of the weapon. Kerren never sold his jewel box to Wilhelm. Arkwright stole the jewel box, as soon as he knew of its existence and the location of the safe in which Kerren hid it. He obtained that knowledge from Dr. Olfrig. To learn more, we should have to return to Bad Homburg, assuming the good doctor has returned from his sojourn to the Friedrichsbad, and induce him to turn over his records of Kerren's 'treatment.'"

"What treatment? Who is Dr. Olfrig?" asked the Prince.

"My brother was having difficulty with his nerves," said Lady Radnar. "Adrian suggested that Dr. Olfrig could help."

"On the first visit," Holmes continued, "the doctor used drugs or hypnosis to extract from Kerren all his grand plans for a super weapon and his hopes for a lucrative sale to the British government. Employing the same techniques, Olfrig then induced Kerren to forget his disclosure. But then Kerren grew worried about his memory, and of course when he realized that his jewel box was missing, and he could not remember where he had put the plans, he returned for a second visit."

"He did say that his memory was returning after he saw the doctor again," said Lady Radnar.

"I doubt that the doctor helped in that regard," said Holmes. "I think it more likely that the effects of the treatment began to wear off. But whatever the cause of the improvement may have been, Kerren did announce that he had begun to recover his memory. You, Arkwright, could not risk having him recall or disclose what Olfrig had done to him. So Kerren had to be killed."

"I did not kill Kerren," Arkwright said.

"I believe you," Holmes replied. "But at the moment we are discussing how you manipulated us into coming here to test this weapon. You engaged the man called Mr. Gruen to impersonate a representative of the supposed criminals who had supposedly stolen the invention. You had Mr. Gruen come to Watson to negotiate for the jewel box. To bolster Gruen's credentials as a potential ally, you had Dietrich and Richter—whom we knew to be hostile parties—abduct Gruen at gunpoint. You provided Dr. Watson with an advance payment. You told Gruen that Dr. Watson had the funds in a satchel and that he would arrive on the train to which you had directed him. Then Gruen took the funds. Whether he did this under your orders or on his own account is not clear to me. But Gruen did offer to produce the jewel box in exchange for another payment. You suspected his loyalties, but you needed a way to confirm your suspicions. You utilized the services of Dr. Olfrig, who interviewed Dr. Watson using the same methods he had employed on Lord Kerren. Dr. Watson revealed Gruen's offer."

So *that* was what I had divulged in Olfrig's office but had been unable to remember! I felt relief, and yet a frustrating degree of uncertainty, for I still could not recall what had happened.

But Holmes was continuing. "You could not allow Gruen to operate independently of your orders. So you killed him. You induced him to come to Tesla's room, and there you overpowered him and pushed him off the balcony to his death."

"Gloat all you want, Holmes," Arkwright said. "It won't change a thing."

Lansdowne turned to Arkwright, his gaze filled with both anger and sorrow. "Adrian, why?" he asked. "You were one of us."

Arkwright glared. "You say 'one of us,' as though that ought to be sufficient compensation to be at the War Department's beck and call every day of every year for the past decade. Wilhelm would have given me far greater rewards. Had Holmes not interfered, I would have become a German duke, with a castle in Bavaria and a fortune in the Rothschild bank. No one would have known of my role in making all of you—all of England—the fools of the century. Each of you would have been turned to dust and vapour." He gave a light little wave of his hand, twisting his wrist within his manacles. "The prevailing winds might well have borne you across the Channel into France, or possibly even to my new home in Germany." An oddly crazed little laugh came from his radiant, now-maniacal face. "I might have *breathed* you, Holmes!"

"We will extract the full truth from you and then put you on trial, after which you will be hanged for treason," Lansdowne said, his voice calm and matter-of-fact.

"You know you will not, Lansdowne. You will release me into the care of the German ambassador, in London."

To my surprise, Lansdowne did not reply.

Arkwright went on, "If you do not release me by the end of this month, an associate of mine will feed the contents of my journal to the ravenous press, whose readers are always hungry for scandal. You may succeed in muzzling the papers in England, but your influence will not extend to those in other nations. The journal contains details of numerous acts I have performed for you in cities throughout Europe, under the cover of my public role as a touring violinist. The journal also contains the names of those individuals who cooperated with me. Your network of spies will be exposed, and *they* will be hanged. The scandal will bring down Salisbury's government. Is that what you want, Lansdowne?"

Lansdowne's face was impassive. "Take him to the garrison," he told the guards.

"Mr. Secretary, if I may have a word," said Holmes. He spoke in a low tone to Lansdowne, who nodded.

"Your Majesty," Lansdowne said, "would you please remain inside with Lady Radnar until we can summon another carriage. Two of my men will stay with you for your protection."

Holmes then said something to Lucy that I could not hear. Her eyes flashed.

We followed as Arkwright was untied, hauled to his feet, and escorted at gunpoint to the front of Kerren House, where the black regimental carriage awaited. The uniformed driver stood ready, holding the bridle of a large black horse. The rear door was open, facing the Channel. The weather had grown darker still, and a fog was beginning to roll in. We could see wisps of grey mist at the edge of the cliff.

Arkwright stopped before the open door, about to speak, but Lucy's voice cut in like the crack of a whip.

"Mr. Arkwright!"

All eyes turned to her. Lucy took a few steps and in a moment stood face-to-face with the traitor. "When you hang," she went on, "I hope your last thoughts will be of Harriet Radnar, the woman whose life ended in sorrow because of your despicable behaviour."

Arkwright showed not the slightest trace of remorse. To the contrary, he appeared amused. "Ah, Miss James. The schoolgirl friend," he said, his tone heavy with insolence. "The orphan who befriended the poor little English girl, who found herself all alone in the great American wasteland—the poor foreigner, who had lost her mother's life and her father's love. Your loyalty is oh-so very, very touching."

As Lucy moved closer, he went on, "Mark my words, Miss Lucy James. These men will give in to my demands and I shall see you again."

His sneering voice trailed off, accompanied by an insinuating leer. But he said no more, for Lucy, in one swift movement, lashed him across the face with the barrel of her derringer.

What happened next was a blur. Arkwright appeared to grapple with Lucy, struggling for the gun. The two stumbled backwards, falling onto the floor of the army carriage. Holmes cried out, "No!" and leaped to Lucy's assistance. For a moment I could see only his shadowy form and the others behind him, locked in deadly struggle. Lucy's voice came from within the van in a loud cry. "He has my gun!" The struggle continued for several interminable seconds.

Then a shot rang out, and the movement within the dark interior of the carriage subsided.

I strained to see into the darkness. One figure stood, and moved away from the other dark shapes. It was Lucy. She walked around them and stood in daylight, at the edge of the doorway. She held out her derringer to me. "Please help Mr. Holmes with the body," she said quietly.

"Only stand clear for the moment," I heard Holmes say from inside. He was on his knees, manoeuvring the motionless body of Arkwright to the edge of the rear platform and the open doorway. An army blanket had been draped over Arkwright's inert form. As Arkwright's torso was tilted up, we could see a great dark stain on the blanket, in the area of Arkwright's heart.

Holmes stepped down from the carriage, then bent forwards, face-to-face with the unconscious Arkwright, placing his hands beneath Arkwright's shoulders to lift him up and pull him out of the carriage. Holmes's legs tensed as he bore the weight and stood upright.

Then from far away, and muffled by the incoming fog, a second shot rang out.

A great spasm went through Holmes's body. He fell away from Arkwright's inert form and crumpled to the ground. My heartbeat roared within my ears as I bent over him. I was aware of Lansdowne and Lucy on either side of me. I strained to focus. Holmes was facing upwards. His cape had fallen open. A bright red sheen of blood was spreading rapidly from a dark hole in the white front of his shirt, just below his left collarbone, very near the lung and heart. The hole was about one inch in diameter. Holmes's eyes widened and his face flushed deeply as he recognized us. His hand gripped my forearm, trying to push me from him.

"You must go," he said, his voice faint. "You must take cover. I insist—" Then his eyelids fluttered, and his hand fell away.

50. AFTERMATH

Lucy would not leave his side.

Gunshots roared around us as Lansdowne's men fired volley after volley into the fog, in the direction from which the shot had come. Lucy and I carried Holmes behind the carriage where we were no longer visible from the cliff. I tore open Holmes's shirt, stifling my reverberating emotions and desperately willing myself to go into that detached professional state my training and experience had made a second nature. I pressed hard around the wound with my fingertips to staunch the diminishing flow of blood. Mercifully, there was not the hot, pulsing, intermittent rush that would indicate an artery had been struck. Lucy had folded her scarf and smock into two pads, which I applied to the entry and the exit wounds. I took off my jacket and we used it as a blanket to keep him warm. I watched for signs of shock, but there were none. Holmes's breathing grew stronger and more even.

The gunshots faded into silence.

"I believe he will recover," I said to Lucy. "The bullet passed through him. Nothing vital was hit."

Lansdowne's men fanned out in the fog, searching the area. They found only the spot where the sniper had lain, and a single spent rifle shell.

We moved Holmes to a sofa in the drawing room of Kerren House. A military ambulance arrived, and I cleansed and dressed the wound with proper disinfectant and bandages. Lucy still would not move away from him. The two of us watched him breathe.

"What did he say to you?" I asked Lucy, keeping my voice soft so as not to wake him.

"He told me to go to Arkwright and pick a fight. Make it physical, he said. I was to get Arkwright into the carriage, and he would help me. He used some pressure technique around Arkwright's neck to make him lose consciousness."

"Carotid artery."

"He said that, yes. There was an army blanket on the floor of the van. He told me to bunch it up and fire my derringer into it, and I did. Then we spread the blanket over Arkwright, covering his face as though he'd died. Holmes poured water onto the blanket before I got up to leave. He had taken a water bottle from a shelf as we were leaving the conservatory. It was all a ruse."

When Holmes awoke, Lansdowne was with us. Holmes immediately asked what had happened to Arkwright.

"Arkwright is alive," said Lansdowne. "But the bullet that passed through you caught him in the face. He'll have a nasty scar, maybe worse. Our ambulance has taken him off to the garrison infirmary. We'll hold him incommunicado until we decide what to do with him. Meanwhile we will announce his death, as you planned. No details of the incident. Memorial service in a few days, et cetera, et cetera. And we will hope that if indeed there is a journal, whoever has it will feel no fear of retaliation. The fellow will think himself free to keep whatever payment Arkwright provided and not take the risk of going to the press."

Holmes gave one of his tight, wry smiles. His voice was only a whisper, but I heard him say, "Mr. Secretary, you must admit that I was correct."

Lansdowne nodded. "There was indeed another traitor. And the actions of you and Miss James did indeed cause him to reveal himself."

At my confused look, Lucy said, "There had to have been an alternative plan. If the bomb failed, the second traitor was waiting to shoot the Prince. And when the bomb went off harmlessly below the cliff, it was obvious that the Prince was still alive."

"So why shoot Holmes?" I asked. "Was he a secondary target?"

"I should hope not," said Holmes. "My hope is that we provoked the shooter to avenge Arkwright's apparent death. I continue to hope that the shooter still wants to do precisely that. Lord Lansdowne, please also let the press know that I was injured slightly, but that I am expected to make a full recovery."

51. AN INTERVIEW AT 221B BAKER STREET

It was one week later, on the first Friday in October. Five long and difficult days had elapsed since we had returned to our rooms in Baker Street, and we were far from being settled into our comfortable, routine existence. Lucy insisted on remaining near to Holmes. She had moved into 221A, the vacant flat on the floor below that adjoined Mrs. Hudson's. During the first few days, Lucy also insisted on taking her turn when the time came to change Holmes's bandages, and on being trained to recognize the signs that would indicate whether his wound had become infected or was not healing properly. Frequently she would attempt to engage Holmes on the many unanswered questions that still remained concerning the events we had experienced in Dover and in Germany. On each occasion Holmes refused to comment, saying that the time was not yet ripe, or that more facts remained unknown, or that speculation would be, as he always says, inappropriate.

On this particular day, Lucy had gone out to the Savoy Theatre for her first rehearsal since she had performed with the D'Oyly Carte Opera Company in Bad Homburg. Holmes was at our bow window, clad in his dressing gown and with his left arm in a sling so that his movements would not disturb the bandages that still covered his upper body. He was peering restlessly into what remained of the morning fog. Then someone on the pavement below rang our bellpull. Shortly afterwards Mrs. Hudson was at our door, handing Holmes a telegram. "The boy is waiting for a reply," she said.

As Mrs. Hudson hovered in the doorway, Holmes scanned the contents and thrust the yellow paper at me. "What do you make of this, Watson?"

I read:

> My husband asks I engage you to help him with a difficult business problem. May I call on you tomorrow afternoon at your Baker Street address?
>
> —Sophia Radnar

"Funeral services for Harriet Radnar and Lord Kerren are being held today, in Dover," Holmes said, as though musing to himself, without giving me opportunity to voice my own opinions. "So Lady Radnar will be occupied there until evening. Mr. Arkwright's memorial service is Sunday, here in London. I doubt that Lady Radnar plans to attend. I shall accommodate her request for a meeting tomorrow afternoon."

He took his pen, wrote "Four o'clock," at the bottom of the message, and gave it to Mrs. Hudson with half a crown. "Tell the boy it is to be sent at once."

He turned to me. "We shall need to make preparations. Watson, might I trouble you to telephone for Lord Lansdowne?"

As four o'clock approached the following afternoon, Lucy and I grew progressively more apprehensive as we anticipated what was about to happen. Holmes, in contrast, appeared calm, even languid, seated in his armchair before the fire. Against my wishes, he had donned a white shirt and his customary black necktie, though Lucy had been required to slit the shirt fabric up the back to allow for the depth of the bandages that covered his wound. He had also insisted on not wearing the sling. In his dressing gown he appeared as normal as on any other occasion. But for a slight stiffness in the way he moved, one might never have suspected that barely a week had elapsed since he had been struck down by a bullet on that seaside cliff in Dover.

The outside bellpull rang. Lucy, who had been sitting, got to her feet. So did I. We heard Mrs. Hudson's voice, then the familiar sound of footsteps on our stairs. "Lady Radnar, sir," she said, ushering in a heavily veiled woman dressed in black mourning garb and carrying a black purse.

"Thank you, Mrs. Hudson. You may leave us."

Our landlady departed. When the door closed behind her, Holmes said, "Please pardon me if I do not get up. I do require medical care from time to time and Miss James here has been assisting Dr. Watson in that regard. I am still not yet entirely recovered from a bullet wound I received last week."

Then his voice took on that silken tone. "I believe it was you who fired the gun, did you not, Miss Harriet Radnar?"

The veiled woman stood mute. I thought I saw movement beneath her heavy black cape.

"Come, Miss Radnar, you really ought to remove your veil. I do not believe you have the capacity for feelings sufficient to warrant wearing mourning garb for others, although you surely ought to mourn your own many misdeeds."

With an abrupt gesture, the woman swept back her veil. The defiant face of Harriet Radnar stared brazenly at the three of us. From the folds of her cape, she had extracted a large long-barrelled pistol of the German style. She now held it trained on Holmes, but her gaze alternated between Holmes and Lucy.

"Which one of you killed Adrian?" she demanded. "That one will watch the other die."

"Arkwright lives," Holmes replied evenly.

"You lie!" She brandished the pistol. "I saw you strike him, Lucy. I heard the gunshot. I saw him fallen inside the army carriage. I saw you and Holmes get out unharmed. Now, answer me! Which one!"

"His death in Dover, like your supposed death in Germany, was merely an illusion. We thought you might be watching from the cliff as we had him led away to the army carriage. We improvised a bit of drama to induce you to show yourself," Holmes continued.

"I do not believe you."

"You will see Arkwright momentarily. However, you should prepare yourself for a change in his appearance. Your bullet, after passing through my torso, did cause him some harm." He turned towards the barely opened door to his sleeping room. "Lord Lansdowne, if you please."

The door opened. Lansdowne emerged. Arkwright followed, his hands manacled behind him, his face bandaged and badly swollen. Behind him came two strapping Army officers, holding their pistols at the ready.

Harriet gasped at the sight of Arkwright's once-handsome face.

"Is it all that ghastly, Harriet?" His tone was imploring.

"I truly thought Holmes or Lucy had killed you," she replied, her face twisted in revulsion. The barrel of her gun, however, was trained on Holmes and never wavered.

"I wish I could have warned you off."

"But you failed."

"But we shall recover. My face will heal, and we will soon be together, away from this accursed little island. We shall play—" His voice broke, though he quickly cleared his throat and concluded, "—beautiful music."

"You will be away indeed, and for a very long time, Mr. Arkwright," said Lansdowne. "But I doubt you will have time or energy for your Stradivarius in the Andaman Islands. Miss Radnar, put down your pistol."

"You will take us both to the German embassy immediately," Harriet said, continuing to hold the gun. "Mr. Arkwright has written a journal—"

"So he has informed us. We are prepared to take that risk. We will bring you to trial, Miss Radnar, for the murder of your father, Lord Radnar, and of Lord Kerren. We will try you, Arkwright, for treason, and for the murder of Sergeant Phillip Stubbs."

The brown eyes widened in Arkwright's ruined face. His tone was one of mock bewilderment and innocence. "Murder a police sergeant? Why would I do that?"

"Come, Arkwright," said Holmes. "You know exactly why. In order to conceal the truth, you even wrote a note for us to find in Miss Radnar's purse. You were smitten with Miss Radnar. You would do anything she asked. She needed you to prevent Stubbs from continuing his attempts to blackmail her stepmother."

"You are absurd, Mr. Holmes," said Harriet.

"To the contrary," said Holmes. "Stubbs was standing guard on the Dover passenger dock one month ago as travellers boarded a steamship bound for New York. He saw the local draper, one Mr. Lampert, coming up the gangplank dressed in unusually fine attire. Mr. Lampert believed he was on an important governmental mission to impersonate Lord Radnar. Quite possibly, Miss Radnar, you showed Mr. Lampert some credentials of yours from the War Office to gain his trust. You may even have asked him to design new military uniforms. In any event, as Lampert boarded the ship for America, he was recognized by Sergeant Stubbs, who heard the ticket clerk read out the name of Lord Radnar. Stubbs thought there was some illegal activity afoot and imagined that he could profit from his knowledge. He approached Lady Radnar. She mentioned the approach in your hearing, Miss Radnar. You could not allow him to tell Lady Radnar what he knew."

"I was nowhere near Stubbs when he was killed," said Harriet.

"But Mr. Arkwright was. Arkwright, you shot the sergeant twice with the rifle Miss Radnar provided from her father's collection. A difficult shot, and the rifle's aim was not as true as it might have been, so neither shot was fatal. When you learned he had survived, you donned your black knit mask—the same mask you had worn here in Baker Street two days earlier—and you broke Stubbs's neck. It was significant that no human hairs were found in the wool fabric of your mask. You then pretended to arrive on the Calais ferry the next morning, and to be surprised by the exploding military balloon as you sat with us in the garrison castle. You had been in Dover all along, however. You may even have helped Kerren with the explosive and the timing device."

"A tenuous web of wild surmise," said Arkwright, airily confident. "You cannot prove any of this twaddle. Lansdowne, I demand to see my solicitor before I say another word."

52. THE INTERVIEW CONCLUDES

Holmes shrugged. "Very well. At this point it is of no consequence what you say or do not say, Mr. Arkwright. However, I know what it is to stand for an extended period while recovering from a bullet wound. Pray take a seat."

Arkwright hugged his manacled wrists close to his chest. At a nod from Holmes, his two military guards propelled him towards our dining table and pressed him down into a chair.

"Thank you, gentlemen," said Holmes. "Now let us return our attentions to you, Miss Radnar. According to the records of the White Star Line, Mr. Lampert plans to return from New York under his own name. His final task was to send Lady Radnar the telegram from New York that induced her to arrange this appointment. You might more conveniently have sent the telegram yourself to arrange the appointment, under the pretence that it was being sent to me by your stepmother. But you had the foresight to realize that such a course of action bore with it an unnecessary risk. You correctly anticipated that I would be cautious enough to telephone Lady Radnar to confirm that her message was genuine. Then this afternoon, you awaited Lady Radnar here. Your accomplices—I would expect them to be our old friends Richter and Dietrich—accompanied you, positioning themselves at either end of our Baker Street block and signalling the arrival of her carriage, so you could enter here without her observing you. I expect you have ordered them to commandeer her carriage and take her away."

"They may already have done so," Harriet said sweetly.

"You have arranged to meet Mr. Lampert next week here in London, in some anonymous hotel. He is expecting you to deliver the final payment for his successful completion of his very, very secret mission. Instead, you plan to kill him and leave his body without identification. You have grown quite accustomed to killing, have you not, Miss Radnar?"

"I shall thoroughly enjoy killing you," she said.

"Your enjoyment would be short-lived. In the pocket of my dressing gown I am holding my Webley revolver. It is aimed at your face."

Harriet flinched momentarily, but she continued to hold her German pistol trained on Holmes.

"You shot your father more than a month ago, on the day he was to depart for America," Holmes continued. "You wrapped his body in a hessian sack and hid it in Kerren's icehouse. When you learned Kerren was returning, you had to dispose of the body. You had noticed the gypsies fishing and seen the smoke from the fire pit below the wire frame they used to cook their fish. Fortunately for you there was a storm coming in. You warned the gypsies of the oncoming storm. They left their campsite, making their fire pit available to you for your grim purposes."

Holmes shook his head, as though saddened by the appalling details he was about to recount. "It was difficult for you to manage, Miss Radnar, but you accomplished all the tasks reasonably required of you to permanently conceal your father's murder. That night, before the storm, you dragged his body to the edge of the cliff and let it fall. You also tumbled some sacks of coal over the cliff. You buried the body amidst the coals in the fire pit, soaked them with petrol, and set the combustible pile ablaze. Had your father's body not been frozen, it would have soon been reduced to ashes and would have vanished into the tide. But the storm intervened. Even so, the Channel waters very nearly concealed your crime. It must have been distressing for you when the charred body washed up on the beach and caused your stepmother to become so very agitated."

"You have no evidence for any of this."

"The coal sacks left dark traces on the white chalk. The measurements I took of the charred body match the records Mr. Lampert, the draper, kept of your father, who was his customer. There were no teeth, which is consistent with your father's dental history. We found his blood intermingled with the sawdust and hessian fibres in the icehouse. We found his bones oddly fragmented, due to the fall from the cliff and the frozen condition of his flesh."

"You still cannot prove I had anything to do with his death."

"We will have Mr. Lampert's testimony. He will no doubt recall the various telegrams you instructed him to send in the name of Lord Radnar. Also, when you warned the gypsies away from the beach, you spoke to a woman in their party, one Madam Drina. You told her that you were Lady Radnar. When I first interviewed Madam Drina, I took her account of that conversation at face value. However, I later thought to bring her to where she could see Lady Radnar from a short distance away, and she assured me that this Lady Radnar was not the woman she had spoken with. I examined your room and found you had removed all the photographs of yourself, so I was unable to obtain positive identification until D'Oyly Carte's assistant provided photographs of you. But Madam Drina has seen them now. She will bear witness in a court of law if requested."

"You are a commoner," Harriet said curtly. "You cannot know what it is to have your father tell you that your birthright has been squandered—that all that is rightfully yours has been spent on lavish parties in order to elevate the social position of a scheming, jealous woman—and to advance the career of her dilettante, self-deluding brother."

"And the Germans would pay handsomely for the assassination of the Prince."

She gave a short laugh. "We even had a forged packet of letters from the Prince's paramours, ready to be released just before the funeral. Fat Bertie's memory would have been disgraced forever."

Holmes's tone was calm and inexorable as he went on. "But you could not live in the manner you desired if the world was looking for you, as it surely would have done if you had simply gone missing. To create the illusion of your death, you first staged your own kidnapping. You left a note on your bed, and another in your purse, this one from Arkwright to distance him from any association with you. The following morning you went to the Baden-Baden railway station in a wheelchair pushed by Dietrich, who had put on the uniform and cap of a nurse. You used a simple white wig and makeup to appear as his wheelchair-bound elderly patient. You timed your entrance to the station to coincide with the departure of the southbound train, when travellers and soldiers were in place to bear witness, and with the arrival of the northbound express. You jumped from the northbound railway platform onto the tracks, and then after shamming an injury until you were no longer visible to the northbound express engineer, you flung yourself to safety and concealment between two cars of the southbound train. Mr. Arkwright was waiting for you, on the tracks between those cars, in the company of an unconscious young woman whose physical characteristics resembled yours."

Arkwright's shoulders slumped. He closed his eyes as Holmes continued.

"Arkwright had drugged the woman on the journey from Bad Homburg, so she could offer no resistance as he moved her from their first-class compartment to the space between the cars. In his locomotive, the driver could not see either Arkwright or the woman, for she was on the left side of the locomotive and the driver's window was on the right. He could see you, of course, up until approximately thirty feet remained between you and the front of the locomotive. With the train advancing towards you at twenty miles per hour, decelerating due to the frantic application of the locomotive brakes, you had one full second for your leap to safety, and for Arkwright at the same moment to push the drugged young woman onto the track. The impact of the locomotive made it impossible to recognize her. She was dressed in your clothes, with your scarf around her neck. Do not waste the effort of a denial, Miss Radnar. I found the Baden-Baden railway timetables in your room. And Mr. Arkwright has already confessed to his role."

"Traitor!" Harriet's eyes blazed at Arkwright.

"I did no such thing!" he replied. "Harriet, I did not tell him! I swear it!"

"Then you tricked me, Holmes."

Holmes shrugged. "And your reaction has betrayed you. Still, the evidence against you for your other crimes is sufficient to warrant a death sentence, so the consequences of my trick will be immaterial to your ultimate fate. But yours was a brilliant plan, fraught with risk and boldly executed. You could have readily assumed a new identity in a new country after the Prince had been assassinated."

Holmes's compliment was clearly intended to induce Harriet to talk, and it succeeded.

"With this plan," Harriet said, "no one would look for me. I was dead, wasn't I?"

"Indeed. And where did you obtain the young woman?"

"She was a London doxy, about to go to prison for practising her trade."

"And was it you, Mr. Arkwright, who secured her release on bail and brought her to Germany? You may as well answer."

"The little fool thought she was about to entertain an English nobleman at the spa hotel," said Arkwright.

I shuddered involuntarily at Harriet's response, for she seemed to find Arkwright's remark amusing. "Well, she lies beside a nobleman now," Harriet said. "In our cemetery plot."

"What was her name?" asked Lucy.

"Her *name*? What does her ruddy name matter to me?"

"Her next of kin should be notified."

"They can rot in hell." Harriet stared hard at Lucy, who had edged closer. "Did you know?"

"I kept recalling an incident at school," Lucy said. "You and I had agreed to meet at the stables. But when I arrived, you weren't where I thought you would be. I realized you weren't where I thought you were at the railway station either." She shrugged. "Also your silver pen was missing from your purse. And you kept calling attention to that purple scarf of yours. I think you overdid that part."

"You think yourself so very clever, Miss Lucy James. But I am still holding this gun."

What Harriet would have done with her pistol at that moment is unknown, for behind her the door from our stairway opened. We saw Lestrade, about to enter. As Harriet involuntarily took her eyes off Holmes to see the new arrival, Lucy lunged forwards, chopping her hand across Harriet's wrist. In the next instant, Lucy wrested the pistol from the smaller woman's grip. One of the military escorts moved to stand behind Harriet, holding his gun to the back of her neck.

Lestrade's narrow face was flushed with pride and excitement. "My men surrounded the carriage, sir," he said. "Lady Radnar is safe. Richter and Dietrich are manacled and shackled. Richter appears to be in genuine pain from his bonds—some kind of skin disorder, it appears, for his face and hands are very red and blistered, as if he'd been in the tropics, perhaps. He had a few choice words to say about you, Dr. Watson—doesn't seem to like you very much. He and Dietrich are also protesting their harsh treatment and claiming diplomatic immunity. Oh, and we found Mr. Arkwright's journal in Dietrich's valise."

"You may leave the journal with me," said Lansdowne. "The War Department will take custody of the two Germans. We may have some difficulty arranging for them to contact their embassy." He added, with a studied casualness, "This is excellent work, Inspector Lestrade. You need not write up a report."

Harriet held up her hands in mocking submission. "Well, I suppose you have captured me too, gentlemen. Now, I feel inclined to write out a full confession. If you let me write it out here in this room, I shall do so. That silver pen of mine is in my purse."

"And if we do not?" asked Holmes.

"If you deny me, I shall enter a plea of not guilty and demand a public trial. I will provide the court and the jury and all in attendance with a full report of Lord Lansdowne's wicked, secret dealings and the Prince's scandalous infidelities."

"Put the handcuffs on her, Inspector Lestrade. If you please," said Lucy.

"And retain her purse," said Holmes. "The silver pen will have a double reservoir. The second reservoir will contain cyanide and strychnine." He spoke as calmly as if he were discussing the ingredients in a plum pudding. "It is the weapon she used to kill Lord Kerren."

Lestrade manacled Harriet's wrists. She stood proudly, nonetheless, glaring at Holmes. "When I get out, I *will* kill you."

"Others before you have said as much," said Holmes.

As Harriet turned to go, Arkwright cried out her name, straining in the grip of the two burly officers as he tried in vain to reach her. His eyes shone with an earnest passion that I had never expected from a man so worldly and cynical. "I still have friends in high places," he said. "We shall prevail. And our love will always be clean and brave."

"Your face is ugly now. And you failed," said Harriet.

She turned away, head held high, clenching her manacled hands into fists and pressing them tight against her waist.

Lestrade led her from the room.

53. A CURIOUS INCIDENT

On the Thursday afternoon that followed, Holmes was feeling much stronger. He and I took the opportunity to see Lucy in a matinee performance of *Iolanthe* at the Savoy. Carte had continued to use Tesla's electrical equipment for the staged lightning effects. It blazed impressively. There were no sinister incidents. The airy frivolity of the production went precisely as planned. Immediately following the performance, I waited for Lucy at the stage door while Holmes went on ahead. Lord Lansdowne was coming to visit at 221B Baker Street, and Holmes wanted to be punctual. I did not know what the Secretary of War intended to discuss when he arrived.

Lucy and I made our way to Baker Street through the fog. We had just stopped on the pavement before our home and were about to mount our steps when a shabbily dressed old woman bumped into Lucy from behind, causing us both to stumble momentarily.

"Oh, beg pardon, I'm sure," the woman said. "Watchin' me own two feet, I was. It's deathly afeared of fallin' I am, at my age. Are you quite all right?"

We both assured her that we were, and then we followed her progress for a few moments as she continued on her hunched, shuffling way.

Mrs. Hudson met us as we entered our lower hall. "You've just missed Lord Lansdowne," she said, "and the Prime Minister himself was just here too, with his great flowing curly black beard and all. They only stayed a short while."

When we reached our upstairs landing, the door opened from within. Holmes was holding a folded newspaper in his hand. He stepped back to allow us to enter. I noticed that the movement also forestalled the possibility of a hug from Lucy, though I do not know whether this was intentional on Holmes's part.

"Did they bring you a medal?" Lucy asked.

He gestured vaguely towards our table, whereon lay an elegantly slim silver box, opened to reveal a white silk lining, a red and blue satin ribbon, and a brightly shining golden disc.

We both offered our congratulations, but Holmes only shrugged. "The Secretary and the Prime Minister did bring some news of interest. Arkwright's trial was a swift, military one in closed chambers. Investigation of his past revealed that ten years ago his sister had committed suicide. She was bitterly disappointed after a brief liaison with the Prince had ended unhappily for her and also for her reputation. Arkwright is now in the brig of an Admiralty battleship bound for the Andaman Islands. His two German accomplices, Dietrich and Richter, are prisoners on the same vessel. Lansdowne wants them out of reach if their government attempts to silence them. He believes that they may yield some useful information if their interrogation is continued over a protracted period. Von Bülow has made an official inquiry as to their whereabouts, but our government categorically denies any knowledge of their presence."

"Was Arkwright the masked man with them on our steps that Sunday morning?" asked Lucy.

"He admitted that he was. Harriet Radnar had telephoned him from Dover, when she learned that her stepmother had induced Lansdowne to send for me."

"What will be done with Harriet?"

"She was sent to Newgate Prison to await trial. Lansdowne said something about poetic justice. I did not press him for details. In a moment I will show you why."

"Did Lansdowne tell you what is to become of the electrical weapon?"

"It will be placed into storage at the garrison. A commission will decide what to do with it, if anything. Wilhelm will not bring the German copy to Dover—assuming, of course, that there is indeed a German copy. The Prince has withdrawn the invitation."

"But Kerren's machine may be workable," said Lucy. "After all, it never received a conclusive test. The power was never turned on after the insulating rubber pads were placed beneath the metal wheels. And the week before, we did see that military balloon go up in flames."

"We also saw that broken tree and the burning artillery vehicle at the *Kurpark*," I said.

"Those demonstrations may have been genuine, but they could just as easily have been false," Holmes replied. "A simple bomb with a timing device could have detonated the balloon. The core of the tree could have been drilled, packed with gunpowder, and then detonated. The armoured vehicle could have been soaked with petrol and lit just after the electrical generator at the *Schloss* had been temporarily slowed. You will note that we were kept at some distance from all three of these events." He shrugged. "However, Lansdowne promised that I could witness any future tests of the machine."

Then Holmes spread out the newspaper, that afternoon's edition of the *Times*, covering the medal. He had drawn a thick black circle with one of his wax pencils around an article on the second page. The heading read:

WOMAN KILLED IN PRISON. FELLOW INMATES SUSPECTED.

The article read as follows:

> Florence Hapgood, a London inmate of Newgate Prison, was found this morning beaten to death in her cell, her injuries so extensive as to render her face unrecognizable. The unfortunate woman had been jailed for nearly a week for failing to comply with the terms of her bond and was awaiting trial on her original offence of soliciting, as well as a more recent arrest for public intoxication. None of her fellow prisoners would admit to seeing Miss Hapgood's attackers. One, however, noted that the woman was deranged, thinking herself to be an aristocratic lady, the heiress to a well-known estate in Kent that will not be named here. Another prisoner said the woman claimed to have knowledge of scandalous crimes committed by personages at the highest levels of the British and German governments. Proof of the impossibility of Miss Hapgood's assertions has been obtained by the *Times*, which has verified that the well-born woman she claimed to be had been buried in Dover several days before Miss Hapgood was incarcerated. Prison officials have promised a full investigation of the attack. A solicitor for the victim's family says they will seek compensation.

Neither Holmes nor Lucy spoke.

"No doubt she antagonized her cellmates with her superior airs and her unfeeling nature," I said.

Neither Holmes nor Lucy replied.

"It is a sad thing," I continued, "that a woman with all the personal and social advantages that Miss Radnar possessed could become so cold and destructive. I suppose we must take into account that at a relatively young age she lost her mother."

"We must also take into account that such an outcome is not inevitable," said Holmes. His eyes were on Lucy.

Lucy's thoughts appeared to be elsewhere. As if something had just occurred to her, she said, "There *has* been a curious incident. Just a few minutes ago, there was an old woman. She bumped into me on the pavement."

We watched as Lucy reached into the pockets of her coat. From the right-hand pocket she pulled out a folded square of paper. "And here is a note. I did not have it in my pocket when I left the theatre."

The notepaper was thick, cream coloured, and of good quality. Within the note was a neatly cut-out copy of the *Times* story that we had just been reading.

Pasted on the notepaper were these eight words, each clipped from a newspaper:

> *Ihre Vater darf nicht wieder stören.*
> *von Bülow*

"'Your father must not interfere again,'" Lucy said. "My, my. It seems that Mr. von Bülow knows who we are." From her casual tone, she might have been talking about a change in the weather.

Your father.

For a moment I felt as if I were falling into a dark void. I realized that Olfrig's interrogation had drawn from me information far more important than the treacherous behaviour of Mr. Gruen. I had unwillingly betrayed the one secret that both Holmes and Lucy needed me to keep. The room seemed to swirl. I put my hand on the edge of the table to steady myself. "Holmes," I said, "I ought to have told you—"

"That you might have revealed Lucy's identity?" Holmes gave one of his brief smiles. "There was no need. I knew of the possibility from the moment you mentioned Olfrig's name, that evening on the plaza. Do not blame yourself, old friend. The great conflicts between nations have been with us for millennia, and human nature is unlikely to change during our generation or the next. We shall continue to play our small role in the cause of justice, for as long as we are able. This clumsy bit of theatricality will not deter us."

He turned to Lucy. "I believe you knew of the possibility as well. I see you remain unafraid."

She had crumpled the note. Now she threw it into the fire.

"I wonder what else they are planning," she said.

The three of us watched the little ball of paper ignite. It blazed brightly for a few moments. Then the flames turned to ash and disappeared amongst the glowing coals.

HISTORICAL NOTES

This is a work of fiction, and the author makes no claim that any of the historical locations or historical figures appearing in this story had even the remotest connection with the adventures recounted herein.

However . . .

1. Albert, Prince of Wales, went on to become King Edward VII, and ruled from January 22, 1901, until just before midnight May 6, 1910. With the exception of the Second Boer War, there was peace during the years of his reign, which has come to be known as the Edwardian era. He played an active role in affairs of foreign policy and defense, although behind the scenes, his chilly relationship with Wilhelm—and England's with Germany—never improved during his lifetime. He died after suffering several heart attacks during his last morning and continuing to work throughout the day, refusing to go to bed. In 1914 Wilhelm blamed him for the outbreak of military conflict in Europe that came to be known as World War I.

2. In 1934, Nikola Tesla began speaking to the press about his work on a weapon to end war that he had begun in the late 1890s. The press promptly dubbed the weapon a "death-beam." Tesla lived until age eighty-six, dying alone in his room at the Hotel New Yorker in January 1943. A week later the FBI ordered his entire estate to be seized by the US Office of Alien Property. His papers have not been made public.
3. Progress has been made in electrical weaponry. Research on a particle-beam weapon based on copies of Tesla's papers was begun in 1945 at Patterson Air Force Base in Dayton, Ohio. The results were not published, and the papers have disappeared. In 1983 under President Ronald Reagan, space- and ground-based nuclear X-ray lasers and subatomic particle beams were part of the Strategic Defense Initiative, dubbed "Star Wars" after the hit film series of the same period. Today the US Army has a portable laser that can shoot down a drone aircraft from two miles away. The US Navy has a more powerful laser weapon that can stop an oncoming speedboat. The latter weapon uses a technology that causes several laser beams to converge when they reach the target.
4. Progress has also been made in electrical medical equipment, with curative devices of all sorts now commonly available, even at Walmart. "Cold laser" treatment is readily available for healing and pain management in both humans and animals.
5. Kaiser Wilhelm II felt animosity towards England throughout his lifetime. Historians have linked this attitude to a pathological need for personal aggrandizement, possibly rooted in his oversensitivity concerning his withered left arm, a result of his bungled childbirth at the

hands of his mother's English doctors. His antagonistic relationship with the Prince of Wales began at the Prince's wedding, when the four-year-old Wilhelm refused to be quiet during the ceremony, biting one of his British relations on the leg and throwing his toy dagger into the cathedral aisle. His resentment towards England is widely viewed as one of the causes of World War I. Two days prior to the German surrender in 1918, Wilhelm abdicated and fled in exile to the Netherlands. He died there in 1941 at age eighty-two.

6. Bernhard von Bülow was named German Secretary of State for Foreign Affairs in 1897, and then Chancellor of the German Empire in 1900. In 1905 he was given the title of Prince (Fürst) von Bülow. He served as Chancellor until 1909, after which he spent much of his time in affluent leisure at his villa in Rome, enjoying a prominent position in literary society. He died there in 1929 at the age of eighty.
7. In 1909 the British War Office and Admiralty created the Secret Service Bureau. By then Lord Lansdowne had left the administration and was serving in a leadership role in the House of Lords.
8. The historical model for Radnar House in this book is the Granville, a fashionable holiday destination situated on a cliff overlooking St. Margaret's Bay near Dover for more than one hundred years. Twentieth-century luminaries such as Noel Coward and Ian Fleming frequented the Granville, and Fleming's fictional James Bond used the hotel for a spot of R & R with his lady friend in the novel *Moonraker*. The building was demolished in 1996, to be replaced by several elegant residential homes.

9. Wilhelm's eccentric manner of culling trees from the *Kurpark* in Bad Homburg is recorded in *The Lost World of the Great Spas* by Joseph Wechsberg. The towns of Bad Homburg and Baden-Baden continue to flourish. Their buildings and parks described in this book can be seen and enjoyed today.
10. The words to the song in Chapter 24 are from Poem #XVIII in *A Shropshire Lad*, by A. E. Housman, first published in 1896.
11. It is possible that Sherlock Holmes may have assisted in the testing of a functioning electrical cannon shortly after the events recorded here. However, the author cannot confirm a rumor that NASA astronauts, exploring near the Sea of Tranquility in 1969, discovered laser burns in the moon's dust. Nor can the author confirm that those laser burns form the initials "V. R."
12. Lucy James will return. Watch for her further adventures with Sherlock Holmes in The Lucy James Mysteries, narrated in her own voice, and in *The Jubilee Problem*, her next adventure narrated by Dr. Watson.

ACKNOWLEDGMENTS

This book owes a great deal to the editorial wisdom and guidance of Jacquelyn BenZekry and her team at Thomas & Mercer, as well as to Anna Elliott and my wonderful wife, Pamela Veley. I'm also grateful for the support and encouragement of Garner Simmons and Dan Matos, and my friend and college classmate Douglas Quelch, who gave me the benefit of his experience in proofreading and naval history. I'm also indebted to Edward Petherbridge and Malcolm Blackmoor for their insights into British theatre in the Victorian era, and to Edward for his brilliant reading of the audio version of this book as well as its predecessor. Both are available on Audible.com.

ABOUT THE AUTHOR

Charles Veley is the author of *The Last Moriarty*, the first installment in this series of fresh Sherlock Holmes adventures. His other books include *Children of the Dark*, *Play to Live*, *Night Whispers*, and *Catching Up*. An avid fan of Gilbert and Sullivan, Veley wrote *The Pirates of Finance*, a new musical in the Gilbert and Sullivan tradition that won an award at the New York Musical Theatre Festival in 2013.

Made in the USA
Las Vegas, NV
24 April 2023